The Whitechapel Murder Mystery

From the journals
of
John Howard Batchelor

March – November, 1888.

Kaleidoscope Press
London

The Whitechapel Murder Mystery

First Published by Kaleidoscope Press 2006

This second edition published 2011

1 10 9 8 7 6 5 4 3 2

Copyright © Rob Hamilton 2006

ISBN: 978-1-84728-856-1

Formatted using Microsoft Word 2007

Typeset in 11/13pt Times New Roman

www.robhamilton.co.uk

'When you have excluded the impossible, whatever remains, however improbable, must be the truth.'

Sir Arthur Conan Doyle (1859 – 1930)

<>

For

H.K.H

Rob Hamilton

Rob Hamilton was born in the Everton district of Liverpool. He has written several scripts for television and radio. *The Whitechapel Murder Mystery* was his second novel, published in 2006. This revised and updated second edition was published in 2011.

The

Whitechapel

Murder Mystery

Monday
March 26, 1888

I closed my eyes and inhaled the smoky atmosphere of the city deep into my lungs. The day had begun much like any other; just another day, another dreary Monday.

Except it wasn't.

This particular day was to be my last. I had finally made my decision and I intended to justify everything my father said about me and bring an end to my pitiful, worthless existence.

Here and now. No more procrastination. No more excuses.

I shuffled to the end of the metal balustrades that jutted out of Westminster Bridge, and stared down into the dark, choppy waters of the River Thames.

The view from my precarious vantage point took my breath away. It was, in fact, a much longer drop than I had envisaged. The bridge did not seem this high when I viewed it from the south bank.

No matter.

A single step forward and it would be over. I had often lain awake in the early hours imagining what drowning would be like. It was an easy way out, providing I didn't break my neck entering the water.

I paused for a moment. A broken neck?

No, that particular outcome was unlikely; I would enter feet first, spear through the first ten feet of river water and then sink slowly to the bottom. Nothing should break on impact, unless I was really unlucky. And I had determined not to hold my breath as I sank through the murky depths. The best course of action (they say) is to breathe the contaminated water into the lungs immediately and thus end it quickly.

But how did they know that? Breathing the water in might prolong the agony. Maybe it *would* be better to break my neck upon entry. That was fairly quick and painless, I would think.

I continued to stare down at the swirling waters far below my feet; the time ticked slowly past. And I did nothing. Five minutes. Ten. And I just stood there, stock-still. Immobile.

The muscles in my legs began to ache; I struggled to control the shivering in my upper body. Unfortunately, I now realised that suicide by drowning actually raises more questions than it answers. Questions like: How long does it take to drown? It is certainly not instantaneous, I knew that. Would I feel anything as I lost consciousness? And what would the authorities do with my bloated body when it washed ashore in some filthy backwater beside London Bridge? I closed my eyes and tried to blot out the image.

I couldn't.

I visualised a poorly dressed mortuary attendant, slouching past my remains with a cheap bottle of ale in one hand, a grubby piece of cheese in the other. Would he sell my cadaver for medical research? I'd heard all the stories. The gruesome images kept coming, one horrible thought after another.

And now, damn it, I was beginning to get cramping pains in my calf muscle. I had to jump soon, before it got any worse.

Another five minutes crawled past. It suddenly dawned on me that all the questions I asked myself were irrelevant. You see, ending one's life requires courage, and my courage, such as it was, deserted me a long time ago and so I did nothing, except stare down into the flowing waters and feel thoroughly ashamed of myself and my abhorrent lack of resolve; a not unfamiliar emotion.

I would find another way.

Tomorrow.

I turned and clambered down from the balustrade, brushed myself down, picked up my battered carpetbag containing my

meagre possessions, and ambled slowly across Westmin
Bridge.

What was wrong with me? It was always tomorrow. Excuse
after damned excuse. I was a past master; but, in truth, what
else did I have other than lame excuses? I hated London, and
everything it stood for. Even in my more lucid and successful
periods, I never quite understood why I had stayed so long in
such a godforsaken place. It was malodorous, overcrowded
and dangerous, and despite what Samuel Johnson wrote, I was
tired of the city and tired of my woeful existence.

Unfortunately, this time I could blame nobody but myself.

My paltry circumstances had diminished to such an extent
that my undignified ejection from a sixpence a night lodging
house the previous evening came as no surprise.

It was difficult to judge how much further I could fall.

Without putting too fine a point on it, Piccadilly Circus is a
thoroughly depressing area, and the whining voices of the
flower girls selling their wares did little to assuage my general
mood. They say that if you remain here for any length of time,
everybody you've ever known will eventually pass by.

I did not relish that particular prospect.

Dishonour is a weighty burden to carry, a burden seemingly
undiminished by time.

'Hello, my lovely,' said a harsh Cockney voice.

A woman in her late forties stepped forward and blocked
my path. Dressed in dark brown skirts with a grey bonnet
perched jauntily on the side of her head, she swung a small,
rolled-up parasol by her side, almost as though it were a cosh
of some sort; which it probably was. She smiled at me without
parting her lips.

'Would you escort me up Regent Street, sir?' she asked, the grim smile still etched on her well-worn face. 'Just sixpence to you.'

I shook my head. 'No thank you, Madam.'

'Ah, an educated gentleman,' she said, seemingly unaware that the dishevelled clothing I wore did not quite match the accent.

'I'm very sorry,' I said, trying to maintain as much dignity as possible, 'but I must forego your services on this occasion. Lack of resources, I'm afraid.'

Her lips parted and a warm smile spread slowly across her face revealing several gaps in the teeth in both her upper and lower gums. She leaned forward and pressed three coins into the palm of my hand. 'Then buy yourself a nice cup of tea. You, sir, are the only person to have spoken courteously to me all day. If you are ever in the Spitalfields area, ask for Emma. Emma Smith. I'll see you come to no harm. Chin, chin.'

She walked away cheerily swinging the parasol by her side and disappeared into the crowds milling around Shaftesbury Avenue. I glanced down at the discoloured pennies nestling in the palm of my hand. It was an odd thing for her to do. A charitable gesture, without doubt, but why would this woman give money to a stranger without prospect of future reward?

Strange, indeed, but not something to dwell upon. In these reduced circumstances, very little in my life made sense. One accepted good fortune and moved on.

I strode absent-mindedly across Piccadilly Circus towards Regent Street, dodging brougham and hansom carriages that missed me by inches; one so close I felt the horse's hot fetid breath searing into my left ear. For one fleeting moment, I even considered standing in the path of a swiftly moving omnibus. Only the thought of lying in a busy thoroughfare, moaning pitifully, while taking an inordinate length of time to die, increased the pace of my steps and carried me safely into Regent Street. Realising there are less dramatic ways to meet one's maker than under the wheels of a speeding omnibus, confirmed to me that the remaining vestige of my sanity was, thankfully, still intact.

I had no idea where I was going, or why. I just walked along in step with the crowd around me, a lost soul among many. Normally, I would be aware of the pickpockets who operated in this particular area of London. However, with just three pennies to my name, and in a worse state than many of the beggars slumped in the shop fronts that lined Regent Street, I was an unlikely target. Nevertheless, force of habit ensured that I remained alert as I strolled through the milling crowds.

And then I spotted him.

A few yards ahead of me a youth of about fifteen walked slowly along the pavement, ungraciously jostling a succession of pedestrians as they attempted to avoid bumping into him. Other than his bad manners, I also noticed his predatory, hawk-like face complete with piercing eyes, which flicked from side to side in a strange, unnatural manner. He appeared nervous and agitated, which only served to attract my fullest attention.

Intrigued, and with little better to occupy my time, I decided to study the boy's every move.

He was up to something.

And then it happened; a choreographed sequence of events, occurring almost simultaneously. And it happened so quickly I almost missed it. A thickset ruffian bumped into a gentleman walking towards me, knocking him sideways out of his stride. The ruffian continued for several paces along the pavement before passing something to a man strolling nonchalantly in the opposite direction. It was a smooth operation.

But not smooth enough.

A sharp cry of *stop thief* rang out. Unfortunately, the three public-spirited citizens who immediately chased after the thickset ruffian were unknowingly chasing the wrong person. The stolen item, passed on twice by the thieves, was now in the possession of the hawk-like youth. He turned and sprinted down a side alley, which I knew led through to Saville Row.

And I, much to my own surprise, found myself sprinting after him.

God alone knows why.

I ran blindly through the narrow confines of an enclosed passageway, noting with some trepidation that it was getting gloomier, narrower and a little intimidating. Trying to run with the heavy carpetbag banging against my right leg was rather a hindrance, but as the youth seemed unaware I was chasing him, I was able to gain some ground on him.

We turned a corner and entered an even gloomier, narrower passage. I could still see the boy's outline several yards ahead of me, although it appeared he was tiring. He must have heard my footsteps behind him as he stopped suddenly and turned to face me, his grimy countenance betraying no emotion. I also stopped abruptly, drew myself up to my full height, which is half an inch less than six feet, and breathed deeply, hoping he wouldn't notice the tremor in my hands.

'You followin' me, Mister?' he said, in a thin reedy voice.

I didn't think this was the time, nor the place, to engage him in conversation. Dropping the carpetbag, I raised both my fists in the classic upright boxing pose, crouching slightly as I stepped forward. My father taught me this method of self-defence during the endless sessions in his drawing room. I advanced confidently towards the boy fully intending to strike him with a left cross followed by a right upper cut to the point of his jaw, rendering him unconscious in the manner my father had knocked me insensible on many occasions.

Unfortunately, the boy ducked expertly under the left cross and swayed gracefully out of range of the right uppercut. Both punches swished aimlessly through the air, missed the target by six inches and sent me stumbling in an ungainly manner to one side. I tried desperately to remain on my feet.

The boy spotted the advantage immediately and stepped forward. He grasped my lapels with both hands, pulled me down to his level and head butted me squarely in the face.

A bright silver flash exploded before my eyes, and I slowly sank to my knees. I could taste the warm, sticky blood seeping from my mouth as a wave of nausea swept over me. Acidic bile gathered at the back of my throat, causing my eyes to water. It is difficult to explain why I didn't just fall to the stinking cobbles and allow the approaching darkness to devour me. It would have been damnably easier.

Through the haze of pain, I saw the boy approaching. He stopped directly in front of me, a sneering expression etched across his face. He drew back his right boot, fully intending to remove the top of my head with a well-aimed kick. Of course, I noted the irony in this situation almost immediately. All morning I had been attempting to kill myself, and here was a fifteen-year-old boy about to do the job for me. However, when I do shuffle off this mortal coil, it will be on my terms and not at the hands of a thieving miscreant. Regardless of my reduced circumstances, a modicum of pride remained intact.

From my kneeling position I quickly realised I didn't have time to stand up and defend myself; it would be all over in a matter of seconds. An instant before the boy's boot connected with my head, I felt my hand brush against the carpetbag, which was lying by my side. I closed my fingers around the handle and with the last ounce of strength in my body, I swung the bag in an upward arc, connecting with the boy's chin and sending him sprawling backward. I stood up, swaying gently as another wave of nausea passed over me, and shakily raised my fists. The boy recovered quickly and moved towards me, only this time he was holding a long slim blade in his hand, which he clearly knew how to use.

He lunged forward, slashing the blade through the air in front of his body. I sidestepped, feinted to hit him with my left and crashed a right cross against the point of his jaw. It felt good to actually achieve something for a change.

The boy slumped to the floor, his breathing shallow and intermittent. I knelt down beside his prone body, at one point having to place my hand gingerly against the sidewall of the passage to prevent myself from keeling over. A quick search through his pockets, revealed a couple of pennies and the item stolen from the gentleman in Regent Street. I eased the item out of his pocket.

Even in the gloom of the passageway, I could see it was a rather elegant wallet made of the finest Italian leather. Across the bottom right-hand corner, embossed in fancy gold lettering, were the initials C.A.L. I slipped the wallet into my pocket, picked up the carpetbag, and quickly headed in the direction of Saville Row. Clearly, the boy's accomplices would be actively searching for him, eager to recover their booty. The sooner I vacated the area the better. If a young boy could inflict so much damage upon my person, God alone knew what his elders and betters were capable of doing to me.

The constant rumbling sound emanating from my stomach was rather embarrassing. Although, it was hardly surprising as I had not eaten a morsel of food in twenty-four hours. With just a couple of pennies to my name the prospects of a meal, or indeed food of any sort, was a forlorn expectation.

I strode away from the boy as quickly as my aching limbs would carry me, and I now sat in a secluded section of Hanover Square waiting for the right moment to check the contents of the wallet. Glancing around me, I surreptitiously withdrew the wallet from my pocket and carefully opened it, savouring the familiar rich leather smell that wafted upward. To my surprise and delight, the first section contained six one-pound notes, an amount which would have taken me more than nine weeks to earn, had I been in employment. The notes slipped easily into my back pocket and I could feel myself salivating at the prospect of a hearty meal. A bed in a decent lodging house for the best part of three months was now within my reach.

At that point, I should have thrown the wallet away and trotted off to find some sustenance in the form of bread, cheese and a large draft of ale. Unfortunately, my curiosity outweighed my better judgement and I continued to search through the wallet like the avaricious vagabond I had become. In the second section, I found a richly embossed, gold-edged visiting card, which I withdrew and studied, before quickly realising that I should not have done so. My pulse beat ever more quickly as my eyes slowly scanned the card. It read:

Charles Aloysius LeGrand
138, Strand
London WC2
Private Investigator

So, in the space of a couple of hours, I had beaten a young boy senseless and deprived a gang of deplorable pickpockets of their intended booty. There was no doubt they would continue to scour the byways of the West End until they found me.

Not content with my morning's work so far, I now pilfered six pounds from a stolen wallet belonging to, of all people, a Private Investigator. The money rested uncomfortably in my back pocket, increasing an irrational belief that the figurative hand of the Metropolitan Police was about to descend upon my grubby collar.

As a moral dilemma, this situation was equal to anything my erstwhile family had ever dreamed up to put me in my place. The thought of my late father peering accusingly over my shoulder as I descended into depraved criminality raised the hairs on the back of my neck. His oft repeated adage, *Circumstances are transient, breeding is permanent* was particularly appropriate at this time. He was a man who believed in upholding a stringent code of honour, be it family or regimental, although the distinction between the two was something he often failed to clarify.

I replaced the six bank notes back into the wallet, feeling inordinately proud that I had not yet sunk to the level of a common criminal, although, given time I would undoubtedly pay a visit to that undiscovered country.

I knocked purposefully on the heavy oak door and stepped back, not knowing what to expect. Number 138 Strand, was situated on the third floor of an elegant, four-storey town house. Probably built in the early part of the century for a wealthy merchant, it was now divided into rooms; some used privately as dwellings, some used for business purposes. Attached to the front door was a large, brass plaque that bore the legend:

Charles A. LeGrand - Private Investigator

I stared at my reflection in the plaque, removed my cap and tried to straighten my dishevelled mop of unruly hair. With some trepidation I noted a pair of black eyes that would have looked attractive on a bare-knuckled boxer, and a bottom lip that had swollen to the size of a large walnut; there wasn't a great deal I could do about my muddied and torn clothing. In truth, I must have cut a rather extraordinary figure as I stood on that third floor landing.

The door opened and I immediately recognised the figure standing before me as the man robbed of his wallet in Regent Street. He was in his late thirties, more than six feet tall, and rather portly. I also noticed his hands, which were as white as porcelain and very smooth; no labourer, this man. He looked at me disdainfully, his eyes flicking quickly up and down, taking in every aspect of my sorry state.

'Yes,' he said, his nose twitching slightly.

Live on the streets for any length of time and there are some things one fails to notice. Like smells, for instance. Judging by Mister LeGrand's reaction, I was polluting the building with a less than fragrant aroma.

In short, I probably stank to high heaven.

'Good afternoon, sir, my name is John Howard Batchelor,' I said, using my best upper crust accent. Despite the ragged clothing and battered face, my cultured accent never failed to impress, a truism that made absolutely no sense in the real world. 'I was in Regent Street earlier and I witnessed the cruel assault and robbery you were subjected to.'

LeGrand nodded thoughtfully, paused for a moment, and then stepped back, indicating I should enter. I walked into a large sitting room, noting that several doors led off into other rooms. It was an elegantly appointed living area, if somewhat shabby in certain aspects of the décor. And there was also something amiss with the ambience of the room, something that suggested expense without style; a faux pas my mother would have fretted about for weeks.

LeGrand moved across the room with surprising agility and sat down behind a large oak desk strewn with various papers, documents and other paraphernalia. He pointed to the upright Regency chair facing him.

'Sit down, please. May I ask the purpose of your visit?' he said, eschewing preliminary conversation. LeGrand's hostile manner quite unnerved me.

I took the wallet from my pocket, placed it on the desk and pushed it toward him. He picked it up, examined the contents and inserted it into his breast pocket. A confused expression meandered slowly across his podgy face, one bushy eyebrow arching upward into a curious half-moon shape.

'The contents are intact,' he said, failing to disguise the tone of amazement in his voice. 'I find that rather odd.'

'Why?'

'Because you could have disappeared, six pounds to the good?'

'I'm not a common criminal, sir.'

'Nor a prize fighter judging by the appalling state of your face. I hope your opponent was equally distressed.' He paused for a moment, the lines across his forehead deepening slightly. 'John Howard Batchelor, you say?'

LeGrand turned in his chair, reached across to the bookcase behind him, and removed a book from the shelf. He placed it on the desk and flicked through the pages. Even upside down, I could see it was a copy of *Burke's Peerage and Knightage*.

'Batchelor? Batchelor? Of course,' he said, running his forefinger down the page. He stopped a third of the way down, tapped the page and nodded his head. 'Sir Richard Howard Batchelor, Colonel, 1st Battalion, Royal Sussex Regiment of Foot. I remember the incident well. Reported in *The Times* at great length. Sir Richard led a counterattack against Madhi tribesmen in the Sudan.' LeGrand stopped suddenly, glanced across the desk at me and then continued to read from the book. 'Killed in action, 26 January, 1885, last day of the siege of Khartoum. Died a hero. Yes, I recall that some of the more robust gentlemen's clubs had a field day with that particular incident. Parliament debated it for days. Are you related?'

'My father.'

'Indeed?' murmured LeGrand, his eyes widening slightly. 'I'm assuming you are estranged from your family.'

'Yes.'

'May I ask why?'

'I had no wish to accept an army commission and then spend my whole career attempting to emulate a father with a defiant disregard for danger. A heroic death did not appeal to my highly-developed sense of self-preservation.'

LeGrand nodded, a slight smile raising the corners of his mouth. 'Eminently sensible, I would say. How long have you been away from home?'

'Three years. I left after news of my father's death reached the household in February '85. I was given the obligatory white feathers and departed through the servants' entrance,' I said absent-mindedly, as though that explained everything.

'How old are you?'

'Twenty-five,' I replied, my thoughts veering off in other directions as I tried to find the courage to raise a rather tricky subject. Unfortunately, circumstances dictated that I broach this particular subject. And I had to do it there and then. I cleared my throat, and the words just tumbled out in a rush. 'I know it is rather vulgar to discuss money but it is customary to offer a ten percent reward for the return of stolen possessions.'

There. I'd said it.

LeGrand placed his elbows on the desk, clasped both his hands together as if praying and slowly closed his eyes. For a moment, I thought he'd fallen asleep, so shallow was his breathing. The meditative state he had lapsed into lasted for less than thirty seconds, but it seemed an eternity, especially as I had just worked out exactly how much I was entitled to claim. Twelve shillings would be a good return for a couple of black eyes and a stroll along the Strand, providing he was willing to pay a reward, of course.

'Mr Batchelor,' said LeGrand, suddenly opening his eyes and leaning back in his chair. 'I pride myself on recognising honesty and integrity in a man's character. You appear to possess both in abundance.' He paused for a moment and slowly tapped his forefinger against his lips. 'I have, for some time, considered employing an assistant. A new wardrobe of clothes, some medical attention for your face and a hot bath, and I do believe you would fit the bill perfectly. What do you say?'

I said nothing. Of all the prospective career moves I had ever envisaged, Assistant Private Detective was certainly not a choice that would have sprung readily to mind. My father, at times of familial calm, did offer constructive advice to me occasionally. *'Always let the other fellow sweat'*, was another favourite adage. I put it into practice and stared at LeGrand for at least a minute without saying a word, a singularly blank expression etched across my face.

Of course, the strategy failed completely.

LeGrand stared back at me, an equally blank expression on his face, 'Two hundred and fifty pounds a year salary and you may share these rooms with me for fifteen shillings a week. You have thirty seconds to…'

'I'll take it,' I said, rudely cutting across him. Well, they do say discretion is the better part of valour, and reasoned judgment is preferable to unwarranted bravado; which is, of course, true. I certainly wasn't going to argue with his offer of two hundred and fifty pounds a year, regardless of what the job entailed. I'd had more than enough of sleeping in cheap lodging houses, scrabbling around for stale crusts of bread and generally sinking into depravity.

However, having said that, had I been aware of the horrific events that were about to unfold around me, I would have refused LeGrand's offer, and returned to the relative safety of the streets.

Monday
April 9, 1888

Lord Lindby wasn't a difficult man to follow, not even for a novice Assistant Private Detective with just two weeks' service under his belt. This particular gout-ridden member of the aristocracy had spent the entire morning wandering around Mayfair with alacrity, servicing two of his mistresses *and* a renowned stage actress who resided in lavish circumstances on the south side of Grosvenor Square.

As I turned into Brook Street, just a couple of yards behind Lindby, I glanced at my pocket watch. Thirty-two minutes past midday and the lecherous Lord had been on his travels, with me in hot pursuit, since eight-thirty that morning. For a man of fifty-five his stamina was commendable, if not a little alarming. No doubt, his Lordship's frequent use of opiates improved his bedside manners no end.

I was only five yards behind him as he turned left into Bond Street and strolled jauntily along, swinging his silver-topped cane in a wide arc by his side. If he followed his normal itinerary, he would now head toward his club in Bourdon Street for lunch, which meant I had at least three hours to formulate my notes and begin drafting an outline for LeGrand. The finished report would be in the hands of Lady Lindby by the weekend, LeGrand would be richer by fifty pounds, and the unfortunate Lord's financial status would be hanging by the finest of threads.

I slumped onto a bench opposite Sotheby's auction house and contemplated my fortune after accepting this particular position, or misfortune, depending on how one looked at things. I had learned very little about LeGrand in the couple of weeks I had worked for him, but what I had discovered was disconcerting. What he was doing was legal, although his manner of conducting business, not to mention his clear breach of normal moral values, left a bitter taste in the mouth.

Some six months previously, LeGrand had been perusing legal documents and had, rather fortuitously, discovered the 1882 *Married Woman's Property Act*. This act allowed a married woman to retain ownership of property that she might have received as a gift from a parent. Before this Act reached the statute books, property and chattels within the marriage would automatically have become the sole properties of the husband. This legislation offered married women full legal control of the property which they owned at marriage or which they acquired after marriage, either by inheritance or by their own earnings. So, should the misguided, lecherous husband run off with the parlour maid and then contemplate divorce, provided the wronged wife could prove her husband's infidelity, she could legally retain the house and most of the items contained within. LeGrand supplied half the titled ladies in Mayfair with written proof of their spouse's indiscretions, which they duly read and then secreted with their respective solicitors.

The position I had accepted, without asking a single question of LeGrand, was not what I had expected. I now spent my days following arthritic aristocrats from one sordid tryst to another. Once again, I could feel the eerie presence of my father standing by my left shoulder, slowly shaking his head in that disapproving way he had perfected over the years. In truth, he had been correct to disapprove of my hedonistic lifestyle, and even now, he probably would have insisted that not much had changed for the better.

I opened my copy of *The Times* and perused the endless columns of fine print. Death and destruction in all parts of the Empire, duly reported in that deadpan style peculiar to this particular newspaper. Somewhere in the North Country, twelve football clubs had formed a professional league and intended to play on a regulated basis; it would never catch on. Cricket was the people's premier game, and always would be.

As my eyes scanned down the newspaper, I nearly missed it. It was headed *Inquest* and I would have normally passed over it except for one thing; the name of the deceased. The opening lines of the article read:

Mr. Wynne E. Baxter, the East Middlesex Coroner, held an inquiry on Saturday at the London Hospital respecting the death of EMMA ELIZABETH SMITH, aged 45, a widow, lately living at 18, George Street, Spitalfields, who, it was alleged, was murdered. Chief Inspector West, of the H Division of Police, attended for the Commissioners of Police.

Emma Elizabeth Smith? Why did that name leap off the page at me? Smith was a common name. I stopped reading and stared at the melee of traffic careering up and down Bond Street. As I glanced back down at the newspaper, my eyes flicking through the tightly written newsprint, it suddenly occurred to me. Of course, the prostitute who approached me in Piccadilly Circus, the one who dropped three pennies in my hand, hadn't she said her name was Emma Smith? If my memory was correct, she had also mentioned Spitalfields. Could it be the same person? Brutally murdered? If so, it was most unfortunate because, despite her occupation, she had appeared to be a most charitable woman.

I continued to read the report, becoming more distressed as the story unfolded. Apparently, Emma Smith had died of a ruptured peritoneum, perforated by a blunt instrument. That seemed a particularly cruel and unusual way to die. Mr George Haslip, the house surgeon at the London Hospital, stated that the deceased had been drinking but was not intoxicated. She had been bleeding from the head and ear, and had other injuries of a revolting nature.

At the inquest, the Coroner stated that from the available medical evidence, which must be true, it was clear that a barbarous murdered had occurred. Margaret Hayes, living at the same address as the deceased, stated that she had seen Mrs Smith in company with a man at the corner of Farrant Street and Burdett Road. The man was dressed in a dark suit and wore a white silk handkerchief around his neck. He was of medium height, but the witness could not identify him.

The inquest jury returned a verdict of *wilful murder*. The police said they were making every possible inquiry into the case, but had not any clue to the person or persons who committed the outrage.

And probably never would have any clues, if I were any judge of the Metropolitan Police. I folded the newspaper, placed it under my arm, and stood up. I needed to clear my head. Murder in the East End of London was not a rare occurrence and the women who worked the streets were well aware of the dangers, but this particular murder seemed different, more brutal, more shocking than most.

I hailed an approaching hansom cab, which clattered to a stop beside me, the horse rearing and bucking against the bridle. Reaching across I pulled up the passengers' door and climbed in.

'138, Strand,' I said, settling back into the polished leather interior, which, for a welcome change, did not reek of stale cigar smoke and perspiration. This was a cab driver with higher standards than most.

The road slowly unfolded in front of me, most of the vehicles that passed across the front of the cab not registering on my consciousness. All I could see was a hazy mental image of Emma Smith, the memory of her kindness when I was at my lowest ebb, filling and expanding my thoughts. The vehicle was halfway down Bond Street when I changed my mind about the destination. Purely on a whim, and without a logical reason in my head, I decided to go to Spitalfields.

'Driver,' I shouted, looking up as the top panel in the ceiling swung open.

'Yes, sir?'

'Change of mind. Go to 18, George Street, Spitalfields.'

'That will be two shillings and sixpence, sir. Minimum.'

'Drive on.'

'As you wish,' he said, pausing for a moment and then scratching his side-whiskers. 'Are you are aware that George Street is in a less than decorous area?'

'If you wait for me, I'll double the fare back to the Strand.'

'Whatever you say, sir.'

The top panel closed leaving me to my own confused thoughts. I didn't really know what I was thinking, except that Emma Smith may have had young children depending on her. If that was the case, they would now be destitute. I wasn't sure what I could do to help, or, indeed, why I should even bother. Perhaps I was shocked at the barbaric nature of Emma Smith's death, or perhaps I was just naïve and less experienced in the ways of the world than most; if so, I was about to learn some very harsh lessons.

The hansom cab bounced to a halt outside 18, George Street, which appeared to be a lodging house of the sort I had become acutely accustomed to over the previous three years; it was a strange feeling to be on the other side of the social divide. I climbed from the cab to the rubbish-strewn pavement, carefully avoiding remnants of rotting vegetables and animal excrement, and glanced up at the driver. He had pulled his neckerchief up over his nose and now had the appearance of a rather dashing highwayman.

'Sorry, sir,' he muttered through the cloth, slotting his whip into the side holder. 'The air around these parts is a bit riper than I would like. That's two and sixpence, if you don't mind.'

'Will you wait for me, cabbie?'

'Yes sir, but I will need the fare in advance. A total of seven and sixpence, if you please.'

I nodded and handed him the money. It was possible that I could disguise this payment within the normal expenses I incurred following lecherous Lords around London. Since I had joined as his assistant LeGrand was now earning so much money from his questionable enterprise that he very rarely queried any expenses I submitted to him.

I pushed the battered front door open and walked into the gloomy interior of the lodging house. I estimated from my own experiences that this particular house, like so many I had frequented over the years, probably catered for between fifty and sixty residents each night, male and female. The foul air that greeted me was a mixture of cheap tobacco smoke, decaying food and unwashed bodies. It was an odour I had grown used to but, after my step up in the world, I had hoped I would never encounter it again.

A notice directly in front of me announced in large letters that a bed for the night was fourpence. To my right an open door led through to the kitchen where a group of surly, ill-dressed men were drinking tea and smoking paper cigarettes in front of a coke fire. Although none of them acknowledged my presence, I had no doubt they had all noted my arrival.

It was dangerous ground.

I moved to my left and stood in front of a small window. A middle-aged woman, a grubby shawl draped around her neck, sat at a small table behind the window counting pennies. She eventually looked up, slid the window open and stared at me without saying a word.

'I'm inquiring about Emma Smith,' I said, removing my hat and leaning forward slightly. 'She stayed here, I believe.'

'Police?'

'No. I'm a friend.'

The woman stood up, moved to her right, and pulled a door open. She beckoned me into her small office. The interior was hot and stuffy due to the large fire roaring away in the hearth.

'Terrible business it was, sir,' she said, indicating that I should sit on the dirty wooden chair positioned on her right side. I sank down onto the chair. The cleaning bill for my soiled clothing would also go onto the Lord Lindby expense account. The woman continued in a halting voice. 'It's very hard to remember the exact details. If you know what I mean?'

I knew exactly what she meant. I placed a half crown coin in front of her. 'Are you the housekeeper?'

She nodded, picked up the coin and dropped it down inside her ample chest. 'I'm the Deputy Keeper. Mary Russell's my name, been here nigh on ten years I have. Seen some things, I can tell you, sir. But I ain't never before seen the likes of what happened to poor Emma.'

'Tell me about it.'

'Can't rightly remember all the details.'

I took another half-crown out of my pocket, showed it to her, and then closed my fist over the coin. 'Tell me what you know and I'll give you this. Either that or I will leave right now and I may even take back the first coin I gave you. Do you understand, Mary?'

She nodded.

'How long had you known Emma?'

'Two years.'

'Did she have any children?'

Mary slowly nodded her head. 'She was a widow woman. Her husband was a soldier, killed in action somewhere and she never got a pension. Cryin' shame, it was. She had two growed up children, both living up in the Finsbury Park area. Neither of them wanted to know their mother, so she never saw them. Broke her heart, it did, not seein' her kids.'

'What happened the night she was attacked?'

'She went out around seven o'clock and come back about four or five the next mornin' in a dreadful state. Her face had been battered about and one of her ears had nearly been torn off.'

'Didn't anybody see anything?'

'Margaret said she saw something.'

I recalled the report in *The Times* that named a Margaret Hayes as a witness. 'Would that be Margaret Hayes?'

'Yes, it would. She stays here when she has the money. Like most of them, she depends on street trade. Said she saw

Emma with a toff. Nice suit, white silk handkerchief, wide-awake hat. Talked a bit like you by all accounts.'

'Like me?'

'Yeah. Posh.' Mary suddenly stopped talking, paused for a moment, took a deep breath and then continued. 'Emma also complained of pains in the, you know, lower part of her body. She was bleedin' from there a lot, too.'

'Are you saying something was inserted into her?'

'I'd rather not talk about this anymore if you don't mind, sir. It's not right, just not right. Whoever did that wicked thing to her was a maniac. It's not normal. Really, it's not.'

A sudden sharp rap on the window halted the conversation. A uniformed police officer was staring through the small window. Mary slid the window open.

'Any problems, Mrs Russell?'

'No, sir. Will you be lookin' around today?'

The officer slowly shook his head. 'Everything appears to be in order. I'll call again next week, maybe. Cheerio.'

I wasn't sure if the officer had seen me, as I was sitting slightly to the right of the window and possibly just outside his eye line; whatever he saw, he failed to acknowledge my presence. I glanced across at Mary. 'Who was that?'

'Superintendent Cutbush, he's in charge of all the lodgin' houses in this area. He can be a bit strange at times.'

'Strange?'

'He takes everythin' so bloody serious, he does. Doesn't do to cross him though.' She paused for a moment. 'That's all I know about Emma, sir. Do I get the other half-crown now?'

I dropped the coin on the desk in front of her. 'Is there anything else you can tell me, Mary?'

'Not really, except I know some of the girls are bein' a bit more careful than usual, if you know what I mean?' she said, shivering slightly and then pulling the shawl up higher around her neck.

'That's understandable,' I replied, mopping my brow with the back of my hand. It was getting hotter in the small office, almost unbearably hot.

'Poor Emma wasn't the first. A couple of months ago another one of the girls was murdered. Annie Millwood. Nice girl was Annie. Police said it was natural causes, but nobody ever believes a bleedin' word they say.'

'What about that Superintendent? The one who was here a moment ago, couldn't he help at all?'

'Old Cutbush?' said Mary, with a dismissive sneer. 'I don't think so.'

'Just a thought. He knows the area, knows the people.'

'Nah, he's as bad as the rest. Don't do to trust any of them coppers. Do you down soon as look at you, they would.' She paused and then took a deep breath. The five bob I had invested was paying dividends. 'Then there was Ada Wilson, another one of my regulars who stayed here on a double when she had a client. You do know what a double is, don't you, sir?'

Three years staying in places like this meant I knew exactly what a double was, although I wasn't about to tell Mary that.

She tapped me lightly on the arm and winked. 'Pay eightpence and get a double bed. Useful for the workin' girls.'

'Yes, very useful,' I said, in a less than convincing tone. She didn't seem to notice, or care, what I thought.

'Ada was a married woman, so she had to be careful,' said Mary, now in full flow. 'Lived over in Mile End, but brought them here to turn a few bob. Anyway, for some reason, she took one back to her place and the bastard - excuse my French, sir - tried to slash her throat. He eventually stabbed her twice in the neck. Neighbours chased him, but he got away.'

'What happened to her?'

Mary pulled a face and then slowly shook her head. 'She recovered, but she's not been the same woman. She's a bag of nerves every time she goes out.'

'Was there a description of the attacker?'

'30-35 years old, dark coat, white silk scarf, wide-awake hat.'

I stood up and moved toward the door. The descriptions Mary had given me were rather vague; except for the wide-awake hat, which intrigued me. The large wide-brimmed hat, usually worn by Quakers, was popular in the early part of the century, but now considered old fashioned.

I pulled the door open. 'Thanks for your help, Mary.'

She pulled the shawl up around her neck. 'You're welcome, I'm sure.'

I walked through the hallway, out onto the pavement and took a deep breath. The heat and foul atmosphere within the house had made me feel unwell. It was good to be back out in the fresh air, although, the word *fresh* was a relative term considering the variety of interesting odours wafting around the Spitalfields area.

It took me several moments to realise that the hansom cab had disappeared from its parking place outside the house.

I glanced up and down the street, in the forlorn hope that the cabbie had moved to a more favourable parking spot. He hadn't, and the cab was nowhere in sight, which sent a cold shiver down my spine. This wasn't the sort of area to wander around on foot. Unfortunately, I had no choice, although I was well aware that I had to get out of this area as quickly as possible. Some fifty yards ahead of me was a railway bridge. I strode quickly down George Street and turned left under the bridge, hoping it would lead out into one of the main thoroughfares winding back toward central London.

I hadn't walked ten yards under the bridge when a man casually stepped out of the shadows, effectively blocking my path. He was average height, shabbily dressed with a white grubby neckerchief tied roughly around his neck and a flat cap pulled down shading his eyes. As I attempted to pass him, he moved to his right or left, depending which way I moved; it quickly became obvious he did not intend to let me pass.

'Now, what would a toff like you be doin' around these parts?' he asked, casually picking at his fingernails with a slim bladed knife. His hard-edged, rasping voice echoed through the gloom of the tunnel. 'Come to see how the other half live, have we?'

Although I could not see the second man who had moved behind me, I could hear his rapid breathing a couple of inches from my right ear. It was pointless answering the first man's question, as it was quite clear he intended to use the knife to rob me and, no doubt, leave me for dead.

I quickly decided that it would be best not to engage either of them in conversation. Regardless of what I said, I would be relieved of my possessions and then killed. But I had to do something. In one fluid movement, I took a step backward, turned my upper body to the right and then swung my elbow in a wide arc. A hot, searing sensation shot up my arm as my elbow connected with the point of the second man's jaw. A loud splintering sound echoed through the gloomy tunnel as the man's jaw shattered. It was gratifying to hear his body slump to the ground behind me.

I glanced back at the first man, who was moving towards me in a strange crouching movement, a snarl engulfing his ape like features. He leapt up and slashed the knife downward, catching the back of my raised hand and opening up an ugly wound from knuckle to wrist. There was no pain, but I felt the blood pumping and immediately began to feel faint. Within seconds, I began to lose concentration and then felt decidedly unsteady as the loss of blood affected my balance. Turning my body sideways toward my attacker, I raised my fists and pushed out a speculative left jab, which caught the man flush on his nose as he moved forward. Far from stopping him, it actually seemed to enrage him, and he came at me with even more ferocity, screaming foul obscenities at the top of his voice. I leaned backward just in time, feeling the blade whistle inches past my left cheek as he lunged at me. He glared at me, his eyes full of malevolence, as he prepared to strike again. I could feel my back pressing firmly against the rough bricks of the bridge wall. There was no escape.

The man held the slim blade out in front of his body and prepared himself to plunge it into my chest. He was taking his time, enjoying himself. This was a game he was winning and he wanted to savour every moment.

A sudden sharp crack startled us both.

Even in the gloom of the tunnel, I could see the astonished look that had slowly spread across the man's face. He dropped the knife and tentatively placed his right hand to his cheek, his features screwed up in astonishment as the blood poured out from between his fingers. A gaping wound had opened up the length of his face. Another sharp crack rang out and the man sank to his knees, unable to comprehend what was happening to him.

The imposing figure of the cabbie suddenly appeared out of the gloom, his neckerchief still wrapped around his nose and mouth. From a distance of about twenty feet, he cracked the long whip expertly against the kneeling man's face again, causing him to yelp in pain and then fall backward onto the cobbles. My would-be assailant scrabbled to his feet and darted off in the direction of George Street, still holding his blood-smeared face.

The cabbie moved toward me, removed his neckerchief and bound it tightly around my wrist. 'Hold that firmly, sir, it's a tourniquet. Used them in the Crimea, we did, very effective for open wounds. It should staunch the bleeding until we get you to a medic. I think you're going to need that wound sewed up.'

I glanced down at my bloodied hand and then up at the weather-beaten, bewhiskered face of the cabbie. Despite his athleticism, I guessed he was probably in his mid-fifties. 'Where in God's name did you go?'

'I'm sorry, sir. I'd never leave a fare stranded like that. A policeman moved me on. Superintendent, I think. An officious bastard, if you ask me. I tried to explain the situation, but he wouldn't listen.'

The cabbie grasped my arm and led me gently towards his vehicle. 'I drove round the block a couple of times and then noticed you were having a spot of trouble.'

I climbed up into the cab and slumped back into the seat. 'What's your name, Cabbie?'

'Cullen Moffat, sir. Colour-Sergeant, 11th Hussars, retired. Most people call me Cull.'

'Thank you, Cull.'

'You're very welcome, sir,'

The last thing that registered in my befuddled brain before I lost consciousness was the sound of a whip cracking and the cab lurching forward.

It never occurred to me that at some point I would have to explain this whole sordid mess to LeGrand.

Tuesday
August 7, 1888

Three months on from my encounter with the two reprobates under the George Street Bridge in Spitalfields and I was still annoyed with LeGrand's attitude. So annoyed, that over the previous several weeks I had even contemplated resignation. A course of action, which, had I followed it through, would have placed me back on the streets. I do acknowledge that a casual observer may perceive me to be many things; recklessly immature, ignobly defiant and sublimely introspective, but a complete fool I am not.

LeGrand had graciously given me just one day to recover from my risky venture in Spitalfields before he asked me to explain myself. He made it quite clear he was not interested in why I had found it necessary to question a prostitute in the East End of London. He was indifferent to my injured hand, and wholly unimpressed with the details of Cull's fortuitous intervention. He just wanted to know one thing. And he asked the same question several times. How did I have the temerity to claim seven and sixpence expenses for a single cab ride?

I didn't have an answer.

In retrospect, the expenses did seem rather excessive, as did the doctor's bill for half a guinea, which I still hadn't shown him. He paced up and down our sitting room at the Strand, his eyes blazing. Occasionally he crashed his fist down on the desktop, scattering papers asunder and making me jump. I sat in the upright regency chair, like a schoolboy in detention. Such was LeGrand's consuming anger, I half-expected him to order me to bend over the desk and receive a damn good thrashing, which might have led to my immediate resignation had he ordered me to do so; fortunately, he did not.

He eventually stopped pacing around the room and stood by the desk, looking down at me. 'I expected more from you, John. You have disappointed me. Seven and sixpence to travel to Spitalfields, when you should have been accounting for Lord Lindby in Mayfair, is outrageous. I'm not happy with your conduct.'

'Charles, three women have been attacked by a lunatic and two have suffered appalling deaths. That is not acceptable in this enlightened day and age,' I said, deciding that if he intended to dismiss me I may as well go down fighting.

He leaned forward, his nose just inches from mine. 'The amount of horseshit on the streets of London is not acceptable, but it is an unpleasant fact, as is the deaths of prostitutes in the East End. Unfortunately, we are not a branch of the Salvation Army,' he said, moving backward and then standing up straight. He shook his head, sat behind his desk and sighed deeply. 'John, I have been most impressed by your work, this last incident aside, and I am, therefore, prepared to give you another chance.'

LeGrand's patronisingly phrased *another chance* consisted of more of the same; trailing perverted aristocrats around London at ungodly hours. The only bright spot was that I had been able to convince him that it made financial sense to pay Cull the Cabbie a daily retainer, rather than pay numerous cab fares every day. Over a period of time, the situation with Cull proved such a success that LeGrand eventually hired him as a full time employee.

And on this particular night, Cull and I found ourselves sitting in his hansom cab surrounded by the eerie gloom of Whitechapel High Street. Only the flickering gas lamps placed at infrequent intervals broke the intimidating shadows of darkness.

The East End of London at four o'clock in the morning is certainly not the most desirable location to place somebody under surveillance; unfortunately, it was part of the job. We were waiting for Lord Milford DeVere to leave the unobtrusive building he had entered approximately five hours previously, having followed him around London all day. Despite various deviations to his route, he had eventually arrived at precisely the location I had expected.

My report for LeGrand would make interesting reading. There is no easy way to say this, but the building we had under surveillance contained an exclusive club for men of a homosexual persuasion. A procession of male prostitutes of the lowest order serviced the patrons, a situation Lady DeVere, now sleeping soundly in her Belgravia residence, had suspected, but was unable to prove. The report would confirm her suspicions, and, more importantly, secure her home and finances.

I exited the cab in order to stretch my legs and quickly noticed that Cull, who had been remarkably silent for the last half an hour, had fallen asleep bolt upright in the driving seat of the cab. He must have sensed my presence, or, more likely, heard my feet shuffling on the uneven paving stones.

'Sorry, John, I *was* asleep,' he said, sheepishly gathering up the reins.

'Don't worry about it. This isn't the Crimea, shouldn't be that many irate Russians around. Although it's hard to tell these days,' I said, smiling up at Cull and then glancing at the building across the road. 'I don't think DeVere is coming out tonight. Anyway, we have all the evidence we need for the report.'

'Back to the Strand?'

'I think so,' I replied, checking the time on my pocket watch. It was 4:20 am.

'It's been a long day,' said Cull, yawning deeply.

He was right. Very shortly, the sun would rise heralding a new dawn. The city of London would slowly come to life and the masses would begin their relentless daily grind. 'I'm going for a pee,' I said, stepping off the kerb.

I pulled my cape tightly around my aching body, strode across Whitechapel High Street, and entered a large archway that led through into a darkened passage. A single gas lamp halfway down the passage gave out barely enough light to read the sign on the wall, but more than enough to ensure I didn't splash my boots. Through the partial gloom, I could just about read the words written on the grubby signboard:

George Yard Buildings

Before I had time to unbutton my flies, I heard a muffled noise emanating from somewhere along the passage. It was a rasping sound, as though someone or something, engaged in frantic activity, couldn't catch their breath quickly enough. The other sound that floated through the early morning air was a methodical thumping, squelching noise, which I found difficult to recognise.

I moved further into the passage, intrigued by the unusual sounds, and stopped at an entrance to a large, open yard that appeared to lead into a building. The scene that greeted me was appalling, and I stood transfixed, unable to comprehend what was occurring before my eyes.

A man of medium height, his back toward me, was hacking at something below his feet, a large butcher knife glinting on every downward stroke. The two sounds I had failed to recognise were that of a knife repeatedly thrust into a prone body, and the rasping breath of a murderer as he manically butchered his unfortunate victim.

Common sense suggested that I should run away from the scene unfolding before me and enlist Cull's help to bring this lunatic to heel, but my fear quickly turned to intense anger. A variety of irrational emotions welled up inside me as I realised the implications of what I was watching. I thought of Emma and the other women who had been in the wrong place at the wrong time, and paid with their lives.

The man was so involved in his frenzied actions that he failed to notice me as I moved forward and grasped his collar in both my hands. I yanked him forcefully backward and hurled him out through the entrance to the yard and into the adjoining passage, my extraordinary body strength fuelled by fear and loathing. He stumbled against the passage wall and then quickly recovered his balance and composure, the bloodstained knife still glinting in his right hand.

We stared at each other for an uncomfortable length of time, both of us seemingly perplexed by the situation. I quickly realised this was the man I had been seeking, the man who had brought unimaginable terror to the East End of London. He was dressed in a dark, expensively cut suit, a white silk scarf tied loosely around his neck and, most damning of all, a wide-awake hat pulled down over his eyes. All this I had noted in a fraction of a second, before realising that if he decided to attack me, I would be unable to defend myself without the benefit of a weapon. He moved slowly forward and positioned himself in the entrance to the yard and I now feared the worst. Hopelessly trapped, my impetuosity and immaturity was about to cost me my life. I had entered the passage to relieve myself, and now, shamefully, I was unable to control my bladder. I wet myself like a small child afraid of the dark.

It was at that moment fortune decided to smile on me.

We both heard it at the same time; muffled footsteps, about thirty yards away, approaching from the left side of the passage. The killer was first to move; he glanced to his right and then ran away down the passage towards Whitechapel High Street.

I quickly followed him, emerging out onto the main road as the first rays of light spread across the eastern sky. To my left I could see him sprinting towards a carriage parked against the kerb less than twenty yards further along the road. I realised I would be unable to reach him on foot before he drove off down the High Street towards central London.

From his position on the other side of the road Cull must have seen what had happened, and having quickly turned the hansom cab in a tight circle, he was now heading straight for me at considerable speed. At the last moment, he reined in the horse and I leapt into the cab, slamming the double half-doors behind me.

'It's the murderer. Don't let him get away,' I shouted, looking up at Cull through the aperture in the ceiling.

A sharp crack of the whip and we were off in pursuit. I grasped the leather handle to my right and hung on steadfastly as the cab bounced and rolled around in a manner the coach builders would never have believed possible.

Another crack of the whip as Cull expertly swung the cab into Aldgate High Street, less than ten yards behind the killer's vehicle, which was also a hansom cab. If there was a better way of moving around the East End in the small hours, blending into the background, but always ready to affect a devious escape, then I couldn't think of it. No wonder the killer appeared to disappear into the darkness with no visible traces.

We were now approaching Bishopsgate only feet behind the killer, whose erratic driving was causing his vehicle to shake and roll precariously on its axle.

Both cabs turned into the corner and veered left towards London Bridge. The horses' hooves pounded out a rhythmic cadence in the morning air as we sped through the cobbled streets, which were still, mercifully, free of traffic. The sun had now risen, but the visibility was only fair as the two cabs cut through the swirling mist that gathered around the bridge.

We were only inches behind the killer's vehicle when it suddenly struck a kerb, rolled over onto its side and skidded across the cobbles. The unfortunate horse continued to pull the upended vehicle, sparks showering outward as pieces of metal sheared off in several directions. Then, with a loud crack, something snapped and the horse galloped madly away across the bridge, trailing reins and bridle in his wake.

Cull stopped behind the upended vehicle, which had now skidded to a grinding halt halfway across the bridge, and we both rushed toward it. The man, thrown from the driving position on the cab, had landed head first on the pavement. We both knelt down beside the body.

Cull felt for a pulse under the man's ear and then slowly shook his head. 'He's dead, John. Broken neck.'

I stared down at the unmarked, almost handsome face. He fitted the description that Mary in George Street had given me; his clothes, his age, everything about him, except he didn't look like a killer. He looked very much like a gentleman to me.

But there was something else that intrigued me about his appearance, and it was blindingly obvious. 'He's sunburnt,' I said, touching the man's leathery face with my fingertips.

Cull placed his hand on the man's forehead and slowly lifted a clump of hair. 'See that?'

I leaned forward and stared intently at the man's head. The sunburn ended abruptly just below his hairline. I recognised it immediately. My own father's hairline was similar.

'Look at the severity of the tan. That line is caused by an officer's cap, probably worn in India over a period of years.' Cull raised the sleeve on the man's jacket to reveal a white upper wrist and arm. 'Officers wear jackets or long sleeve shirts most of the time. And did you notice his hands?'

'No,' I said, shaking my head.

'There are calluses on his right forefinger and thumb. I've seen that before, in the Crimea.'

I shrugged my shoulders, completely bewildered.

Cull continued. 'They're the marks of the scalpel he used to operate on an endless stream of wounded men. In a front line field hospital, it could go on for days, weeks, or months. This man is an army surgeon, probably a Surgeon-Major.'

'It doesn't excuse what he's done,' I said, staring down at the body. I wanted to feel anger and hatred toward him, but I couldn't. I suddenly felt very empty.

'Of course, you're right, there is no excuse. But there may be mitigation,' said Cull, searching carefully through each of the man's pockets. He found nothing and then slowly shook his head. 'We will never know what this man has seen. Most certainly, he witnessed the unnecessary deaths of many young men grotesquely mutilated by grapeshot or slashed to ribbons with sabres, men he was unable to save from death. Can you imagine that, John? Accepting the blame for the ravages of war. Ask yourself if we have the right to judge this man?'

I touched Cull's arm. 'What are you trying to say?'

'Revealing what we know and disgracing his family, friends and regiment won't bring back the people he's murdered. It will just distress innocent people. Is it worth it?'

I stood up and nodded. 'All right, I take your point.'

Lying next to the body was the large bloodstained butcher knife used by the killer. I picked it up, flung it over the wall of the bridge and watched as it spiralled through the air, hitting the water with a gentle splash. It disappeared into the depths of the Thames.

Cull patted me on the back, walked to his cab and climbed up into the driving position. I took one last look at the body and followed him. As we pulled away from the scene and headed across the bridge, I glanced back through the rear window of the cab. Two vehicles had stopped and a uniformed policeman had arrived and taken control of the situation. It was now just another of the many road traffic accidents that occurred on the congested streets of London.

I relaxed into the gentle rocking movement of the cab as Cull drove sedately back to the Strand. Everything had worked out perfectly.

Or so I thought.

Common sense should have told me that my life was not destined to run this smoothly. What I had thought was the finale of the gruesome Whitechapel murders played out on London Bridge was, in fact, not even the beginning. In less than four weeks, another homicidal maniac would appear in the East End of London and *his* victims would die in an even more terrifying manner. Yet again, we would find ourselves in the middle of horrific events beyond our control.

Even as we made our way back to the Strand, the man who would eventually reveal himself to the world as *Jack the Ripper* was skulking in the Whitechapel shadows.

And he was preparing to strike.

Wednesday
September 5, 1888

Trying to glean personal information from Cullen Moffat was akin to pulling teeth with a large pair of pliers. I had learnt, by constantly badgering him, that he was the oldest of eight children, and had grown up in Liverpool before escaping the poverty and joining the army as a fourteen-year-old boy soldier. He had risen quickly to the rank of Colour-Sergeant in the Hussars and I suspected he had been present at the charge of the Light Brigade at Balaclava, but he simply refused to talk at any length about his service life. He had never married, but I was sure my father would have approved of his stoic patriotism and penchant for hard work. Cull was a man you would want by your side in times of crisis.

He was carefully grooming his horse, Domingo, having rented a mews stable adjoining our Strand apartment. LeGrand had offered him the use of a spare room in the apartment for fifteen shillings a week, earning a tidy sum of money from the pair of us. Cull's salary was on a par with mine, two hundred and fifty pounds per annum, which was far in excess of what he earned as a cabbie. We had both accepted the situation with resignation, although my feelings about LeGrand were still somewhat ambivalent. I had moral and ethical reservations about both him and his business practices, although I couldn't quite understand why I felt so uneasy.

Five weeks had passed since our encounter with the murderer on London Bridge, and at my insistence, we had decided not to tell LeGrand anything about it.

Cull threw a blanket over Domingo, closed the stable door and stepped out into the yard. 'Do you know what LeGrand wanted to talk to us about?'

I shook my head and glanced at my pocket watch. 'Ten o'clock he said. We have five minutes to get back to the apartment. It's probably another job following a rheumatic Earl around the gin palaces of old London town. I can't wait.'

'Would you rather live on the streets?'

'No, of course not, but there has to be a better way of earning a living.'

'Maybe we could start our own detective agency,' said Cull, a mischievous smile spreading across his whiskery face.

'And investigate what?'

He shrugged his shoulders. 'Anything. We'd probably do a damn sight better job than the Metropolitan Police.'

'You think so?'

'I do. Saw it in the army for nigh on thirty-five years. It's all about class, John. Half a dozen prostitutes slaughtered; who cares? One single businessman robbed or murdered and the forces of law and order swing into action immediately from the Commissioner of Police downward. That can't be right, can it?'

'You'll never change society, Cull. Set in stone, I'm afraid.'

'I've been around long enough to know that *some* things can be changed. You have to believe.'

We exited the mews, walked out onto the Strand and entered our apartment building. 'You didn't know my father by any chance, did you?' I asked, sarcastically. 'You sound awfully like him at times.'

'I knew many fine officers. Good men, proud of their country. One day you'll understand.'

'I doubt it. Never cut out to be a soldier, despite what my father thought. And, by God, he tried his best to get me into uniform.'

'What are you cut out to be?'

'Good question,' I replied, shrugging my shoulders. 'I wish I knew, Cull. I really do.'

We entered the apartment to find LeGrand sitting at the dining table with another man. They both stood up as we entered.

'This is Mister George Lusk,' said LeGrand, introducing a short, middle-aged man. The only noticeable aspect of his appearance was the thin, excessively trimmed and pomaded moustache, which seemed fussy in the extreme. 'George, this is John Batchelor and Cullen Moffat, my two assistants.'

Cull and I shook hands with the man and sat at the table. We were eager to discover what lurid new venture LeGrand had dreamed up for us this time.

'Mister Lusk is about to set up *The Whitechapel Vigilance Committee*. The Metropolitan Police's poor response to the brutal murders in the East End of London is causing unrest among the lower orders. It has to be addressed before the situation gets out of hand.' LeGrand paused for a moment, glanced at Cull and I in turn and then continued, unable to disguise the self-righteous tone in his voice. 'Gentlemen, we have been appointed to investigate the murders. Mister Lusk and I are fellow members of the Churchill Club in Bond Street and we have been discussing this situation at length. Would you care to elaborate, George?'

I glanced at Cull who avoided my gaze and stared blankly at the table. It was an interesting turn of events. Some months ago, when I had mentioned to LeGrand about the East End murders, he informed me that the Salvation Army did not employ me, and it was none of my business. Now, with a fee involved, it was acceptable to investigate anything. LeGrand's hypocrisy was beginning to grate against my better judgement.

Lusk leaned forward in his chair and addressed us in a tone of voice he probably reserved for political meetings in smoke filled back rooms. 'Gentlemen, five prostitutes have been brutally attacked and only one, Ada Wilson, escaped with her life after having her throat slashed with a butcher knife.'

I glanced at Cull who, except for a slight flicker in his eyes, remained stone faced. These figures were wrong, surely. By my reckoning, *four* prostitutes were attacked, only one of them survived.

Lusk continued. 'The last two murders, Martha Tabram at George Yard Building and Polly Nichols at Buck's Row were the most brutal of all. A postman on his way to work discovered Martha Tabram's body just before five o'clock in the morning. She had suffered thirty-nine stab wounds, mainly concentrated on the breasts, stomach and groin area. A truly gruesome murder, gentlemen.'

I could feel my heart pounding as Lusk spoke, and I now fervently wished I had told LeGrand the truth about that final night in Whitechapel. Cull's flushed face told the same story. It just didn't make sense. If we had left the murderer of Martha Tabram and others lying dead on London Bridge with a broken neck, who killed Polly Nichols? And Why?

Lusk tapped the table with his forefinger to emphasize his point. 'It's a terrible business. The killer cut Polly Nichols' throat through to the vertebrae, almost severing the head from the body. The lower region of the body was also mutilated. In the coroner's report, the word *disembowelment* is used. It does not make pleasant reading, gentlemen.'

'When did the last murder happen?' I asked, trying to keep an even tone in my voice.

Lusk consulted an elaborate leather diary. 'Polly Nichols was murdered just five days ago, on Friday, August 31. They discovered the body at 3:35 am. The police, seemingly, have no leads, no suspects and, apparently, no interest in solving these murders. This is why I have decided to set up *The Vigilance Committee*. We cannot allow this state of affairs to continue.'

LeGrand stood up and nodded his head in the self-righteous way he had perfected. 'Rest assured, we won't let you down.'

Lusk shook hands with us all and exited, obviously convinced he had struck a favourable deal with LeGrand. It would have been interesting to know just how much he was being charged for the dubious services we were about to render him.

LeGrand regained his seat at the table and glanced at each of us in turn, a smug, self-satisfied expression on his face. 'Well, gentlemen, I have secured yet another lucrative contract for us. One close to your heart, John, I would imagine, considering your vicarious interest in East End prostitutes.'

His derogatory comment wasn't worth a response.

LeGrand continued. 'Unfortunately, I will be engaged in other business matters. I want you both to conduct inquiries in the East End until further notice, and provide George Lusk with a weekly progress report.'

I began to feel an anger rising within me, although I spoke slowly and calmly, disguising my emotions rather well, I thought. I glanced across the table at LeGrand. 'Charles, do you sincerely believe either Cull or I have the experience or knowledge to investigate such brutal murders.'

LeGrand slowly shook his head and made a silly tutting sound with his tongue. 'John, my dear boy, you have missed the point entirely. If I may so, I pay you both an excellent salary, and all you have to do is ask a few questions around the East End area. Just investigate the murder sites and provide a weekly report for George Lusk. Not that difficult, surely? A couple of week's work at most. What you put in the report is your concern; just make it interesting reading. Do you follow?'

'So, you don't really care if the murderer is apprehended or not?' I asked, once again managing to contain my emotions.

'No,' said LeGrand, looking puzzled. 'Do you?

It just wasn't worth the effort responding to LeGrand's inane platitudes, and by the expression of Cull's face, it was obvious he thought the same.

'Oh, and a couple of other things,' said LeGrand, leaning back in his chair. 'Mister Lusk has organised accommodation for you both in Whitechapel, giving you better access to the area. You can move in this afternoon. It's a six-month lease, which *I* will be paying. Any questions?'

Both Cull and I shook our heads in unison. There seemed little point in discussing anything with LeGrand, as his vision of the world was set in stone; and because he paid our salaries, *he* was always going to be right, regardless of moralities or principles. I was disgusted with myself, but I had to go along with whatever he said. Other than a beggar's life on the streets of London, I had no other choice.

Cull suddenly took a deep breath and stared directly at LeGrand. 'Won't the local police be rather disconcerted to find two private detectives wandering inanely around the Whitechapel murder sites asking impertinent questions?'

'Yes, I have dealt with that possibility,' replied LeGrand. 'Another member of the Churchill Club, a good friend of mine actually, is an officer in the Metropolitan Police. Executive Superintendent Charles Cutbush is directly responsible for the policing of common lodging houses in the Whitechapel area. He is directly involved in the murder investigation, and has agreed to offer you privileged information with regard to the murders. He has also agreed to sanction your presence within the area with the local constables. You have carte blanche to do as you wish, gentlemen.'

I glanced at LeGrand and then shrugged my shoulders. 'Why, in God's name, would he do that?'

LeGrand sighed, stared at each of us in turn and then spoke slowly, annunciating each word in a precise manner, as though addressing a pair of bedlam inmates. 'The Metropolitan Police have lost the confidence of the people in the East End and they are struggling to glean any information at all. If this situation continues, the area will become a powder keg waiting to explode. The consequences do not bear thinking about.'

He stopped talking and paused for a moment, presumably to allow his unadulterated pearls of wisdom to sink into our thick skulls. Under any other circumstances, I might have stood up and punched him full in the mouth. Judging by the scowl on Cull's face, I would have been second in the queue.

LeGrand continued. 'The Metropolitan Police need all the help they can get to solve these murders and quell the growing unrest in the East End of London. But I'm not particularly interested in that, all I want you to do is provide a weekly report for George Lusk. I mean, how difficult can that be?'

I wasn't sure if LeGrand's final remark was rhetorical or not, but we were about to find out how difficult it would be, not to mention how dangerous. So dangerous, in fact, that both Cull and I were about to place our own lives at risk while our employer enjoyed his afternoon soirees with his well-heeled cronies at the Churchill Club.

Number 27, Church Lane, Whitechapel, was acceptable as living quarters. It was a clean, well-appointed, self-contained house, with two large bedrooms, a sitting room and kitchen. At the rear, there was an expansive stable, and a covered yard for the hansom cab.

We travelled to the East End of London and moved into the accommodation that same afternoon. After sorting out who had which room and where we should stow our belongings, Cull prepared a meal for us both. We sat at the table and ate the food in silence.

After ten minutes, I could stand it no longer. 'Where do we start?' I asked, cutting into the fine piece of mutton Cull had cooked. 'We're not really detectives, are we?'

'It depends how we interpret LeGrand's instructions.'

I placed my knife and fork on the plate in front of me. 'That's not too difficult. He gets a substantial fee from George Lusk and we provide a stream of meaningless reports. Nobody who moves in LeGrand's pampered circles really cares about prostitutes being brutally murdered, or who the murderer may be.'

'I agree, but we could simply ignore LeGrand's instructions and investigate the murders. To hell with concocting weekly reports, let's do it properly. Think about it, John. We have to assume that every murder that occurred before Polly Nichols was probably the work of the man who died on London Bridge. You even threw the murder weapon into the Thames. Remember?'

I nodded.

'So, now we have another murderer, and his first victim is Polly Nichols. Is this a random killing of another unfortunate prostitute? I don't think so. There has to be a reason, a motive behind this. And, if you think about it, we actually know more about these murders than the Metropolitan Police.'

'That's true, but how do we handle it?' I asked, digging my fork into the remaining piece of mutton on my plate.

'We find out all we can about Polly Nichols. Then we check out the murder scene. We need to establish a clear motive.'

'You seem well informed for a retired Colour-Sergeant and former Cabbie.'

'I read a lot of novels. *Penny Dreadfuls*, mostly.'

'Really? Didn't think you'd have the time. Oh, by the way, you know Executive Superintendent Cutbush, don't you?'

Cull slowly shook his head. 'No, should I?'

I nodded. 'Yes. He moved you on while you were waiting for me in George Street. I believe you may have referred to him as an *officious bastard*.'

'Oh, excellent. I can't wait to meet *him* again,' said Cull, scowling slightly at the memory.

Thursday
September 6, 1888

The gateway entrance to the old stable yard in Buck's Row stood between a boarding school and a row of terraced cottages. They found Polly Nichols' body directly outside the closed gates of the stable yard, her almost severed head resting against the wooden frame.

I knelt down and closely examined the cobbled access path that ran from the road, under the gate and into the stable yard. There were no obvious bloodstains, or indeed anything that might indicate something untoward had taken place on this spot. Unfortunately, the only information available to us came through newspaper reports, never a particularly reliable source considering the sensationalist style some of these publications used.

Cull was standing over me, studying a copy of *The Times*, one of our more reliable sources, which he clumsily held open in both hands. 'According to this account the body was found exactly where your left knee is resting.'

I flinched slightly, feeling a cold shiver run through me and I stood up. 'Any evidence that was here will be gone by now. Bloodstains, footprints, everything will have been cleaned up or washed away by the weather. It has rained since last Friday, hasn't it?'

Cull nodded. 'One of the worst summers since records began, apparently.' He paused for a moment, a thoughtful look passing across his face. 'There probably wasn't that much blood.'

'If her throat was severed almost to the vertebrae, there must have been plenty of blood.'

Cull shook his head. 'As a soldier you are taught how to kill. It's a lesson you don't forget. In armed combat, how you use your knife is very important.'

'Are you saying the murderer is a soldier?'

'No, but if the victim was strangled there would be very few bloodstains on the floor.'

'How do you prevent a body bleeding all over the place?'

Cull closed his eyes and inhaled a deep breath. He was obviously very uncomfortable talking about things like this, but we had to discuss it. He moved forward, reached out and grasped my jaw firmly in his left hand. His voice was cold and disjointed as he spoke. 'They probably had sex standing up, so we must assume they were facing each other. The murderer grasps Polly's jaw in one hand, her neck in the other, and twists in opposite directions.'

The intense pressure on my neck increased as Cull slowly tightened his grip on my neck and jaw.

'*No*,' I shouted, grasping Cull's wrists. I immediately felt the pressure decrease as the big man relaxed his grip. 'Dear God, I nearly passed out.'

'Unbearable, isn't it. And I wasn't using all my strength.'

I held my hands up to my throat. 'Do you know what that feels like?'

'No, but I can imagine,' said Cull, his expression remaining cold and calculating. 'Polly's neck is broken, and her heart stops pumping within seconds. It doesn't matter what the murderer does now, there's only going to be a trickle of blood. He probably cuts the throat from right to left, dragging the knife towards him.'

Cull took a deep breath and turned away.

'Does the report say who found the body?' I said, trying to defuse the intensity of the situation.

'Yes, a man called Charles Cross was first on the scene. He was joined by a Robert Paul, both of them on their way to work.'

'What time was that?'

Cull struggled to hold open the flapping newspaper and find the exact part of the article he needed. 'There has to be an easier way of doing this.' He paused for a moment, his eyes scanning the columns of fine print. 'Got it. They found the body at 3:35 am. Robert Paul said Polly Nichols was still warm, which meant she hadn't been dead very long. A police constable, P.C. Neil, joined them and then went off to get a Dr. Llewellyn, who lived close by. They returned quite quickly, and at 3:50 am, approximately, the doctor pronounced life to be extinct 'but a few minutes'. That's interesting, isn't it?'

I shrugged my shoulders. 'Why?'

'According to this report, P.C. Neil is not the beat constable for Buck's Row,' said Cull, folding the newspaper in two halves, 'a P.C. John Thain is.'

'Sorry, I still don't get it. Told you I wouldn't make a very good detective, didn't I?'

'No, it's not about detection. This only strikes me as odd because of all the years I spent on either patrol duty, or organising patrols in some godforsaken colonial outpost. It's about timings.' Cull paused for a moment and took a deep breath. 'At 3:15 am, P.C. Thain passes down Buck's Row on his beat and sees nothing unusual.'

I leaned back against the stable door and closed my eyes; my brain ploughed through the endless series of facts and timings Cull threw at me, and tried to put it all into context. 'So, Polly Nichols was killed between 3:15 and 3:30. That gives the murderer roughly fifteen minutes to do the deed and then disappear into the darkness. That's more than enough time, isn't it? Or am I missing something?'

'No, you're not missing anything, because I haven't told you yet,' said Cull, tapping the newspaper with his forefinger. 'It says here that P.C. Thain's beat around Buck's Row is a very short one, and quickly walked over would occupy no more than twelve minutes at the most.'

I nodded. 'Right. Go on.'

'If he passed the stable yard at 3:15 am and saw nothing unusual, he should have completed his beat twelve minutes later at 3:27 am and definitely seen something. He should have stumbled over the murderer in the act, or at least found the body, having missed the suspect by seconds. He did neither, and he still wasn't near Buck's Row when the two workmen found the body at 3:35 am. Where was he?'

'So, what are you saying? That the Metropolitan Police are involved in some chicanery? You think they're covering up or withholding evidence.'

'Anything is possible,' said Cull, his eyes narrowing as he attempted to put his thought process into action. 'There are three possibilities. Policemen are very much like soldiers, give them an opportunity to skive off, and, believe me, they will. So, the first possibility, and the most likely, is that P.C. Thain stopped for a quick cup of tea somewhere along his beat and innocently missed all the action. The second possibility is that he did actually encounter the murderer.'

'And?' I said, intrigued by Cull's logical approach.

'The murderer is somebody he knows.'

'Like who?'

Cull shook his head in frustration, his tone of voice rising slightly. 'How should I know? A friend, maybe. Or another policeman, I'm only speculating.'

'That's not very likely, is it? What's the third possibility?'

'P.C. John Thain is the murderer.'

'Good God, Cull, that's even less likely.'

He shrugged his shoulders and pointed his finger at me. 'After thirty-five years of military service, I have seen things that you would not believe. I would suggest that absolutely *anything* is possible.'

'There is a fourth possibility,' I said, trying not to diminish, or impinge on, Cull's experiences of life. I could see by the angry look in his eyes that I was beginning to annoy him. 'What if all these timings are utter rubbish? Witnesses to the same event often tell conflicting stories and some timepieces

56

are not very reliable. At that ungodly hour in the morning people are very tired and prone to mistakes.'

Cull nodded. 'I agree, except for one thing.'

'Which is?'

'Every witness interviewed by the police agreed that they heard the sound of the luggage train passing by. That's why the residents in Buck's Row did not hear screams, or indeed, anything out of the ordinary. A woman is possibly strangled and disembowelled underneath their windows and they heard nothing.'

I shrugged my shoulders. 'It still doesn't pinpoint the exact time though, does it?'

'The 3:07 am luggage train from New Cross passed Buck's Row at 3:30 am, which confirms all the timings, because *every* witness mentioned the train. Does that help?'

I nodded and raised my hands. 'I suppose it's even possible that Polly Nichols was killed elsewhere and her body dumped here.'

Cull sighed deeply and then slowly scanned the area before shaking his head. 'I don't think so.'

Regardless of Cull's experience, I wasn't sure what to think. Buck's Row was a very narrow, cobbled street. Apart from the stable yard and school, it had a terrace of small, two storey houses on one side of the road, and a row of tall warehouses facing them. Even in the middle of the day, the road was gloomy. At night, with just a single gas lamp at the end of the road, it would have been pitch black.

'There's something else,' said Cull, glancing at the wall that ran between the schoolhouse and the stable yard. 'I think the murderer knew this area well. Let's suppose Polly Nichols propositions a client on the Whitechapel Road, and they go into one of the nearby side streets for sex.' Cull took a deep breath. Despite his many years of active military service, it was obvious violent death still affected him, even more so as he attempted to work out the circumstances of this particular murder. He continued, his voice wavering slightly. 'The man tries to strangle Polly, as I've mentioned. Perhaps she fights him off, maybe she sees the knife. Whatever happens, she runs for her life and is eventually caught in Buck's Row.'

'Right. So he kills her and then runs off.'

'No, he doesn't,' said Cull, slowly shaking his head.

'He has to get away quickly, or he's seen.'

Cull shook his head again. 'That's the point. If he was a stranger to the area and he chased her through a series of back streets, eventually he wouldn't know where he was in relation to the Whitechapel Road. If he goes left, he runs into one of the beat constables. If he goes right, he runs straight into the men on their way to work. Somebody must see him, distressed and bloodstained. He'll look suspicious, to say the least.'

'But nobody did see him. He just disappeared into thin air. That's not possible.'

'Yes, it is,' said Cull, pointing at the wall. 'Despite chasing Polly through several darkened streets, I think he knew exactly where he was.'

'How can you know that?'

'Because he went in there,' said Cull, pointing at the wall.

I stared at the wall. 'He went over the wall?'

'No, he went through it. Have a closer look.'

I walked toward the area of the wall Cull indicated. As I approached it, I suddenly noticed a small gap leading into a side alley. It blended in so well with its surroundings, it was almost invisible. This was the middle of the day and I couldn't see it until I was standing right next to it. How could the killer have seen it in the darkness?

I followed Cull as he walked slowly into the gloomy alley, his eyes flicking from one side to the other. The alley was about fifteen feet in length and high enough to allow me an inch of headroom. Cull, a good four inches taller than me, had to stoop slightly as he moved about. The residents of the cottages had obviously tried to keep the area as clean as they could, and apart from the pungent odour of boiled cabbage, nothing seemed amiss.

'I presume the police searched this alley,' I said, examining the area around my feet.

'Never presume anything, especially if it involves the Metropolitan Police,' said Cull, kneeling down on one knee. He picked something up off the stone floor and showed it to me. It was a small coin, tarnished and dirty.

I shrugged my shoulders. Again, I missed the point. 'It's a half-penny. Why is that important?'

'What if it were polished to look like something else?' said Cull.

'Like what?'

'A half sovereign. Would a working girl accept it?'

'In the heat of the moment, who would notice?'

Cull stood up, nodded his head and then dropped the coin into his pocket. 'Precisely.'

After leaving Buck's Row, we spent the rest of the afternoon scouring the local pubs and lodging houses of Whitechapel talking to working girls; we must have bought and distributed around two gallons of cheap gin to the girls.

Cull suggested I try to tone down my accent, as it seemed to attract unwanted attention from certain types of East End ruffians, their violent intentions deterred by Cull's size and obvious military bearing, but still an irritant. It was never explained to me how I was supposed to instantly adjust my accent, and attempting to emulate Cull's rough-edged North Country military twang was completely beyond me. I decided, after the third hostile public house we entered, to allow Cull to do all the talking. I stood silently by his side looking suitably unintelligent.

It wasn't *that* difficult.

Over the course of the afternoon, lubricated by an endless supply of gin, the women we interviewed provided detailed descriptions of the various types of men who regularly frequented the Whitechapel area as paying clients. Both Cull and I quickly noted that the same two descriptions cropped up repeatedly.

The first description was: forty-years-old, short and Semitic looking, with an exceptionally thick neck and a bushy black moustache. Many women described the man's movements as *silent and sinister*. Apparently, he also had gleaming eyes and a *repulsive smile*.

The second description was that of a man of about forty-five years of age, average build and height, sandy coloured hair, grey eyes and a florid complexion, with a thick drooping moustache. He wore tailored clothes, including a billycock or bowler-type hat and a white silk scarf wrapped loosely around his neck. The women described the second man as either *cultured* or *refined*, several referring to him as a *proper gent*.

Despite the well-reported deaths of several prostitutes in the area, none of the women seemed deterred from earning their living on the streets, until it occurred to me that they had little choice. I noticed that many of them now carried a weapon of some sort, usually a penknife, to defend themselves against possible attack.

It seemed churlish of me to suggest that any resistance to deter the murderer would be futile, given that this was a man whose avid hatred of prostitutes led him to strangle and disembowel his victims in the most gruesome manner.

This was not just another murderer at large; this was a man with a serious problem.

The uncooked piece of beef sat on the kitchen table, almost mocking me. Arrays of raw vegetables, peeled and unpeeled, bought earlier in the Middlesex Street market, lay haphazardly around the kitchen.

'You haven't the faintest idea how to cook, have you?' said Cull, staring menacingly at me with the stern Colour-Sergeant face he adopted occasionally. 'Or organise a kitchen. I leave you for less than ten minutes, and look at the place. I've never seen anything like it.'

'I'm cooking roast beef, a variety of vegetables and boiled potatoes. Don't panic. Everything is under control; it is not a problem. Although, I must admit, I'm not up to Mrs Beeton's standard.'

'Who in God's name is Mrs Beeton?'

'She wrote a very good cookbook. Home management, that sort of thing. It was always lying around the kitchen at home.'

'Really,' said Cull, patting the piece of beef. 'And when did you last cook anything resembling food?'

I shrugged my shoulders in a non-committal way.

'Answer the question.'

I bit my lip and remained silent for as long as I possibly could. Unfortunately, the big man's piercing stare demanded a response. 'Well, I've *never* cooked anything like this before, but I've seen it done. Not very hard, is it?'

'Did you have servants in your house in Gloucestershire?'

I nodded, unable to decide upon the correct response. I cleared my throat before answering. 'Only a maid; well, four of them really, but they all had very different duties.'

'And a cook?'

'Obviously. Everybody has a cook, don't they?'

'No, John, everybody does not.' He paused for a moment. 'Did you have a driver?'

'Of course not,' I said, testily.

'But your father did?'

'Well, yes, *he* did, but he was married to the cook.' It was getting harder to justify something I wasn't particularly proud of, and even harder to justify my appalling syntax. 'The driver was married to the cook, you understand. My father was never married to her.'

'Of course,' said Cull, lighting the oven and then filling a pan with water. 'Would you prefer me to cook dinner?'

'Yes, I think so. I'll just watch, and learn.'

'Good. You read the note while I cook.'

The note in question was inside an envelope pushed under the front door whilst we were out. I ripped it open and studied the contents. 'It's from Executive Superintendent Cutbush. Why does he use his full rank?'

Cull placed the piece of beef in the oven, and slammed the door shut. 'He's a conceited idiot, that's why. What does he want?'

'Apparently, he has some important information reference a suspect in the Whitechapel murder enquiry. Calling on us tonight at 8:00 pm.'

Cull dropped several potatoes into the boiling pan of water. 'What time is it now?'

I glanced at my pocket watch. '7:05 pm.'

'He'll arrive just in time for dinner,' said Cull, pausing for a moment and then looking thoughtful. 'We have to be careful what we say to him.'

'Why?'

'I don't understand anything about him. Why would a serving police officer supply us with confidential information? It doesn't make sense.'

'Internal politics, who knows? How much do we tell him?'

Cull dropped a large handful of vegetables into another pan of boiling water and then sat down at the kitchen table. 'As little as possible.'

Cutbush placed his knife and fork on the plate, dabbed the corners of his mouth with a napkin, and nodded. 'Excellent meal, Mr. Moffat.' He paused for a moment before continuing. 'I seem to recognise your face from somewhere. Have we ever met?'

'No, I don't think so. I'm sure I'd remember.'

I glanced at Cull and thought back to the George Street incident, barely suppressing a smile as I remembered the fruity comments he had directed at the Superintendent.

'You were in the army?' said Cutbush, leaning back in his chair.

'That's correct. I served with the 11th Hussars. Thirty-five years service.'

'Balaclava?'

Cull nodded.

'Really? Weren't the Hussars one of the regiments involved in the Charge of the Light Brigade?

'Yes.'

'Were you there?'

'I was.'

'May I ask in what capacity?'

'Provost-Marshal's office,' said Cull, leaning forward in his chair. 'I was seconded into the M. M. P.'

Cutbush paused for a moment, glanced at me and then turned his gaze back to Cull, his brow furrowed. 'Mounted Military Police?'

'Correct,' said Cull, picking up a toothpick. He stared across the table at Cutbush, his tight-lipped expression making it quite clear he had nothing further to say on the matter. 'May I ask the purpose of your visit?'

'I understand your scepticism, gentlemen. However, it is much simpler than you would imagine.'

'Sorry Superintendent, it doesn't appear that way,' I said, refilling Cutbush's glass with port. 'We don't understand why the Metropolitan Police would want to share information with us. I'm sure you can cope quite well without our help.'

Cutbush sipped from his glass of port, savoured the wine and then nodded approvingly. 'I share an office with Inspector Frederick Abberline. He's in charge of the enquiries into the Whitechapel murders, which, as we speak, stands at four. He has made no significant progress at all.' Cutbush paused, sat up straight and pushed his shoulders back. 'Gentlemen, I should be leading this enquiry.'

Both Cull and I stared at the Superintendent without saying a word. My guess regarding internal politics wasn't far off the mark. I glanced at Cull who refused to make eye contact with me. He obviously realised it too.

Cutbush continued. 'Abberline has a highly developed sense of his own self-importance. Unfortunately, his performance has been abysmal.' He paused for a moment, obviously trying to phrase his criticism of a fellow officer in an acceptable manner. 'His incompetent investigation into these matters is causing concern at the highest level. The reputation of the Metropolitan Police is at stake. There is rumour of a *Vigilance Committee* being implemented, a state of affairs which would completely undermine police authority. I cannot allow this to continue.'

Cull refilled all the glasses and glanced across at Cutbush. 'You have information regarding a suspect?'

The Superintendent nodded. 'I have a name. For reasons best known to Inspector Abberline, he rejected this suspect out of hand. Personally, I believe this lead should be investigated.'

'Do you have a description of this man?' asked Cull.

'I do,' said Cutbush, reaching inside his breast pocket and withdrawing a small leather notebook. He flicked open a page and began to read. 'About forty-five-years-old, average height and build with…'

'…sandy coloured hair,' said Cull, interrupting Cutbush in mid-sentence, 'grey eyes and a florid complexion with a thick, drooping moustache.' Cull leaned back in his chair and took a sip of his port.

'Very good, Mister Moffat, you have been busy.'

'Simple legwork, Superintendent.'

Cutbush took a deep breath. 'A description of this man has appeared after every single murder. I do not believe that is a coincidence. Abberline's team has *not* investigated him, and I think they should. And with due respect, if you gentlemen have also obtained this description, I would suggest that this person be placed under scrutiny as quickly as possible.'

'We also obtained another description,' I said, glancing at Cull, who nodded his head almost imperceptibly. I continued. 'A short, 40-year-old man, Semitic looking, with a thick neck and a bushy black moustache.'

Cutbush nodded. 'Yes, they know about him. His name is John Pizer, otherwise known as *Leather Apron*. At some point, if they haven't already done so, they intend to release his name to journalists. Of course, he's innocent.'

'Why would they release the name of an innocent man?' I asked, making brief eye contact with Cutbush. He looked away almost instantly.

'It gives the intolerable press something luridly interesting to write about for several issues, rather than concentrating on Metropolitan Police inefficiencies. Politics, gentlemen.'

'What shall we do about the first man?' I asked, refilling all the glasses from a freshly opened bottle of port.

Cutbush picked up his glass and swilled the port around. 'Find out anything you can about him. I understand you will be producing weekly reports for George Lusk, but I would be grateful if we could keep this particular information between ourselves. It is rather sensitive, gentlemen. I will, of course, endeavour to make your stay in Whitechapel as pleasant as possible.'

Cull glanced fleetingly across the table, making brief eye contact with me, before looking down. We both realised the implied threat in Cutbush's words; he wasn't the subtlest man either of us had ever encountered.

'What name do you have?' asked Cull, a barely repressed scowl flitting across his face.

'He's a respected North country merchant,' said Cutbush, reading from his notebook. He removed a crumpled piece of paper and laid it on the table. 'I also have this.'

It was a police artist's impression of a round-faced man, with a moustache, wearing a billycock hat. I studied it for a moment and then pushed it across the table.

Cutbush continued. 'No, you may keep that. It may be of some use to you. The gentleman concerned conducts most of his business in London, but actually lives in Liverpool.'

Cull placed the drawing into his pocket. 'And the name of this gentleman?'

Cutbush burped extravagantly, patted his chest and said in a low, almost whispered voice, 'James Maybrick.'

Saturday
September 8, 1888

The shimmering blood-red glow from Cull's pipe lit up the interior of the hansom cab, enabling me to see the time on my pocket watch. It was exactly four minutes past midnight. Cull had parked the cab opposite the house in Middlesex Street into which James Maybrick had disappeared two hours previously. Our experience following miscreant peers around London had stood us in good stead, having spent six hours successfully following Maybrick from one side of London to the other.

Despite our relentless activity over the previous several hours, something Cull had said to Cutbush still bothered me, and this was my first opportunity to raise the subject. 'Why didn't you tell me you were a Military Policeman?' I asked, unable to meet Cull's piercing gaze. I continued to stare into the darkness beyond the doors of the cab.

Cull sighed. 'It was a secondment for a short period, less than five years, in fact. Now, could we possibly talk about something else?'

'Fine,' I said, covering my mouth and coughing gently, 'your tobacco stinks to high heaven.'

'I agree that it certainly has a more pungent aroma than most other brands. I bought several pounds of it from Afghani tribesmen. They may have added something to it.'

'Probably horseshit.'

'I don't think so.'

'Well, it certainly isn't extra Virginia tobacco.'

We were sitting next to each other staring through the darkness. Both cab doors opened outward, allowing Cull to stretch his long legs. Unfortunately, I slipped forward every time I moved. 'These seats are too buffed. I like polished leather as much as the next man, but I could use these in place of my shaving mirror.'

Cull puffed contentedly at his pipe, blowing streams of smoke in all directions. 'If you make a list of your grievances, I'll attend to it when I have a few spare minutes. You know, people have asked me why I never married.'

'Really. And what do you say to these people?'

'Tact, diplomacy, and thirty five years of Army discipline forbids me to furnish an answer to that question.'

An awkward silence lasting more than a minute followed. He was stalling. I had to ask him the question again. 'Why didn't you tell me you were a policeman?'

Before Cull could answer, a policeman appeared out of the darkness. We hadn't even heard his footsteps.

'Evening,' said the constable, peering into the interior of the cab. He swung his bulls-eye lamp around, practically blinding the pair of us. 'May I ask exactly what you two gentlemen are doing?'

I almost replied with a flippant remake. I wanted to say, at least we are not doing what you expected, but decided to hold my tongue at the last moment. No point in exacerbating relations with the local beat Bobbies. 'I'm John Batchelor and this is Cullen Moffat. Executive Superintendent Cutbush may have mentioned us with regard to certain investigations in this area.'

The constable paused for a moment, lowered his lamp and then shook his head. 'No, I didn't hear anything.'

'I suggest you talk to your desk Sergeant,' said Cull, leaning forward. 'We are on police business, which your continued presence is not helping.'

'I'll be checking that out when I get back to the station. Now if I could just…'

'Constable?' said Cull, in a low, officious voice.

'Yes, Sir.'

'Please find something else to do.'

The constable sniffed, pulled his hat further down and stood back. 'Good evening,' he said, disappearing into the darkness. No doubt, we would hear more about this encounter.

'We need one of those,' said Cull, stifling a yawn.

'One of what?'

'A lantern.' He leaned forward, removed something from under the seat, and passed it to me. 'And you may find this useful, as well.'

It was a heavy wooden truncheon. 'What am I supposed to do with this?'

'Hit people,' said Cull. 'Remember George Yard Buildings? You were lucky. Next time, defend yourself.'

I nodded and then sighed, allowing the air to escape from my mouth slowly and petulantly. 'I'm bored, tired and irritated. How long do we have to stay here? He probably won't come back out tonight.'

'Unfortunately, suspected murderers do not work office hours. We stay here until sunrise, just in case.'

'What time would that be?'

'5:25 am, officially.'

'Oh my God,' I said, sliding back into the seat and rubbing my eyes. 'That's five hours.'

I didn't even realise I'd been asleep until Cull dug his elbow firmly into my ribs, and I jumped forward in the seat.

'He's just left the house.'

'Who?' I asked, trying to gather my muddled thoughts from the depths of sleep.

'Maybrick. Who do you think?' said Cull, pushing me out of the vehicle. 'Follow him on foot. I'll be behind you in the cab. Go on, before you lose him.'

I stumbled across the Middlesex Street cobbles almost in a trance, stepped onto the opposite pavement and followed Maybrick through the darkness, keeping as far back as I could. I could hear the reassuring clip clop of Domingo's hooves as Cull followed behind. Maybrick was about thirty yards ahead of me. He walked on the right side of the pavement, passing out of shadow and into the light of each successive gas lamp as he strolled along.

He turned left into Whitechapel High Street and disappeared from my sight. Even at this ungodly hour of the morning, several carriages were moving about, and I also noticed odd movements in the shadows between the buildings. Of course, that could have been my mind playing tricks. If I had not heard Domingo trotting behind me, I would have panicked and fled the scene. The unrelenting darkness, which engendered a strange feeling of vulnerability, made my nerves tingle.

I turned into the High Street, keeping close to the buildings that ran down my left side. With slightly better lighting in the main road, I could see Maybrick striding along ahead of me, seemingly without a care in the world. After covering a couple of hundred yards at a brisk walking pace, he turned left and disappeared into a side road.

The hansom pulled alongside me and drove at walking pace. 'That's Brick Lane, John. I'm going to get ahead of him. We may lose him if he dodges into another side street,' said Cull, flicking the reins and urging Domingo forward.

The cab turned into Brick Lane and disappeared from sight. Now I did feel vulnerable. My imagination worked feverishly as I strode along; every dingy alley, every pool of darkness, contained some unimaginable horror waiting to spring out at me. I quickened my steps and turned left. Maybrick had vanished and so had Cull. I began running along the uneven pavement, risking a turned ankle, or worse.

Reaching Hanbury Street, I leaned forward, hands on knees, and tried to regain my breath. It wasn't just the darkness that spooked me; it was also the complete silence. So quiet was it away from the main roads, I could actually hear my own heart thumping against my chest.

After inhaling several deep breaths, I managed to control my breathing. I removed my pocket watch and raised the glass face. It was too dark to read the time on the dial, so I gently ran my fingertips across the two hands of the watch; it was 5:10 am.

Somewhere in the darkness, I heard a slight movement, followed by a muffled female voice. I stepped backward into the alley behind me and stared across the road, waiting until it was possible to distinguish the movement of the two people in the ever-lightening gloom. After two or three minutes, I saw James Maybrick. He was standing less than ten yards away from me, talking to a woman, who, judging by her slovenly appearance, was probably a common prostitute.

As daybreak approached and the darkness slowly dissipated with each passing second, I began to feel more confident. I clearly saw the couple open a door opposite my position and enter the building. With my pulse racing, I crossed the road and tentatively pushed open the same door. A damp, unlit passage, led through the interior of the building and out into a small yard. The smell of neglect and decay hung heavily in the fetid air. Cull's erudite words about not facing danger until I was in a position to defend myself fleetingly crossed my mind.

I withdrew the truncheon from my side pocket and took a deep breath to steady my nerves. How in heaven's name had I found myself in a situation like this? I entered the passage and walked slowly along, treading carefully as each step found another creaking floorboard underfoot. The palm of my left hand brushed against the clammy, mildewed walls of the passage as I tried to steady myself and avoid the debris and mounds of stinking refuse that lay beneath my feet.

Somewhere in the gloom, I heard a man's voice say, 'Will you?'

A woman's voice replied, 'Yes', quickly followed by the sounds of a scuffle. If I didn't do something now, it would be too late. I increased my pace and entered a small yard through a door that opened outward. A woman was standing with her back to the dividing fence, facing me; Maybrick was standing directly in front of her adjusting his clothing. I stepped forward onto the step and brought the truncheon down in an arc towards Maybrick's head. He must have heard something moving and he turned sideways to look behind him. The truncheon missed his head and caught the edge of his shoulder, inflicting no injury at all.

Realising he had been caught in a compromising situation, he moved very quickly, barging me roughly out of the way with his shoulder, and then running out into the passage. I glanced at the woman, who was standing with her hands on her hips, glaring at me. Her skirts rode up around her waist, revealing distinctive red and white striped woollen stockings.

'Oh, thank you very much. That's a shillin' you owe me,' she said, holding her hand out toward me.

Ignoring her, I turned and sprinted down the passage, dragged open the front door and emerged out into Hanbury Street. In the distance, I saw the fleeing figure of Maybrick turn left, his footsteps echoing against the cobbles. I followed him into a gloomy alley, and listened intently. The sound of laboured, irregular breathing was evident somewhere very close by. Several yards in front of me, a brick wall effectively blocked off the alley.

It was a dead end. Mister Maybrick was going nowhere.

Although it was getting progressively lighter, it was still dark enough to hide in one of the many nooks and crannies dotted around the alleyway, or even in one of the adjoining yards. I held my breath and listened. I could hear laboured breathing somewhere in the darkness.

'I know you're here,' I said, holding the truncheon out in front of me, and slowly scanning the small area. I could feel myself shaking with fear, and my voice sounded high-pitched and reedy in the enclosed space. 'I'm staying here until you show yourself.' The words made me sound much braver than I felt. I wasn't quite sure what I would do if he jumped out and waved a very large butcher knife under my nose. Probably run very quickly in the opposite direction, if I'm honest.

I heard a shuffling sound behind me and I turned quickly to face the unknown threat. Had Maybrick managed to sneak past me under cover of the darkness? Did he have a couple of accomplices we didn't know about? As ever, my imagination ran wild, conjuring up all sorts of scenarios.

I raised the heavy truncheon, which felt reassuring in my hand, and prepared to stand my ground.

'Is he here?' asked Cull, appearing like an apparition out of the gloom.

I breathed a sigh of relief. 'He's hiding in one of the yards.'

Cull took a deep breath and addressed his words into the darkness. 'Listen, Mister Maybrick, there's a good gentleman. I have a service revolver in my hand and if you do not show yourself, I'm afraid I'll have to shoot you. Do you understand, sir? No mercy, straight through the back of the head. Imagine what that is like, if you will, bits of your brain and skull flying everywhere. Surely, the rope is preferable. Much cleaner.'

No response. I turned my head and stared at Cull, who was now standing slightly in front of me. I could not see a service revolver in his hand, but judging by the intense look on his face, he meant every word he said.

He frightened me at times, he really did.

Cull took a step forward. 'Mister Maybrick, you are a respected Liverpool merchant. Please conduct yourself in the manner expected. Step forward now, sir, and I'll hand you over to the police.'

'It would be preferable if you didn't shoot me,' said a quietly cultured voice. 'I haven't actually done anything.' The now familiar figure stepped out of one of the backyards to our left, dishevelled and distraught.

Cull nodded. 'I'm a man of my word, Mister Maybrick. I won't shoot you.'

'Thank you.'

'You're quite welcome, sir,' said Cull, stepping forward and landing a perfectly executed right uppercut on the point of

Maybrick's chin. He turned his head and glanced across at me. 'Can't take any chances, John.'

At that very moment, I made a swift mental note never to cross or annoy Cull in any way. Ever. 'What are we going to do with him?' I asked, glancing down at Maybrick, who had slumped to the cobbles in an unconscious heap.

'Hand him over to Cutbush, who will, of course, claim full credit for the arrest of the Whitechapel murderer.'

'Does that bother you?'

'No. I have certain reservations about the Superintendent, that's all. Couldn't possibly explain what the reservations are, there's just something odd about him.'

'It's over. We did it.' I paused for a moment. 'Where's the gun?'

'What gun?'

'The service revolver.'

Cull shook his head and then reached down and grasped Maybrick's collar. He dragged the prone body effortlessly across the cobbles in the filthy alley and out into the main road. By the time we reached Hanbury Street, Maybrick had regained consciousness. Cull pulled him roughly to his feet.

'Why did you do it?'

'I don't believe that's any of your business.'

'I think it is. Answer the question.'

'If you really must know, I enjoy engaging with prostitutes,' said Maybrick, gently tapping his bleeding lip with a white silk handkerchief. 'It's rather less expensive than financing a mistress.'

'You're a cold fish, and no mistake,' said Cull. 'Do you not regret what you have done?'

'Regret? Why should I regret anything?'

'How many do you admit to?'

'I have no idea what you are talking about,' said Maybrick, anger and bewilderment sweeping over him. 'Would you care to enlighten me?'

'Prostitutes.'

He slowly shook his head. 'I mean, does it really matter? Hundreds. I don't know. Are you a pervert, sir?'

I could see a thunderous scowl beginning to form on Cull's face. 'Would you go back and speak with the girl?' I said, trying to calm the situation. 'I'll stay with Mister Maybrick.'

'That was more than fifteen minutes ago. She'll be gone.'

'A bed for the night costs at least fourpence, Cull. She probably doesn't have it.' I held my hand out in Maybrick's direction. He rummaged in his pocket and then dropped a florin into my hand.

I passed the coin to Cull. He shrugged, turned on his heel and walked back towards the front door of number 29, just a few yards further down Hanbury Street.

Maybrick took a deep breath. 'May I ask who you are?'

'We're engaged on police business. You, sir, are one of the main suspects.'

'Suspected of what? Importuning prostitutes?'

'No, killing them. One, at least, possibly more.'

'What? Are you deluded?'

Before I could answer, I noticed Cull standing at the open door beckoning to me. I grabbed Maybrick by his elbow, marched him down Hanbury Street, through the doorway and into the passage that led to the backyard.

The sight that greeted us in the yard was one of bloody carnage. Maybrick took one look, leaned to his right and vomited violently, his whole body shaking. He continued to retch, until he sank to one knee, completely exhausted.

The woman's body was lying with her head against the fence, her feet facing away from the passage door. Her clothing was in a state of bloodied disarray. Her left arm hung loosely across her left breast; her legs spread-eagled at an odd angle, the knees turned outwards. The woman's swollen tongue protruded between her front teeth in a grotesque manner, indicating strangulation. The killer had then used a jagged incision to virtually sever the head from the body. As was the case with the previous murder, it was mutilation on a grand scale.

Cull was kneeling beside the body. 'Good God, John, I've served in many theatres of war, but I've never seen anything as brutal, or as demeaning, as this. Just butchery, as simple as that.' He paused for a moment, and then continued, his voice calm and even. 'Again, there's not much blood because this unfortunate woman suffered a broken neck. It's the same killer, John. There's only one weapon that can cause injuries like this; an infantry bayonet.'

I wanted to walk away and breathe some fresh, unsullied air, but I needed to look at the body, and I needed to understand how anybody could perform such vile and utter desecrations upon another human being. What lay before me had to be imprinted on my brain, the horror had to register, had to stay with me. And, more than anything else, I wanted to find the person responsible for this carnage, and bring them to justice. I also wanted to be there when this monster swung from the Newgate gallows.

I forced myself to stare down at the body. The killer had cut straight up from the pubic area, ripping open the whole stomach. Why in God's name would anybody remove the intestines and internal organs and then carefully arrange them around the woman's shoulders?

Cull removed a small knife from his pocket and used it on the woman's black coat. He slit the bottom seams of both coat pockets and placed an array of items on the floor in a neat line.

I took a deep breath and tried to compose myself. 'What are you looking for?'

'Coins,' said Cull, moving various items around. 'And here they are.' He held three halfpenny coins in the palm of his hand and then placed one into his pocket. The other two he dropped at the woman's feet among an array of other items, which included a scrap of muslin, two combs and a couple of pills in a crumpled envelope.

Cull then did something that surprised me. With some difficulty, he removed a brass ring from the woman's finger and dropped it into his pocket.

'We need to take as much evidence as we can. I guarantee that the police will not investigate this murder properly.' He paused for a moment before continuing. 'So, we are going to do it for them. Look at her finger.'

I squatted down beside the body.

Cull held up the woman's hand. 'Can you see the white imprint on the ring finger? The mark is still reddened, which means the murderer probably removed a ring.'

He was right. The woman's hand and fingers were very grubby, except for the white marks on the fingers. It also appeared that the killer had removed two other rings from the woman's fingers.

'Well spotted,' I said.

Cull nodded, stood up and faced Maybrick. 'Please accept my apologies, sir. We nearly made a dreadful mistake.'

Maybrick shrugged. His mouth dropped open as he stared down at the eviscerated body, but he said nothing. He just turned and retched feebly into the corner.

I knew exactly how he felt.

Drinking Irish whiskey at 7:05 am is something polite society frowns upon. But, frankly, after what we had witnessed some hours earlier, none of us gave a damn what polite society thought. James Maybrick picked up the half-empty whiskey bottle and refilled all three glasses.

After leaving the house in Hanbury Street, Cull had driven us back to the rented house in Church Lane. We heard the shrill sound of the police whistles as we crossed Whitechapel High Street, but by then, we were far enough away not to attract any undue attention.

Cull leaned forward in his chair. 'Mister Maybrick, why do you travel from Liverpool to engage with prostitutes?'

'I don't travel just for that purpose,' said Maybrick, sipping from his whiskey glass. 'And please, call me James.'

Both Cull and I stared blankly across the table at him, neither of us saying a word.

Despite his confident demeanour, Maybrick looked slightly uncomfortable as he attempted to explain himself. 'I have business interests in London and I often call upon my brother, Michael. He's quite famous, you know.'

I nodded. 'We followed you around London for several hours. You're not very discreet.'

'One tries.'

'One does not try hard enough,' I said, leaning forward. 'Why does a man of your social standing feel the need to use Whitechapel prostitutes?'

'As I said previously, it is a more financially viable option than funding a mistress. I prefer London prostitutes.'

'Liverpool is not lacking that particular service,' said Cull, looking decidedly unimpressed with our guest. 'I do not believe you, Mister Maybrick. Whitechapel prostitutes? I think not. A man attaining your position would use Mayfair call girls. You're lying, sir.'

Maybrick swallowed a mouthful of whiskey and looked down at the table, his eyes nervously flicking from side to side. 'Yes, you are correct. This is rather embarrassing for me. I'm afraid if I reveal my true intentions I will attract your derision.'

'Oh, I wouldn't worry about that. A couple of hours ago, had the murderer not struck at that particular moment, you were bound for the Newgate gallows,' said Cull, draining his whiskey glass and refilling it. 'Less mendacity, more reality, if you please, Mister Maybrick.'

'My brother Michael has always been the favoured son. He is very talented, and I have to compete with him, or at least try to equal his formidable achievements. I have been doing that all my life. Do you see?'

Both Cull and I stared at him. Even if we did understand his problem, I doubt if either of us really cared at that moment.

Fuelled by alcohol we listened to his debased story with polite disinterest.

'I have no musical talent of any sort. So, I presumed to write a novel,' said Maybrick. He waited expectantly for our comments. Unsurprisingly, neither Cull nor I spoke. Maybrick continued. 'At the least, I was expecting derogatory remarks.'

I shook my head. 'Why? That seems a perfectly respectable undertaking to me. What would this novel be about?'

'It will tell the fictional story of the Whitechapel murders in diary form. The protagonist is 'Sir Jim'. I haven't actually written anything yet, bar a brief outline of events, but I have accumulated a considerable amount of material.'

Cull suddenly sat upright in his chair, a frown creasing his forehead. 'How long have you been engaged in this exercise, Mister Maybrick?'

'Eight months, or so.'

'In your opinion, how many of these murders have been committed?' asked Cull, surprising me with his intensity.

For a moment, Maybrick seemed taken aback. He leaned forward, giving himself more thinking time, and refilled all the glasses. 'I think Annie Millwood was the first. Then there was Emma Smith, Martha Tabram, Polly Nichol and the poor girl this morning. So, I would say five.'

'Were you in the vicinity of all these murders?'

Maybrick shook his head vigorously. 'Not all of them. I was one of a group of men who chased the assailant after he stabbed Ada Wilson in the neck.'

Cull nodded sagely. He then raised his whiskey glass and downed the contents in one go, his eyes remaining steadfastly on our guest. 'You know, don't you?' he said, reaching for the bottle and refilling his glass.

Maybrick remained silent for a moment, unable to meet Cull's piercing stare. Several uneasy and awkward seconds passed in reflective silence before Maybrick eventually sat back in his chair and took a deep breath. 'Yes. I know who the murderer is, or should I say, I know who the murderer *was*. He was killed in a road traffic accident on London Bridge.'

'Was he really?' I said, unable to keep the sarcasm out of my voice. Mister Maybrick didn't quite know it all.

'You also have a name for this man. Correct?' said Cull.

'Yes. Surgeon-Major Nathan Bromley, 6th Dragoon Guards, retired. He was a veteran of the Indian campaign. He was also a member of my club in Cavendish Street. Most embarrassing, really.'

It suddenly occurred to me who the approaching figure in George Yard Buildings may have been. If the murderer had not heard the footsteps, he probably would have stepped forward and finished me off. 'Were you in George Yard Buildings at the time of Martha Tabram's murder?' I asked.

Maybrick nodded. 'I'd been following Bromley, but I'd lost him somewhere on Whitechapel High Street. Then I saw the commotion in the alley. I'm really not sure what happened after that, except for the unfortunate accident on London Bridge, which I chanced upon whilst driving home.'

Cull finished his whiskey, placed his glass on the table and then leaned in Maybrick's direction. 'Why did you allow those women to die? If you knew who the murderer was, why did you not inform the police?'

'I'm sorry, Cull,' said Maybrick, holding his head in his hands. 'I'm so ashamed.'

'So you damn well should be.' Cull stood up, towering over both Maybrick and myself. I could see the anger burning brightly in his eyes. 'And you, sir, will address me as Mister Moffat. Do you understand?'

Maybrick nodded his head, but remained silent, thoroughly chastised. He could not even bring himself to look in Cull's direction.

'Please leave this house. And do so immediately, if you will, sir.'

Maybrick swallowed hard and then stood up. 'I may be able to help with your investigations.'

'Damn your eyes, man, you are a disgrace to everything a gentleman holds dear. Get out before I forcibly eject you.'

Maybrick placed his empty whiskey glass in the centre of the table and stood up, trying desperately to maintain his shredded dignity. He dropped a calling card onto the table. 'That is my home address, gentlemen, if you should need me.'

It was a pitiful sight as he turned on his heel and marched rigidly out of the room, his face burning brightly. I waited for the sound of a slamming door before speaking. 'The man is a fantasist.'

Cull sat down and sighed deeply. 'No, John, the man is a complete buffoon. I hope history records his ignominious actions and damns him to hell, but I fear it won't.'

Forewarned by the ominous black clouds passing across Cull's face, I deemed it wiser, at that particular moment, to keep my own counsel and remain silent. I refilled both glasses with whiskey, sat back in my chair and contemplated what had just happened. Of course, I didn't know it at the time, but this was not the last occasion Cull and I would encounter the oleaginous Mister Maybrick and his dilettante attitude.

Unfortunately, our paths were destined to cross one more time.

Monday
September 10, 1888

Monday morning started with a bang. The first brick thrown through the window showered the sitting room with shards of glass and splinters. Luckily, both Cull and I escaped injury as we were taking breakfast in the kitchen at the time. The second brick, an unusually large and heavy one, was heaved against the front door with enough force to cause a deep split from the top of the door to the bottom, tearing it clear away from the frame.

While I sat immobile at the breakfast table fearing for my life, Cull sprang into action. I presumed he would go and confront the brick-throwing roughnecks face to face. He didn't. He went into the back yard, presumably to check that Domingo had not sustained any injuries.

A couple of moments later Cull strode through the dining room with some purpose. Face distorted with anger, eyes blazing, he passed me on his way to confront the mob at the front of the house. Through the kitchen window, I could see Domingo, securely tethered and chomping at the contents of a nosebag.

This disturbance should not have come as a great surprise to either of us. Noises emanating from the unruly mob had echoed around the streets of Whitechapel most of the previous evening, keeping respectable people awake and in a state of trepidation. I was rather intrigued as to why we had suddenly become the focus of such abject hatred.

Several minutes passed before Cull returned. He sat down at the table and calmly poured himself Earl Grey tea, delicately cutting a thin slice of lemon and dropping it into the cup. His face relaxed into a picture of calm serenity as he sipped the tea.

'Bastards,' he muttered, gently placing the cup onto the saucer.

'What happened? I mean, was Domingo injured?' I asked, trying to avoid Cull's incisive stare.

'They threw rocks at him, John. *Rocks*. They missed, but he could have been seriously injured.' Cull's voice took on a tone of quiet disbelief. 'They threw large rocks at him. *My* horse.'

'But he's fine, isn't he?'

'Bastards.'

'What did you say to the mob at the front door?'

Cull raised his cup and sipped more tea. 'I said if they didn't disperse I may lose my temper. A couple of Bobbies arrived and moved them on. Which was fortunate as I was about to throttle the life out of their pox-faced ringleader.'

'Good morning, gentlemen,' said Superintendent Cutbush, appearing from nowhere like a third rate vaudeville magician. 'Do I detect the aroma of freshly brewed Earl Grey?'

The superintendent sat at the table and poured himself a cup of tea, without, I might say, the courtesy of an invitation. Both Cull and I stared at him with disdain,

'Don't worry about the damage to the door, gentleman,' he said, delicately sipping his tea. He raised his little finger in the prescribed manner. 'My officers will organise a replacement within the hour.'

Cull's top lip curled upward as he attempted to suppress his anger, displaying a row of white teeth beneath his luxuriantly thick grey moustache. He spoke slowly and clearly. 'How did that mob know we were involved in police business?'

'Mister Moffat, you've been asking awkward questions in the neighbourhood for several days now. This is a tightly knit community. Information spreads quickly among the lower orders. Welcome to the difficulties of law enforcement in the East End of London, gentlemen.'

'Would this be the same law enforcement employed at the Trafalgar Square demonstration November last? You must remember that particular day, Superintendent, you supervised the police action against defenceless men. One innocent person killed; many more clubbed and beaten senseless by officers under *your* command, officers who were patently out of control. Not a proud day for the Metropolitan Police.'

Cutbush shrugged his shoulder. 'I am but a small cog within the organisation, Mister Moffat.'

I wasn't quite sure what point Cull was trying to make, but whatever it was had gone straight over my head. As for Cutbush, he affected an unrepentant, almost uncaring attitude, except for the persistent tic in his right eye, which told another story.

I suspected Cull had deliberately touched a raw nerve within the Superintendent. How raw that particular nerve was would become apparent over the next couple of weeks.

On the pretext of wanting some fresh air, Cull marched out into the back yard, leaving the Superintendent to finish his tea alone. I followed him and then watched as he bridled up Domingo to the hansom. Within minutes, we were heading towards Whitechapel High Street at a fierce trot. I should have guessed our destination would be a murder site.

We pulled up against the kerb outside 29 Hanbury Street. A dishevelled and bored looking police constable stood at the front door, his hands buried deep inside his trouser pockets. It was common knowledge that standards of decency within the public services were slipping beyond reproach.

We had also heard rumours that local people were charging a penny to view the murder location, unhindered it seemed by any police intervention, which saddened, rather than surprised me.

I stepped out of the cab and moved toward the constable, who belatedly stood up straight and saluted me in what I deemed to be a rather perfunctory manner.

'You're John Batchelor, aren't you?' he mumbled, handing me a sealed envelope.

His sneering attitude was very disconcerting, but I nodded politely and took the envelope from him. Before I could open it, Cull brushed passed me and stood toe to toe with the constable, a menacing expression etched across his face; an expression, I have to say, I had seen many times before, which made it no less intimidating.

'Where's your pride, man?' said Cull, poking his finger into the constable's chest. 'You are a disgrace to your uniform. If I see you standing on duty in such a slovenly and undisciplined manner again, I'll send a written report to your superiors. Do you understand?'

The constable stood to attention and saluted. 'Yes, sir, it won't happen again.'

Cull pushed open the front door and entered the building without saying another word. I followed him into the gloomy passage that led through into the backyard. The odour of decay and neglect was still prevalent and the rubbish still strewn around underfoot. A brutal murder is committed, but nothing changes and life just goes on as before. At times, I found myself despairing of human nature.

The ugly, black stains on the yard stones told their own story. What we could possibly learn by revisiting this place was beyond my imagination.

Cull leaned against the fence and stared down at the bloodstains for an interminable amount of time. Eventually he raised his eyes and glanced across at me. 'What do you think?'

'I don't understand the mutilation.'

Cull answered without hesitation. 'I think I can explain that. The same person probably murdered the last two victims, Polly Nichols in Buck's Row and Annie Chapman right here, because we know Surgeon-Major Bromley was responsible for the previous murders.' Cull paused for a moment before continuing. 'What do you know about the Masons?'

'Nothing. Do you think there is a Masonic connection?'

Cull shook his head. 'No, but that's what we're supposed to think.'

'Why?'

'The mutilation; intestines over the left shoulder, various organs removed from the body. This is supposed to suggest a ritual slaying.'

'And it does. It's very specific, isn't it?'

Cull slowly moved his head from side to side. 'Depends how gullible you are.'

I glanced down at the pool of blood, which had spread and then slowly dried, leaving a wide area of the paving darkly stained. 'Obviously, I am clearly more gullible than most because I believe only a deeply disturbed person would be capable of an atrocity like this.'

'Hold your hand out.'

I extended my hand. Cull placed what looked like a gold coin into the palm of my hand and then slowly closed my fingers over it.

'What value coin was that?'

'It was a half sovereign,' I replied, confidently.

Cull opened my hand to reveal a highly polished halfpenny coin.

'We are in daylight and you failed to recognise it. What chance would a working girl have standing in the shadows?'

'Polly Nichols and Annie Chapman both had halfpennies in their possession. That's a good lead, isn't it?'

Cull didn't look convinced. 'There's something about these two murders that bothers me. It's almost as though somebody is playing a game.'

'And we don't know the rules.'

'No, we don't, not at the moment' said Cull, staring down at the bloodstains. He paused for a moment before continuing. 'And I don't think it's going to stop at two.'

86

'What can *we* do about it?'

He ignored my question, his face a mask of concentration. 'Open the letter the constable gave you.'

I reached into my inside pocket and removed the crumpled envelope. An unsteady hand had scrawled the words across the page. 'It's from George Lusk. Two things. He wants to know why he hasn't received his weekly report. And he wants us to go to an address on the Whitechapel Road. The inaugural meeting of *The Vigilance Committee* is taking place at seven o'clock this evening.'

Cull took the note from me and read it, his eyes moving slowly across the crumpled piece of paper. 'He's beginning to annoy me.'

'But how did he know we'd be here? We could have gone anywhere in Whitechapel.'

'It's an Army trick. Leave several notes in different places, one of them will be found. It is interesting, though.'

I inhaled a deep breath. 'Cull, I'm starting to experience profound feelings of general inadequacy.'

'Why is that, dear boy?'

'I can't keep up with your logical reasoning. Everything you encounter is revealing or interesting and I rarely understand anything, or see the relevance, until you painstakingly explain the details. Do you think my gullibility has something to do with my background? No, don't answer that. What is so interesting about George Lusk? Just tell me.'

Cull smiled, only the second time I'd seen him do so since I'd first met him. It faded as quickly as it had appeared. 'If George Lusk uses an Army trick, chances are that he was, at sometime in the past, connected to the Military. Would you not agree?'

'Yes.'

Cull turned on his heel, stepped up onto the step and pulled the door open. 'Which means he's a suspect because I think the murder weapon is a bayonet. And if that assumption is correct then we may be looking at a conspiracy of some sort.

We have to find out if George Lusk is a Mason. I'll guarantee Superintendent Cutbush is, and that makes it very interesting.'

'What about LeGrand? Good Lord. What if the…' I stopped mid-sentence and glanced around me. Cull had disappeared. I went through the open door, along the passage and out into Hanbury Street. When I emerged from the passage he was sitting atop the hansom cab, whip in hand, waiting to go. The constable was still standing on duty, and he immediately stood to attention and saluted sharply as I passed him. A lesson quickly learnt, and not just by the constable.

The address on Whitechapel High Street was a former Christian meeting hall, now the new home of *The Whitechapel Vigilance Committee*. Cull jumped down from the driving position, tethered Domingo to a holding post, and gently slipped a nosebag over the horse's head.

I stepped out onto the pavement to face a throng of rough looking characters, some leaning against walls, and some swaggering straight through the entrance to the hall while ignoring everything around them. Every man who passed appeared to be dressed in a grubby muffler and cap, almost as though it were some sort of uniform. As each group crowded into the building, several of the men directed sneering looks at me. Why such animosity? It confused me. I turned to face Cull, who was tying up Domingo's nosebag. 'Don't they know we are trying to help them?'

'We're perceived as authority. It doesn't matter what we're trying to achieve, or how we go about it. We're outsiders, John; nothing is going to change that.'

We entered the building and followed the crowd along a dimly lit passage that led into a large hall. Several rows of battered chairs stood either side of the room, all of them now occupied. I stood next to Cull at the back, barely able to breathe as clouds of acrid tobacco smoke engulfed me; it didn't seem to bother Cull. Indeed, I noticed him taking a deep breath from time to time. He eventually filled and lit his own pipe, adding an extra dimension to the malodorous fug of smoke that surrounded us.

The diminutive figure of George Lusk suddenly appeared on the stage at the front of the hall, his head barely visible above the lectern. 'Gentlemen, you all know me, I'm sure, but for those who don't, my name is George Lusk and I am Chairman of *The Whitechapel Vigilance Committee*.' Lusk paused and nodded regally as a small ripple of applause rolled around the room.

'Get on with it, Lusk,' shouted a gruff voice. 'We 'aven't got all bleedin' night.'

'Gentlemen, there have been several horrible murders in the Whitechapel area and the Metropolitan Police have done nothing to apprehend the person responsible.' Lusk paused for a moment and then slowly scanned the sea of nodding heads before continuing. 'I'm afraid we have to do their job for them. Each of us has to go out and patrol the streets of Whitechapel in order to protect our own.' Lusk's voice had slowly risen to a crescendo, encouraging the burst of applause that followed. He paused, a slight smile creasing his lips, and then continued. 'Gentlemen, *we* ourselves must catch this maniac because we cannot rely on the incompetent, and indeed, corrupt officers, who are responsible for the policing of this great city. Every single one of you has been let down by the system. Why? Because they simply don't care about you or yours.'

Cull turned his head slightly, glanced at me and raised his eyes as almost everyone in the room applauded wildly.

Lusk tapped his finger on the lectern in front of him and then raised both hands. 'Gentlemen, please. I requested the presence of a senior Metropolitan Police officer at this meeting tonight. They declined. Can you believe that?' More applause. 'However, we do have a private detective in the hall tonight, who is working in conjunction with the police. I'm sure he would relish the opportunity to explain the situation to you. Please welcome Mister John Batchelor.'

To say I was surprised would be an understatement. Lusk was now pointing directly at me and every head in the room had turned towards me. I could feel my face glowing.

Lusk was still pointing at me. 'Mister Batchelor, speak to the good people of Whitechapel and explain why the police are so inept.'

I walked down the centre aisle between the rows of chairs, clambered up onto the stage and smiled sweetly at Lusk. As I turned to face the rows of hostile, bewhiskered faces, I quickly realised I didn't have one relevant thought in my head. Not a single idea came to mind, and I just stared blankly through the shifting clouds of tobacco smoke.

'Oi, pretty boy,' shouted a voice. I was unable to pinpoint the owner of the voice among the sea of faces, but whoever it was continued unabated. 'Is it true you have a big posh house up West?'

Before I could answer, another voice piped up from the centre of the room. 'Too bloody right he has. House, servants, he's got the bleedin' lot. What you doing here, mate? Bit of slummin', is it?'

'Now that's just ridiculous. I'm here to help because it's…' I began. My words were lost as a shrill voice emanating from the front row shouted me down.

'Are you a Nancy-Boy, John? Look what I got for you.'

A rising gale of laughter swept around the hall, completely drowning out my response. Some of the men were standing up waving their caps above their heads, obviously enjoying every second of my immense discomfort.

A deep voice, two inches from my left ear, suddenly boomed out. 'No, he bloody well isn't.' It was Cull. He gently moved me to one side and slapped his hands onto the lectern. 'And neither am I. Do any of you scrimshanking bastards want to argue with that?'

Although nobody responded directly, I think the answer was probably *no*, as the whole room had gone silent. All the men had regained their seats, and were all staring sheepishly at the snarling face of Cull.

'There's a murderer out there. Nay, a lunatic.' Cull took a deep breath, and slowly moved his piercing gaze around the audience. 'And he's mutilating and killing *your* women; wives, mothers, sisters. If you want to stop this animal, we have to work together. Anybody who disagrees with that, please leave now.' Cull paused. Nobody moved. 'When we catch this bastard, he's going to swing from the highest gallows Newgate has ever seen. If you have any information, you know where I live. And it isn't up West. Got it?'

A ripple of applause started at the back of the room and slowly spread, until it was echoing around the whole building. I glanced over my right shoulder at George Lusk, who was standing in the wings looking exasperated. His attempt to humiliate me had rebounded on him and he didn't look best pleased. Cull moved away from the lectern, approached the rear of the stage and whispered something into Lusk's ear.

I followed Cull from the stage, through the crowd and out into the passage. 'What did you say to Lusk?'

He stopped and turned to face me, an expression of anger still deeply engraved across his face. 'I told him his card was marked.'

'My father had a saying that fits Lusk perfectly.'

'Really?'

'Yes. He would have said George Lusk was all gong and no dinner.'

Cull shrugged his shoulders, turned on his heel and walked briskly toward the exit door. He was facing away from me, and I couldn't be certain, but I think he was smiling.

Friday
September 28, 1888

Following Cull's inspirational words at the stormy meeting of The Whitechapel Vigilance Committee, we expected to find ourselves inundated with information about suspicious characters and possible suspects for the murders. In fact, three weeks had passed, all the leads had petered out and, surprisingly, no further murders occurred. We had provided George Lusk with his weekly reports, which tested my fictional writing skills to the limit, but the man himself failed to call upon us, or query any of the reports we sent him. Also conspicuous by his prolonged absence was Superintendent Cutbush, who had seemingly vanished off the face of the Earth.

Cull and I were sitting in the yard of our rented house in Church Lane, enjoying a flagon of fine ale on a very pleasant and balmy evening. If I had any complaints at all, it was that Cull was still smoking his malodorous Afghani tobacco.

'Does this tobacco bother you?' he asked, lighting another bowlful of the damned stuff.

'No, not at all.'

'Good,' he said, drawing heavily on the pipe and blowing a cloud of dense smoke up into the evening sky. 'I've been thinking and I may be wrong.'

'Yes, okay, the stuff still stinks to high heaven, but I am getting used to it.'

Cull raised his eyes. 'I'm not talking about the damned tobacco, man. Dear Lord, give me strength.'

'Sorry. What are you talking about?'

'I assumed the last two murders, Polly Nichols and Annie Chapman, were probably the first of a series,' he said, taking a deep breath. 'Obviously, that is not the case. Suggesting that the ritual mutilations had some sort of Masonic connection also seems a bit foolish now. Maybe I was looking for motives that weren't actually there.'

I refilled both tankards with more ale. It was surprising, to say the least, that Cull should admit he might have been wrong about anything. He wasn't normally so introspective; that was my job.

'Did you hear that?' said Cull, turning his head to one side.

'What?'

He stood up and walked to the end of the yard, leaving a wispy trail of tobacco smoke behind him. 'I can hear a tapping sound.'

Cull slipped the bolt on the gate and slowly inched it open. A tall, slender woman, possibly in her late forties, stood the other side of the gate. She was a striking woman, with a deathly pale complexion and dark brown hair flecked with grey.

'Mister Moffat, is it?'

Cull nodded.

'Pleased to meet you, I'm sure,' she said, inclining her head slightly. 'I've been told you were wantin' information about those wicked murders.'

Cull opened the gate fully and indicated that the woman should enter. 'John, would you get the lady a chair?'

I walked briskly into the kitchen, retrieved a chair and placed it down in front of her. 'Good evening, my name is John Batchelor,' I said, bowing slightly. The woman had distinctive grey eyes that sparkled in the evening light. She appeared to be a cut above the normal streetwalker, if that's what she was.

She sat demurely on the chair, straightening her grubby skirts slightly. 'I don't know where to start.'

'The beginning is usually a good place, Madam,' said Cull, tapping his smouldering pipe on the heel of his boot. 'Perhaps you should tell us your name.'

'I'm sorry, sir. I'm very nervous.' She paused for a moment, her eyes downcast. 'My name is Elizabeth Stride. Liz. It's about my boyfriend, he's very violent.'

Cull nodded. 'Yes, go on.'

'I haven't seen sight or sound of him since the night poor Annie was murdered.'

'You knew Annie Chapman?' I asked, noticing that the lady's hands were shaking slightly.

She nodded, but kept her eyes downcast. 'I also knew Polly Nichols.'

Cull filled his pipe, tapped the tobacco down and lit it. 'How well did you know them?'

I glanced across at the woman and studied her actions. She had brought her hands together in her lap and intertwined her long fingers to control the shaking. She looked so nervous, and took so much time to answer the question, I got an impression that she was about to jump up and flee the yard.

'I didn't know them very well, sir. I shared a space with them at a lodgin' house for a few weeks. That's all.'

'In Whitechapel?' asked Cull, blowing smoke out of the side of his mouth.

'Flower and Dean Street. There were five of us, including the two women who were murdered, and we shared what we had, you know? It wasn't much.'

Cull suddenly sat upright in his chair. 'Five, you say? What were the names of the other two?'

The woman continued to stare at the floor. She spoke without looking up. 'Catherine Eddowes and…'

The gate, which Cull had neglected to bolt, suddenly crashed open, drowning out Liz Stride's words. A ruffian of medium height staggered into the yard. He had an open bottle of ale in one hand and a small penknife in the other.

'I thought you might be here, you fuckin' bitch,' said the man, throwing the bottle to one side and advancing unsteadily down the yard.

Cull was first to rise. He said nothing, just stared at the stumbling figure that had burst into the yard.

The ruffian poked Cull in the chest. 'I've no argument with you, big man. That's my woman and she's comin' with me, but I'll fight you if that's what you want. Is it?'

Cull slowly shook his head. I had difficulty in swallowing as my throat had suddenly gone very dry. I remained seated. The ruffian grasped hold of the woman's arm and dragged her from the chair. He bundled her roughly down the yard.

'I didn't say anythin', Michael. Honest, I didn't.'

'Shut up, you whore,' he said, shoving her out of the yard. The gate slammed shut behind them.

Cull turned on his heel and stared down at me. 'Must you sit there looking like you're about to organise a sewing circle?' he said, rather ungraciously, I thought. 'Grab that truncheon. We're going to follow them and find out where our new friend Michael lives.'

'It's still light, Cull, they'll see us.'

'He's so drunk I doubt if he'd see a bright yellow omnibus before it mowed him down.'

I picked up the truncheon, which was resting against the wall, and stomped out of the yard behind Cull.

Sewing circle, indeed.

By the time we had followed the bickering couple along Church Lane, across Whitechapel High Street and into Goulston Street, the light had faded completely, leaving us at the mercy of the infrequent gas lamps.

We were about twenty yards behind the couple when they suddenly stopped. Cull grasped my shirt collar and dragged me into a side alley out of sight. I leaned forward and peered through the gathering darkness as the couple struggled on the pavement. Michael had grasped Liz Stride by her throat and was slamming punch after sickening punch into her face.

'I'm going to stop him, Cull. This is not right.'

'No.'

'But...'

'We need to know his full name and where he lives. And that means following him home.'

'I don't think so,' I said, pushing Cull aside and moving across the pavement toward the couple, who were still grappling with each other. Even in the poor light, I could see copious amounts of blood streaming from Liz Stride's mouth and nose.

Enough was enough.

Michael had his back turned to me and I brought the truncheon down on the right side of his head with all the force I could muster. Unfortunately, he didn't go down. He just turned to face me, a blank expression installed deep within his drink sodden eyes.

'Who the fu...'

I didn't wait for the end of his sentence. This time I hit him full on the side of his left temple, opening an inch long gash across his forehead. And heaven only knows why, but he still didn't go down.

'Good grief,' said Cull, moving out of the shadows. 'Can't you do anything right.'

In one swift movement, Cull stepped forward and smashed a right cross into Michael's jaw. This time the ruffian went down like a sack of potatoes and sprawled backwards across the pavement, his battered boots hanging over the edge of the kerb.

I helped Liz to her feet. She slowly raised her right hand and stepped backward, her whole body shaking violently.

'I'm fine, sir. Thank you,' she said, wiping the blood from her mouth with the back of her hand.

'What's his full name?'

She shook her head.

'We can help you,' I said.

Cull stepped forward and grasped the woman firmly by her shoulders. 'What's his name, Liz? Tell me.'

She paused for a moment and then said, 'Michael Kidney.'

'Do you live with him?'

She nodded.

'Address?'

'38, Dorset Street.'

'Thank you.'

It was at that moment I heard running footsteps. At first the sound appeared distant, certainly more than one person, although it was difficult to determine from which direction the sound was emanating. They emerged from the alley to my left and were upon us before either of us could move. There were four, maybe five ruffians, all poorly dressed, and all carrying sticks or cudgels of some sort.

I raised the truncheon and attempted to hit the first man as he ran toward me, but he simply caught my upraised arm, twisted it backward and head butted me squarely in the face, opening up a gash across my left eyebrow. The blood immediately spurted from the wound and cascaded down my face, impairing my vision. Strangely, I felt no pain, but I could not prevent my knees slowly buckling, and I sank to the pavement with all the grace of a downed pheasant filled with buckshot.

Somewhere in the distance, I could hear Cull's voice shouting something that sounded like *cover up*, but by this time, I didn't really care. The relentless kicks and punches aimed at my body didn't seem to matter. I was no longer lying on a filthy pavement in Whitechapel. I was swimming underwater in clear blue water, heading slowly towards a bright light somewhere near the surface. It all felt quite serene and tranquil, almost enjoyable.

And then everything faded to black…

Sunday
September 30, 1888

My eyes were tightly closed, and I wasn't about to open them just yet. It was difficult to judge what had brought me back to the verge of consciousness; the pungent aromas of boiled cabbage and stale urine, or the throbbing pain in my left temple. I decided on the latter as the pain behind my eyes slowly increased and my senses became more acute, which, in turn, caused me to take a sharp intake of breath. Unlike my father, who had appeared to relish the odd Sabre cut or stray bullet wound to the fleshy parts of his anatomy, I'd never been remotely capable of dealing with pain, even minor toothache. Unfortunately, I had a dreadful foreboding it was all about to change.

Dried blood caked the area above my left eye. I didn't need to examine it to know that; I could feel it. Tender and sore. And still I couldn't bring myself to open my eyes. Trepidation, fear of the unknown, it was difficult to quantify exactly what I felt. Maybe I was blind and my eyes *were* open. Perhaps I wasn't seeing anything because I'd lost my sight. Dear God, not that. Not blindness.

'So you are alive then?'

It was Cull's voice, tinged with the normal irony, but thankfully not very far away. I slowly opened my eyes and forced myself to focus on the gloomy surroundings. I was lying on some sort of wooden bed or cot, in a brick-walled double cell. A shaft of sunlight speared through a small barred window high up the wall, highlighting a patch of the hideous green paint adorning the bricks. Cull was sitting on a similar

98

bed some six feet away against the opposite wall, filling his pipe.

'What time is it?' I asked.

'Midday.'

I raised myself on one elbow, and turned my head to face the big man. The aches and pains in all parts of my body counteracted the wave of nausea that suddenly swept over me; I had to decide which was the lesser of two evils. 'Midday? Good God, have I been asleep all night and all morning?'

'No. It's midday Sunday. You've been unconscious for two days.'

'*Two days*? Where are we?'

'A Metropolitan Police cell, Whitechapel.'

'What?'

Cull nodded. 'The police doctor checked you over and concluded that you are suffering from mild concussion. You'll live.' He paused for a moment, lit his pipe and continued. 'It would appear that the Whitechapel area is crawling with undercover police officers. Apparently, we were beaten up by policemen.'

'Bastards.'

'It could have been worse.'

'How much worse?' I said, holding my head in my hands. The throbbing across my left temple continued unabated.

'Beaten to death on a Whitechapel pavement. How does that sound?'

I paused for a moment, and tried to ignore the waves of nausea passing over me. I took a deep breath 'Why are we still here? What are we charged with?'

'Drunk and disorderly, disturbing the peace, resisting arrest. I'm sure they'll find something interesting. I did manage to take two of them down. They won't be patrolling the streets for a while.'

I nodded, lay back on the bed and stared up at the ceiling. This whole situation didn't make much sense to me. If Superintendent Cutbush had informed police officers working in the Whitechapel area about Cull and I, why would they launch such a violent attack upon us? Unless they were under orders to do so, of course. Other than Cutbush, I was at a loss to know who would have the authority to order such an attack. It could have been a mistake, but even I, as gullible as I am, didn't believe that.

I lay back on the bed and drifted off into a light sleep. The sound of jangling keys and then the cell door clanging open brought me back to my senses. Thirty seconds or even thirty minutes could have passed, it was difficult to judge as I was losing track of time. I opened my eyes to see a uniformed constable beckoning Cull and I out of the cell. He ushered us into a drab corridor, the brickwork painted with the same horrendous green paint as the cell. With an expression of practised disdain on his face, the officer locked the cell door and marched us down the corridor towards the charge room some twenty yards further along.

We were positioned in front of a large desk, behind which sat the rather intimidating figure of the Charge Sergeant. With my dirty and dishevelled clothing, and a face covered in dry blood and ugly bruises, I probably looked uncannily like most of the miscreants that stood before him on a daily basis. Cull, however, stood rigidly to attention, clicked his heels together and stared impassively across the desk at the Sergeant. How the big man managed to keep his eyes so cold and devoid of emotion was something I would have to ask him about at a more convenient time.

I, on the other hand, felt like weeping.

'Gentlemen, you were arrested for common assault.'

I was stunned for a moment as the words slowly sank into my befuddled brain. '*What*? Are you serious?'

The Sergeant leaned forward. 'I'll tell you when to speak, *Mister* Batchelor. And this is not the time.' He paused for a moment and turned over several pieces of paper on the desk, before placing them into a grubby file. 'The victim, Michael Kidney, has decided not to press charges.'

'*Victim*? What the fu…'

Cull dug his elbow into my ribs before I could finish the sentence.

The Sergeant, seemingly unaware that I'd just had the wind knocked out of me, picked up the file and placed it into a drawer. 'No charges are being laid. You're free to go.'

'Thank you very much,' I muttered, with as much sarcasm as I could muster.

'Careful, Mister Batchelor,' said the Charge Sergeant, rising from his chair, 'these cases can be reopened.

I didn't doubt that. I smiled at the officer, just about managing to move my blood-caked lips, and then followed Cull out of the building.

As we made our way back to the house in Church Lane, I sensed a general feeling of unrest on the streets. Although, it was only as we approached Berner Street that we noticed the increased activity. A large crowd had gathered around a building halfway down the street, the women shouting various obscenities at the lone police officer standing guard outside the entrance gate.

I followed behind Cull as he pushed through the crowd and stood before the officer, whom I immediately recognised. We had encountered the same police officer at Hanbury Street after the murder of Annie Chapman. Cull's dressing down had obviously made an impact, as there was nothing slovenly about the officer this time. The man was standing rigidly to attention, staring straight ahead, completely oblivious to the baying mob that had surrounded him.

He nodded his head in my direction as soon as he noticed me. 'Good Afternoon to you, Mister Batchelor. Blimey, what happened to your face?'

'I walked into a door.'

'Some door.'

'Yes, indeed.' I pointed in the direction of the building. 'What happened?'

'Another murder, I'm afraid.'

'May we go in?'

The constable slowly shook his head. 'Sorry, sir, orders.'

'Whose orders?'

'Superintendent Cutbush. Nobody is allowed to enter the building or inspect the scene of the crime, and that includes you or Mister Moffat. The Super's orders were quite clear.'

Cull stepped forward. 'There's been an improvement in your attitude since I last saw you. Well done, lad.'

'Thank you, Sir.'

'Do you know the name of the victim?'

'I do, but I can't reveal that information either. Sorry.'

'If I say a name, would you say yes or no?'

The constable nodded. 'Oh, I think I could do that, sir.'

'Elizabeth Stride.'

'Bloody hell, how did you know that?'

'Lucky guess?'

The constable leaned forward and lowered his voice. 'There was another murder last night about an hour after this one. It was on City Police territory, Mitre Square. I can tell you the name of that victim.'

Cull took a step forward. 'Catherine Eddowes?'

The constable's mouth dropped open.

'What's your name, lad?'

'Albert Stephens.'

'Albert, you have the makings of a good police officer, or a soldier. If you need any career advice, you know where I live.

'Appreciate that, sir.'

'Could you possibly forget that you've seen us here today? We'd prefer certain people not to know.'

A wry smile spread across the constable's face. 'It has been a busy day, sir. Can't be expected to remember everything that happens, can I?'

Berner Street was only a couple of streets away from our house in Church Lane. The first thing Cull did when we arrived back was to feed and water Domingo, who didn't seem any the worse for Cull's prolonged absence.

I brewed a pot of Earl Grey tea and now sat facing Cull across the sitting room table.

'How did you know?' I asked.

'Know what?'

'The victims' names.'

Cull dropped a slice of lemon into his tea. 'Elizabeth Stride told us. It was as simple as that. She knew something, as did Catherine Eddowes. We have to find out exactly what that something was.'

'Is this a conspiracy?'

'Possibly, but we need more information on the last two murders before we can make a judgement like that. There's been four murders since Nathan Bromley died on London Bridge, and, according to Elizabeth Stride, all the victims knew each other. I think that's significant.'

'It's also circumstantial.'

Cull nodded. 'It is, but there was one other thing that Elizabeth said to us.'

'I missed that as well. Sorry.'

'Don't apologise, and don't make judgements about people, listen to them.' Cull sipped from his cup and then continued. 'Elizabeth said there were five women sharing a space in that lodging house, but she never named the fifth woman, because, unfortunately, Michael burst into the yard at that moment. We need to know that fifth name.'

The sound of a horse's hooves interrupted the conversation. A hansom cab had pulled up outside the house, clearly visible through the sitting room window. I moved across to the window and peered through the curtains. Charles LeGrand had exited the cab, walked up the path and opened the front door.

'It's our erstwhile employer,' I said, moving back to the breakfast table. 'Wonder what he wants?'

LeGrand entered the room with a flourish. 'Good afternoon, gentlemen, this won't take long.' He paused for a moment, glanced disdainfully around and then stared straight at me. 'I'm dismissing you both from my employ.'

Cull picked up his cup and sipped the tea, his face a blank canvass. Only a slight twitch of his right eye indicated he was containing his anger.

'May I ask why?' I said, pouring a cup of tea for myself but quite deliberately not offering LeGrand a cup; rude under most circumstances, but certainly justified here.

'Incompetence. I have taken on a new assistant and we will investigate the latest two murders ourselves as it appears that little or nothing in the way of new information is forthcoming from this quarter. I also have to say that George Lusk is less than impressed with you both.'

'Well, fuck George Lusk,' I said, casually dropping another slice of lemon into my Earl Grey tea.

Cull nodded. 'Quite so.'

LeGrand dropped two small packets onto the table. 'Your vaudeville humour is quite passé. Those envelopes contain your final salaries, gentlemen, paid up to date. I require you to vacate these premises by the end of next month. October 31, to be precise. Good day.'

LeGrand exited the room in his usual ostentatious way, his cape swirling behind him like some moustache twirling theatre villain. Once again, we heard the clopping of hooves as the hansom pulled away from the kerb.

I ripped open my envelope and placed the single bank note on the table. 'One bloody pound. The fleecing, scrimshanking bastard.'

'John, would you please contain yourself. Listen. This is very interesting. I think we may have touched a raw nerve somewhere. Undercover policemen attack us in the street. Why? Was it a warning? Cutbush, Lusk and LeGrand are members of the Churchill Club, all have similar agendas, and they have used us for a purpose we have yet to discover.' Cull paused and stared at the table. 'I would wager the contents of my envelope that all three are members of the same Masonic Lodge.'

'Never mind that. We only have two pounds between us. We are going to starve.'

'We won't starve. Will you please address the matter in hand?'

I shrugged my shoulders. 'It's not our problem anymore, is it? I mean, is it really worth continuing with this?'

'That's up to you,' said Cull, leaning back in his chair. 'Just remember who started this investigation in the first place. If you hadn't gone to George Street that day, we would never have met. I can go back to driving a cab anytime, what are you going to do?'

It was a good question. I reached into my inside pocket, produced my wallet and removed three white feathers. I placed them on the table. 'I would like to return these to my family.'

'Don't be so melodramatic. You're not a coward. Maybe a bit naive at times but that's no crime. Not yet, anyway.'

'Thank you.'

Cull continued. 'But there's more to this than your honour, don't you think? Remember the day you hailed me in Bond Street? You felt the need to be involved because the senseless murder of an innocent woman disturbed you. Events have moved on since then, the truth is still hidden but the need to be involved is as strong as ever, is it not?'

He was right. Emma Smith gave me three pennies when I was at my lowest ebb. She was a good woman, and probably the first to die a horrible death; how insignificant that incident had appeared at the time. How long ago it now seemed.

'We are close to discovering something of importance,' said Cull, pouring himself another cup of tea, 'something related to these murders, and there are certain people who do not want that to happen.'

'Who are these people?'

Cull shook his head. 'I don't know, but on reflection, you may well be right about the conspiracy theory.'

'Thank you. That's very encouraging. I'm not right about much, you know,' I said, basking in the unfamiliar glow of appreciation.

Of course, I didn't realise it at the time, but the big man was closer to the truth than he could ever have realised. *The Daily News* was about to publish something in their morning edition that was destined to shock the whole country. Even as Cull and I sat in that house in Whitechapel, the Fleet Street presses were rolling. A text that would come to be known as the *Dear Boss* letter was about to be printed in full.

The Central News Agency had received the letter earlier in the day. Written in red ink, it contained the name that would forever strike fear into Londoners.

Jack the Ripper.

Monday
October 1, 1888

I could barely contain my excitement as I spread The Daily News across the breakfast table.

'Do you want me to read out the whole letter?'

Cull shook his head. 'Just the relevant pieces will suffice. Is it dated?

I ran my finger down the page and across the text of the letter. 'Yes. 25 September.'

'Written a full six days before the latest murders. That's a good trick.'

'It certainly is.' I paused for a moment before continuing. 'The first couple of paragraphs are just baiting the police. He talks about *Leather Apron* and how he's laughing at the efforts to catch him.' I quickly scanned the next paragraph before continuing. 'He goes on to say he's down on whores and won't stop ripping until he's buckled, whatever that means, and then he says what grand work the last job was. Now, this bit is interesting. He says he's going to clip the lady's ears.'

Cull nodded. 'So we have to find out if either Elizabeth Stride or Catherine Eddowes had their ears clipped.'

'Do you know what strikes me about the text of this letter?'

'No, but I think you'll probably tell me anyway.'

I sat down and stared across the table at Cull. 'The words are phrased in quite an odd way, almost like an educated person trying to appear semi-literate.'

'That's a very good point. What if...'

The sound of heavy knocking on the front door interrupted the conversation. I stood up, walked through the hallway and opened the door. The young policeman we had encountered at various sites, now dressed in civilian clothing, was standing on the doorstep looking very self-conscious.

'Good morning,' I said, looking down at him. 'It's Arthur, isn't it?'

'Albert, sir, Albert Stephens.'

'Yes, of course it is. Please come in, Albert.'

Cull stood up, nodded at the young man as he entered the room, and then indicated that he should take a seat at the table.

'Tea?'

'No thank you.'

'What can we do for you, Albert?'

'I'm sorry, but I don't know how to put this,' said the young man, hesitantly.

Cull stood up, walked to the cupboard and retrieved a bottle of whiskey. He placed the bottle and two glasses on the table.

'It's a bit early, but you look in need of a pick-me-up,' he said, filling both glasses.

'Thank you, sir. I worked a double shift last night.'

'Take your time, lad.'

'Some of the constables down the station have been talking about these murders, and we're not happy at the way they've been investigated. Of course, it's not our place to question senior officers, but it's not right.'

'Go on.'

'We've been told not to discuss this with anybody, but I think it's scandalous. I noticed several words chalked on a wall in Goulston Street. I wrote them down in my notebook because it struck me as odd.'

Albert dipped into his pocket, produced the notebook and pushed it across the table.

Cull picked it up, glanced at the open page and read the contents aloud. 'The Juwes are the men that will not be blamed for nothing.'

'How odd. A double negative and grammatically incorrect,' I said, sitting at the breakfast table. 'Why would anybody write that on a wall?'

'Is the spelling correct?' asked Cull.

Albert nodded. 'I made sure of that, sir. I always keep good notes, known for it. People are saying that it was the Ripper himself who wrote that on the wall after the murder of Lizzie Stride.' He paused and glanced first at Cull and then at me before slowly shaking his head. 'Couldn't have been.'

'Why not?' asked Cull.

'I saw those words written on that wall three hours before the murders happened. Apart from anything else, the murderer wouldn't have had the time to stop and scrawl on a wall.'

Cull glanced down at the notebook. 'Interesting.'

'But it was evidence and it was erased before they could take any pictures of it,' said Albert. 'That's not good enough. The City Police wouldn't do that. They do the job properly.'

Cull leaned forward in his chair. 'Who ordered the epithet to be erased?'

'The newspapers are saying it was Sir Charles Warren.'

Cull's face creased up in disbelief. 'The Metropolitan Police Commissioner was in Goulston Street?'

Albert nodded. 'It wasn't him who gave the order, although he will probably take responsibility.'

'How do you know that?' I said, slowly sipping my tea.

'I was there when it was erased. The Commissioner wanted it photographed. He was furious when he arrived on the scene and saw the bare wall.'

'So, who did give the order?' asked Cull.

Albert picked up his glass and swallowed a large mouthful of whiskey. 'Superintendent Cutbush,' he said, shuddering slightly.

Albert led us down Berner Street, a narrow street that runs north to south, and stopped outside the gates leading into the yard of Number forty. He pushed open the heavy gates and Cull and I followed him into a surprisingly large courtyard. The surrounding building was an old two-storey edifice that looked as though it had seen better days.

'They print a newspaper journal here,' said, Albert, waving his arms around expansively. 'And hold meetings in the hall.'

'What sort of newspaper is it?' I asked, glancing around the yard.

'*The Worker's Friend* is a radical Jewish paper that seems to attract the worst type of Anarchists and Communists. A lot of strange people come through these gates, I can tell you.' Albert stopped talking for a moment and glanced around. Although he seemed to be enjoying his spell in the limelight, he also appeared uneasy. 'The C.I.D. tried to close it down on several occasions, but as usual, they failed. I really don't know why they bother.'

Cull began pacing around the courtyard, deep in thought. He stopped suddenly, stared into the distance and spoke slowly and clearly, as though thinking aloud. 'A murder is committed on the property of a Jewish newspaper. A chalked message mysteriously appears on a wall some time before the murder occurs. And, interestingly, the message contains the Masonic spelling of *Jews*. What do you think, John? Is somebody trying to tell us something?'

I shrugged my shoulders. 'I'm not sure. I think the more pertinent question is why would Cutbush erase it?'

'If our conspiracy theory is correct and Cutbush, LeGrand and Lusk are involved in some way, then the murder of Liz Stride was unexpected and probably shocked them.'

'As would the message on the wall,' I said, glancing at Cull who was slowly nodding his head in agreement. 'Particularly if you are correct about the Masonic connection.'

Cull turned to face Albert. 'What's your view? You were on the spot.'

'I don't think this was a Ripper murder.'

'Why not?' said Cull.

'I was here when the doctor examined the body. Being a bit of a nosey beggar, I listened to what he was saying.' Albert paused for a moment, swallowed hard and continued. 'Liz Stride's throat was cut just below the angle of the jaw. According to what the doc said, it was a clean cut and she died of blood loss due to the severing of the carotid artery. I think that's how you say it. There were also deep bruises on both her shoulders.'

'Was that the extent of her injuries?' asked Cull.

Albert nodded.

'No mutilations?'

'Nothing. Course, the murderer could have been disturbed. Some witnesses saw Liz Stride arguing with a man around the time of the murder. Perhaps he didn't have time to do what he normally did to the bodies.'

'No, I don't believe that,' I said, walking slowly across the courtyard. 'It's twenty paces across, and it was dark. He could have dragged her into a corner and done anything he wanted. Nobody would have seen anything. He's done it before.'

Cull nodded. 'You're right. This is different from the other murders. Albert, do you know if her ears were clipped?'

'That's a good point, Mister Moffat. The killer did *not* clip Liz Stride's ears. But I spoke to a mate of mine in the City Police and he told me that Catherine Eddowes ears *had* been cut, just like the Ripper said he would do in that letter.' Albert walked across the yard and leaned against the left side of the gate. He pointed down at paving stone nearest to the wall. 'She was found here lying on her back, head towards the rear of the yard. Her face was turned towards the wall and she was still warm.'

Cull approached the wall and knelt down. 'Was anything found on or near the body?'

'She had some grapes and sweets in her hands. She also had some cachous in her pocket. Oh, and she had a fresh flower attached to her dress. I found that a bit odd.'

Cull stood up and slowly paced around the yard for several minutes. He looked so engrossed in his thoughts I decided to remain silent, and wisely, so did Albert.

'The grapes and sweets had to be gifts,' said Cull, suddenly stopping halfway across the yard. He placed his hands on his hips and stared directly at the two of us. 'The Cachous are used to disguise the smell of alcohol on her breath. She has a fresh flower in her dress; what does all this tell you?'

Albert swallowed hard and then shrugged his shoulders. 'She was turning a trick, and it went wrong?'

Cull shook his head. 'No, it indicates that she was meeting a friend, a lover, somebody she cared about. She wanted to be at her best. She wouldn't care if it were just another threepenny trick. No, Elizabeth got dressed up for her new boyfriend.'

Albert looked confused. 'Why would her new boyfriend cut her throat?'

'I don't think he did. It wasn't the new boyfriend she was seen arguing with; it was the old one,' said Cull. 'And he would have been very jealous.'

'My God, Michael Kidney,' I said, feeling my heart racing.

Albert looked more confused than ever. 'Who?'

'Liz Stride had an obsessive, not to say, maniacal boyfriend by the name of Michael Kidney. Have you heard of him?' asked Cull.

Albert slowly shook his head.

'He called on us a couple of days ago without the benefit of an invitation,' I said, glancing at Albert. 'I'd like to talk to him about this.'

'Oh, so would I,' said Cull, clenching and unclenching his fists.

We arrived back at the house in Church Lane and Cull immediately bridled up Domingo to the cab, having decided to drive to Dorset Street. We hoped to find Michael Kidney at home and discover exactly what he knew about Liz Stride's death. In less than five minutes, we were on our way across Whitechapel.

Unfortunately, Albert had to leave us to report for his afternoon duty. He promised to call on us when he was next off duty, or if he had any new information to impart. I knew the young man's enthusiasm had impressed Cull. If we'd had the means to do so, we would have paid him for his inside knowledge and expertise, but with just two pounds between us, that was out of the question.

Cull drew the cab to a halt outside 38 Dorset Street. This particular location, on the north side of Whitechapel, was a striking example of how unchecked criminality can prosper. The police, who considered it beyond the pale, very rarely patrolled this street. It was full of barely concealed criminal lairs, opium dens and other such undesirable residences. The derelict, decrepit houses and back alleys that lined both sides of the street reminded me of the foul Rookery slums that had existed in the Westminster area in the 1830's, most of which had now, thankfully, been demolished.

I stepped onto the pavement and knocked on the front door of number 38, causing several pieces of ancient paint to flake off the battered door. Cull had hitched Domingo to a bridle post and was now standing behind me, his eyes flicking quickly from side to side. Although the street appeared to be completely deserted, the feeling of prying eyes boring into the back of my neck was overwhelming. I could see that Cull felt the same way.

The front door slowly creaked open to reveal a bleary-eyed Michael Kidney. Considering it was the middle of the afternoon, it was indicative of the nocturnal lives led by these rapscallions that he should be sleeping at such an hour. My mother usually served tea and cucumber sandwiches to her guests at this particular time of the day.

'What the fu...' began Kidney, before recognising the two figures standing before him. He quickly tried to slam the door shut, but Cull reacted instantly. He sprang forward, pushed me out of the way and smashed his shoulder into the door, knocking Kidney backward into the hallway.

The odour emanating through the open front door was simply indescribable, and as I entered, I had to raise my handkerchief to my nose to dampen the malodorous stench. The poorly lit hallway was a hovel, and even that word is inadequate to describe the true horror of what lay before us.

Cull seemed unaffected as he grasped Kidney by his collar and hauled him into what I presumed was the sitting room, which turned out to be no less disgusting than the entrance. Except for a table and one chair, there were no other pieces of furniture in the room, although a filthy blanket lay in one of the corners. Several orange boxes completed the ensemble.

No cucumber sandwiches served here.

Cull had lifted Kidney up by the throat and placed him against the wall, leaving the man's feet dangling a couple of inches from the ground.

'Michael. I'm sure you remember me.'

'Fuck off,' said Kidney, spitting the words out through clenched teeth.

'John, will you remove the knife from Mister Kidney's right trouser pocket,' said Cull, turning his head slightly towards me.

I stepped forward and gingerly placed my hand into the greasy depths of Kidney's trouser pocket. With the tips of my fingers, I grasped the handle of the knife, slowly removed it from the pocket and placed it carefully into Cull's left hand.

It was a bone handled, wickedly sharp Wharf man's knife with a stained seven-inch blade. I immediately wondered if this was the knife used to snuff out Liz Stride's life. Sadly, the only thing I remembered about her was the distinctive grey colour of her eyes, and the way they sparkled in the evening light. It was a shame, a damned shame.

'Michael, tell me what you fear most?' asked Cull, keeping Kidney effortlessly pinned up against the wall. 'It's not death, is it? That would be far too easy.'

'You'd better fuckin' kill me, cos if you don't I'll come lookin' for you, by God, I will,' said Kidney, speaking with increasing difficulty. Cull was slowly applying more pressure to Kidney's neck, causing the criminal's eyes to bulge.

'I'll tell you what you fear, Michael.' said Cull, raising his left hand and slowly moving the tip of the knife towards Kidney's reddening face. The blade stopped a fraction of an inch short of the criminal's right eye. 'You fear blindness. Am I right?'

Cull relaxed his grip, but Kidney remained silent.

'I'm going to ask you once. And then I'm going to push this knife through both your eyeballs, one at a time and very slowly. Tell me what happened last night?'

He needed no thinking time. He slowly nodded his head.

Cull released his grip on Kidney's neck and shoved him into the corner. 'Sit there, and don't move, Michael. If you so much as twitch a muscle, you know what will happen. Did you kill Elizabeth Stride?'

Kidney shook his head.

'Tell me about it.'

'The bitch said she was leavin' me for a new boyfriend, some rich bastard from up West. So, she gets all dolled up, flower and everythin' and meets him in the Bricklayer's Arms. I follow them around, and it was only when they started kissin' and huggin' in Berner Street that I got angry.'

'And you slit her throat. If you can't have her, nobody else will, right?'

'No, it wasn't like that. I grabbed her by the shoulders and shook her around a bit, and yes, I was a bit rough. But I was just tryin' to make her see sense. Listen to me, big man, as God is my witness, I never killed her.'

Cull glanced across at me and then turned his gaze back to Kidney. 'Carry on with the story, Michael. I believe you.'

Kidney sniffed and then wiped the back of his hand across his nose. 'I walked back to the pub, had a few more ales and then went home. Liz still wasn't back by half twelve, so I went out to look for her. As I was walkin' down Berner Street, I had a feelin' she might be around that area somewhere, I heard screams. She was bein' attacked by a bloke I'd never seen before. I don't know what happened to the fancy Dan she'd spent the night with, but he'd disappeared. Well, I wasn't havin' that.'

'What did you do, Michael?' asked Cull.

'I ran towards them, but they scarpered. Poor Lizzie was lyin' there in the yard with her throat cut. I got out of there pretty quick cos I knew I'd get fingered for it.'

'What do you mean *they* scarpered? Was there more than one person attacking her?'

Kidney slowly nodded his head. 'There was a bloke pullin' her around, and another standin' on the opposite side of the street just lookin' on. Maybe he was a lookout, or somethin', I don't know. He was smokin' a white clay pipe as though he didn't have a care in the world.'

I walked across the room and squatted down in front of Kidney. 'Can you describe the two men?'

'Yeah. The one with the knife was about 35-years-old. He was short, brown hair, fair skin, small reddish moustache, dark jacket and trousers, and a blue cap with peak. You know, like those stupid anarchist types wear.'

Cull looked thoughtful. 'What about Mister Pipe-Smoker?'

'He was a good bit older, early fifties maybe, tall, black bushy moustache, waxed at the ends. He was wearing a long dark overcoat and a hard felt hat. Looked like a copper, if you ask me.'

Cull walked slowly toward Kidney, towering over him as he cowered in the corner. 'Anything else you want to tell us, Michael?'

'You know about the chalk message on the wall?'

Cull nodded.

'I was in the Bricklayer's Arms last Friday and some bloke gave me ten bob to write a message on a wall in Goulston Street. Said it was a joke. Told me to do it around half past midnight on the thirtieth, but I couldn't be bothered waitin' around until that time, so I wrote it about eight in the evenin'. Couldn't see how the time would make any difference, know what I mean?'

'How did you know what to write?' asked Cull.

'He gave me a bit of paper and said I had to write on the wall exactly what was on the paper.'

'And you did?'

Kidney nodded his head.

'Can you describe him?'

'Not really,' said Kidney. 'I had a few ales that night, and I never really noticed. I mean ten bob is bloody good money for doin' bugger all, isn't it?'

'Are you going to tell the police what you know, Michael?' asked Cull.

'Not bleedin' likely. We don't talk to the coppers around here, not worth the bother. Who can trust those bastards?'

Cull glanced across at me and then slowly nodded his head.

Michael had posed a good question.

A very good question.

Wednesday
October 10, 1888

Hyde Park is a fashionable meeting place for the great and good of London. Abutting Kensington Gardens, it forms a vast open space a mile and a half in length and three quarters of a mile wide. Without the wide-open spaces of Hyde Park, London Town would surely suffocate under its own obnoxious odours.

Cull and I entered through the south side at Albert's Gate, one of eight entrances that led into the park. After a short, but bracing walk in the winter sunshine, we arrived outside the Humane Society establishment, located discreetly on the north side of the Serpentine Lake.

Somebody had slipped a typed note under our front door in the early hours of the morning, rather too surreptitiously for my liking, requesting that we meet an unnamed person at this particular time and location. I had been in favour of declining the invitation. Cull, however, had successfully argued that any information we received, regardless of the source, could only benefit the ongoing investigation.

We had been at the meeting point for no more than two or three minutes when a short man in his mid-forties suddenly appeared, and stood before us grinning inanely. His attire was slovenly, his slouching, oleaginous demeanour reminiscent of the sleazy salesmen who inhabited the less salubrious tailoring establishments in the Soho area.

His gaze rested upon me. 'Mister Moffat is it?' he asked in a rasping south London accent.

'No, I'm John Batchelor.' I raised my hand and indicated Cull. 'This is Cullen Moffat. And you are?'

The man removed his billycock hat and bowed, inclining his shining baldhead slightly more towards Cull than me. 'Uriah Garrett, chief crime reporter, *Evening News*. Pleased to meet you, gentlemen.'

'Why do you require these clandestine arrangements, Mister Garrett?' I said, grasping the clammy hand he proffered and shaking it as briefly as possible. 'You could have knocked on our front door and we would have spoken to you.'

'You're missing the point, sir. I've been investigating these murders for several weeks and your names crop up repeatedly. I suspect you're becoming an irritant to the authorities, and I see no point in giving them more information than necessary. Hence this meeting in the park.' He tapped the side of his nose twice.

'You have something to tell us, don't you?' said Cull, filling and lighting his pipe in one smooth movement.

'Yes. I have been authorised to offer you a payment,' said Garrett, pausing for effect. Cull and I stared at him with blank expressions lodged upon our faces, a look we had perfected over many months. Garrett continued in the same rasping tone of voice. 'My newspaper will pay you thirty pounds per month as a retainer, plus a lump sum should your information lead to the arrest and conviction of Jack the Ripper. I intend to be the reporter who writes the exclusive story. It will be the pinnacle of my career. I shall probably retire forthwith.'

'Why do you think *we* can help you?' said Cull, blowing a stream of foul Afghani smoke up into the chill morning air.

'I'd wager that you both know more about these murders than probably anybody else in London, bar the murderer, of course. Would I be correct in that assumption, gentlemen?'

I shook my head. 'Mister Garrett, I do not think that…'

Cull raised his right hand, cutting me off in mid-sentence. 'Anybody can claim to be a reporter, Mister Garrett. For all we know, *you* could be Jack the Ripper.'

Garrett shrugged his shoulders and nodded in agreement. 'You're right, sir, and I did expect this response. However, I can prove who I am.'

'Really,' I said, 'and how do you intend to do that?'

Garrett reached his grubby hand into an inside pocket and produced a battered copy of *The Illustrated London News*, which he handed to Cull.

'No doubt you remember the case of the corrupt Scotland Yard detectives tried at the Old Bailey back in '77. Several Metropolitan Police officers colluded with two of the most consummate rascals in the annals of crime. I broke that story, gentlemen. Without my investigations, the evidence would not have stood up in court. I'm rather proud of this edition.'

Cull unfurled the paper and scanned the front page, a wry smile slowly creeping across his face. He nodded and then handed the soiled newspaper to me. Several melodramatic line drawings covered the entire front page, including a very good illustration of '*Famed Fleet Street Reporter, Uriah Garrett*'. Even in a favourable drawing, the image was that of a bald headed, poorly dressed caricature. It was, however, irrefutable; the man was definitely who he said he was.

I offered the newspaper to Garrett, who carefully folded it and placed it back into his pocket. 'Gentlemen, it may be advantageous to the investigation if we pool our knowledge,' he said, passing a large envelope to Cull. 'This is your first payment.'

Cull placed the envelope into his pocket without checking the contents. 'How much do *you* know about these murders?'

Garrett shook his head and shrugged his shoulders in an insouciant, world-weary manner. 'Surprisingly little, actually. Certain officers within the Metropolitan Police appear to have embarked on a conspiracy of silence. Either that or they have no ideas about anything; which is probably closer to the truth.'

I glanced at Garrett as he spoke; I thought it unlikely that he could contribute anything worthwhile to our investigations. A slovenly appearance usually indicated a slovenly mind, and I had taken an instant dislike to the man.

'How many murders do you attribute to Jack the Ripper?' asked Cull, struggling to light his pipe in the stiff breeze now whipping across the lake.

'Seven in total. Ranging from Annie Millwood in March to Catherine Eddowes the other night. I have no direct evidence, and I could be wrong, but I'm not convinced the same person committed all the murders. It just doesn't feel right. Purely my intuition, of course.'

Cull slowly nodded his head. 'Shall we take a constitutional through the park? I'll explain to you why it doesn't feel right.'

We set off on a north-easterly path, heading towards Marble Arch at a leisurely walking pace. Although I remained a step behind them, I could hear every word they said. Cull slowly and painstakingly outlined the whole story, as he knew it. The various expressions that flitted across Garrett's grey-stubbled face were priceless. He heard how we had unmasked Surgeon-Major Nathan Bromley as the original killer, a man who had brutally slain Annie Millwood and poor Emma Smith. Cull also recalled the gruesome events at George Yard Buildings, where Bromley butchered the unfortunate Martha Tabram, leading to the hair-raising cab chase through the dawn streets, and culminating in the untimely demise of the murderer on London Bridge.

Cull described our relationship with James Maybrick and his particular involvement in events. He also related, and it was at this point that Uriah Garrett's jaw dropped, how we believed LeGrand, Cutbush and Lusk were possibly involved in a Masonic conspiracy. Cull made it quite clear that most of this was supposition; we had little proof of anything.

We eventually reached the north-east corner of the park and all three of us sank gratefully onto a bench overlooking the Park Lane thoroughfare, which stretched away beyond the newly painted, green railings.

'That's quite a story, Mister Moffat.'

Cull nodded. 'Indeed. However, according to Liz Stride, five women shared a lodging house space in Flower and Dean Street, four of whom have succumbed to the murderer. If we are to prevent another murder, we urgently need to discover the name of the fifth woman.'

'I will begin working on that immediately,' said Garrett, writing in a small notebook.

'There is much we have yet to discover,' said Cull, once again lighting up his foul tobacco. 'Do you have details of Catherine Eddowes' murder?'

'I do. The City Police are far more accommodating than our friends in the Met, and, I have to say, far more skilled in the art of criminal investigation, or so it would appear.' Garrett flicked through the pages of his notebook and then slowly read out the details. 'Catherine Eddowes' body was found by a P.C. Watkins at 1.45 am in Mitre Square, which as you know, is on the edge of the City of London Police boundary.'

Cull nodded knowingly; as an ex-cabbie, he was well aware of boundary lines. A conversation regarding police jurisdiction ensued, although I felt excluded and slightly intimidated by the verbal dexterity demonstrated by both men. Strangely, I found myself beginning to warm to Uriah Garrett, who was far more profound and intelligent than he had first appeared. Cull had warned me on numerous occasions about first impressions and again, I had been guilty of making an instant judgement based purely on appearance.

It suddenly occurred to me that I had not contributed anything to the conversation for some time. I was also aware of the growing rapport between the two men seated to my left, which in truth could only help the investigation.

'Did the murderer pick Mitre Square deliberately?' I asked, attempting to sound as erudite as possible. It was a thankless task at times.

'A good observation,' said Garrett, nodding. 'Committing the murder just outside the Metropolitan Police area ensures more interest. Somebody lured the victim to her death at this carefully selected location. This was not a random murder.'

'Was Catherine Eddowes mutilated?' asked Cull, tapping his smouldering pipe against the heel of his boot.

An expression of sadness moved slowly across Garrett's face. 'Her throat was cut through to the bone. The mutilation was extraordinary, by far the worst of any recent murder. The murderer crudely butchered the victim's face, indeed a piece of the ear dropped off as the body was undressed at the mortuary. The mutilation of the ear was probably done to justify what was written in the *Dear Boss* letter.'

Cull inhaled a deep breath and then slowly exhaled. His face reddened in anger. 'Were any internal organs removed?'

'The intestines had been pulled from the body and placed over the right shoulder. The left kidney and part of the womb were also missing.'

'The damned Masonic connection, yet again,' said Cull, an expression of distaste spreading slowly across his face. 'Could you possibly check if LeGrand, Cutbush and Lusk belong to the same Masonic Lodge?'

Garrett made another entry in his notebook.

Cull paused for a moment before continuing. 'It might also be worth researching Masonic rituals, particularly the business of placing the intestines over the shoulders.'

The reporter mouthed the words *rituals* and *intestines*, and then continued scribbling in his notebook.

'Were there any witnesses to Eddowes' murder?' I asked.

Garrett glanced up from his notebook. 'Three gentlemen leaving the Imperial Club at 1:30 am saw a woman they identified as Eddowes standing with a man in Mitre Square. They described the man as being about 35-years-old, short, fair complexion with a small reddish brown moustache. He was wearing a dark jacket and trousers, and a blue cloth cap with a peak. They only noticed his appearance because he seemed agitated.'

'Interesting,' said Cull, lighting yet another pipeful of his disgusting tobacco, 'that describes the same man who was seen with Liz Stride minutes before she was murdered.'

Garrett nodded and closed his notebook.

Cull and I arrived back at the house in Whitechapel a little after midday. We were surprised to see a glum-faced Albert Stephens sitting on the doorstep, a large carpetbag lying by his side. He immediately scrambled to his feet as we strode up the path.

'Begging your pardon, Mister Moffat, sir, but I had to call without the benefit of an invitation', he said, breathlessly. 'I'm sorry, but I really don't know how...

'Calm down, lad,' said Cull, opening the front door and ushering Albert into the house. 'You'll have a seizure.'

I strode through into the kitchen and immediately began brewing a pot of Earl Grey. Cull, as was his midday custom, retrieved the bottle of whiskey and two glasses from the cabinet and poured two large drinks for himself and Albert.

'Right, lad, let's hear it.'

Albert downed his glass of whiskey in one gulp. 'I've been dismissed from the force. Ordered to clear off this morning after I finished my duty, no notice, nothing. Lost my room at the Station House, too.' Albert sighed, reached for the whiskey bottle and refilled the two glasses before he realised what he had done. His face reddened and he looked suitably embarrassed.

'What reason did they give you?' asked Cull.

'Cavorting with known criminals, the Superintendent said.' Albert downed another slug of whiskey and slowly shook his head. 'I don't cavort with criminals, Mister Moffat. I don't even know what *cavorting* means.'

I placed the teapot on the table and covered it with an elaborately knitted tea cosy. I had filched the cover from the kitchen in Gloucestershire the night I had left the family home. It was a small piece of my past life I carried around with me; mawkishly sentimental, I know, but strangely comforting. I turned my thoughts back to the present and addressed Albert.

'It means associating with undesirables, people like us, in fact. What do you intend to do now?'

'I'm not sure, sir,' he said, glancing across the table at Cull. 'I was thinking on what you said, Mister Moffat. I don't have any family and I'd quite like to join the Army.'

'I'll speak to some people for you, don't worry about that.' Cull pushed his whiskey glass aside and poured himself a cup of tea. 'How much did you earn as a constable?'

'Sixteen shillings a week, plus board.'

Cull slowly nodded his head. 'In the meantime, how would you like to work for myself and Mister Batchelor?'

'I would, sir. Thank you.'

'Steady on, lad. I haven't told you the salary, or explained your duties. Don't sell yourself cheap, you're worth more than you think.'

'Right, sir,' said Albert, sitting up straight and effecting what he probably thought was a forceful tone of voice. 'So, what salary are you offering and what duties will I be expected to undertake?'

'Twenty-five shillings a week, plus full board, and your duties will be anything we...

Albert raised his hand before Cull finished. 'I'll take it.'

I leaned across the table and shook hands with the young man, who I estimated to be of a similar age to myself. With his police training and improved attitude, he would definitely be an asset to our investigations.

The sharp rapping sound on the front door caused Albert to leap out of his chair like a jack rabbit, and move swiftly towards the hallway. It would have been an understatement to say he looked extraordinarily keen to take up his duties.

Albert returned a moment later and passed a Post Office telegram envelope to Cull, who tore it open and quickly read the message. 'No reply, give him threepence.'

Albert nodded, turned on his heel and left the room.

'Who would send us a telegram?' I asked.

'Uriah Garrett. Rather good work this, John, and achieved in record time, too. He confirms that Cutbush, LeGrand and

Lusk are all members of the Cleveland Street Masonic Lodge, located in the West End of London.'

'You were right about the Masonic connection.'

'Yes, but that's not the half of it,' said Cull, glancing across the table. 'When Cutbush saw that writing on the wall in Goulston Street, his heart must have skipped a beat. The word *Jew*, spelt out in Masonic text, would have unnerved him. As a freemason he is honour bound to help fellow masons in any way possible.'

'I'd wager half the senior Met officers are masons,' said Albert, who had returned and taken his seat at the table. His face reddened and he sipped slowly from his teacup. 'And the Prime Minister, too… probably.'

'Yes, but who wanted those words written on the wall in the first place?' I asked.

'Listen to this. In Masonic texts, there is reference to King Solomon sacrificing three Jews who murdered the master mason, Hiram Abiff. He's the man who built the Temple of Solomon in Jerusalem.'

'Very interesting,' I said pouring another cup of tea for myself, and refilling Albert's cup. 'How does that help us?'

'I haven't finished,' said Cull, gently tapping the telegram with his forefinger. 'Apparently, and I quote, 'The three men had their throats cut from right to left, their breast burst open and their innards scattered about the corpses.' Unquote. Sound familiar?'

'Just like the Whitechapel murders,' said Albert, who now appeared to be gaining confidence with each passing exchange

Cull nodded. 'You're right. It's exactly like the Whitechapel murders. If we can locate the fifth woman, she might be able to shed light on this. It's possible that when the five women were staying at the lodging house together, they overheard, or discovered something.'

'And it was something important enough to cost them their lives,' I said, feeling a chill run down my spine. 'What could that possibly be?'

'That's what we have to discover. Right, gentlemen, I have a plan,' said Cull, pouring himself a large whiskey and then mischievously grinning at me. 'It's relatively dangerous, John, but I think you'll like this idea.'

I doubted that.

Thursday
October 11, 1888

I was right. I disliked Cull's plan intensely, even after I had agreed, under protest, to do it. To further our investigations, we required information about the elusive fifth woman, who remained tantalisingly out of reach. We urgently needed to know her name and what she knew. The only lead we had was the information supplied by Elizabeth Stride before she met her unfortunate end. She had told us about the common lodging house at Flower and Dean Street; regrettably, most of the miscreants in the area now knew us, and we could no longer just walk into a lodging house and ask questions.

This is where Cull's plan came into effect.

Against my better judgement, I had agreed to dress as a vagabond and spend the night at the lodging house in question. I had only concurred after learning that Albert, who would also dress as a vagrant, would accompany me.

Both Albert and I were now standing in the yard rubbing our clothes down with horse manure, kindly supplied by Domingo. Apparently, this produced an authentic street odour, although during my entire three years spent living rough I do not recall reeking of horse manure; there were, however, several less odious aromas I would gladly admit to.

'Is this really necessary, Cull?'

'I'm afraid so. You smell too sweet, my friend. Soap and water are not substances recognised by people who frequent lodging houses.'

'How do we go about this? Asking direct questions would not be prudent,' I said, wrinkling my nose as the odour from Albert wafted across the yard.

'With your accent I would suggest you allow Albert to do the talking. They'd tumble you within seconds. Perhaps you could be a deaf mute; say nothing, hear nothing. Improvise.'

I nodded. It made sense. 'Yes, I can do that. I performed in a Shakespeare production at University. *Romeo and Juliet*. I received a literature credit, you know.'

'Well, that will certainly help you survive an East End lodging house,' said Cull, raising an eyebrow and then turning toward Albert. 'Don't ask questions; listen to conversations. The Whitechapel murders have intimidated both men and women. You'll hear plenty of stories, true and false, it doesn't matter; make mental notes of everything you hear. I think you can do this, Albert.'

Albert nodded vigorously. 'Yes sir, I can do it.'

'Good lad. If you both arrive together around nine o'clock, you should get beds for the night.'

Cull, an optimist of the first order, made everything sound so damned easy. Of course, it never was.

Albert and I arrived at the lodging house a little after 9:30 pm. I had previously stayed at several different lodging houses around the London area, but certainly not one as far down the social scale as this. If a person could not afford a bed in such a place, the alternative was the street and certain death in a filthy gutter or rat-infested alley.

All for the want of three pennies.

Rows of terraced houses, neglected by the authorities for many years, bounded both sides of Flower and Dean Street; every single property appeared to be on the verge of collapse. I had no doubt toolers, kidsmen, forgers, and all manner of criminal elements inhabited these houses. It was common knowledge that patrolling policemen would never venture down such a street, not even in groups of three or more. It was yet another sad indictment of the Metropolitan Police.

We entered the lodging house through a door that had probably not seen a lick of paint in the previous twenty years, and passed through into a rubbish strewn reception area. It was plain from the excruciating expression on Albert's face that he had never sampled the delights of an East End doss house. He did manage to avoid wrinkling his nose as the pungent odour of unwashed bodies and rotting food assailed our senses, although his eyes conveyed everything one would ever need to know about malodorous lodging houses.

We stepped forward and stood in front of the little window. A scowling, bull-necked man slowly slid the window open and stared at us for a moment, as though making some sort of judgement. His raised upper lip revealed several blackened and broken teeth, and his obnoxious, foul breath was evident even from a distance of five feet. After several seconds of silence, an expression of benign boredom slowly drifted across his unwashed and unshaven face.

'Threepence a night, no discounts, no hard luck stories. If you don't have it... fuck off.'

Albert slowly counted six pennies onto the small ledge in front of the window.

The man stared directly at me. 'What's wrong with him?'

'He's a deaf mute.'

'Bit simple, is he?'

'No.'

'Cos I ain't havin' no trouble in here, right? Respectable house, this is.' The man picked up the coins. 'Your beds are on the second floor, right-hand corner. Make your tea in the kitchen. Out by nine in the mornin', no bleedin' arguments.' He slammed the small window shut and disappeared.

Albert shrugged his shoulders, turned on his heel and walked away. I followed him through an ill-lit passage that led into a large, sparsely furnished kitchen. There was an open cooking range, blackened by years of misuse, with several battered kettles and pots strewn around. A long wooden table ran down the centre of the room.

The three surly men sitting around the table stared at us as we entered. None of them said a word, but their eyes followed our every move. We sat on a bench that ran along the sidewall, and tried to avoid making eye contact with anybody in the kitchen, including the nervous young man who sat on the bench that ran down the opposite wall. He was no more than about 18-years-old. His eyes flicked anxiously around and he fidgeted relentlessly. It was a most disconcerting sight.

The silence continued for a minute or two, the atmosphere edgy and hostile. I could feel my heart thumping in the centre of my chest.

'Bedlam let out then, has it?' said one of the men, breaking the awkward silence. He gazed malevolently across the room at me. 'We got a couple of lunatics in the house tonight, lads. A penny each to look at 'em.'

A gale of sarcastic laughter echoed around the kitchen.

Albert stood up and moved toward the table. 'Can I make some tea?' he asked, ignoring the animosity directed at us. The more I saw of Albert, the more he impressed me.

'Your mate don't say much, do he?' said one of the men.

'He's deaf and dumb. He can't say much.'

A bald man with a filthy bandana tied loosely around his neck stared at Albert, a sneer playing around the corners of his mouth. He appeared to be the ringleader of the little group. 'You got any tea?'

Albert shook his head.

'Sugar?'

'No.'

'Then you ain't brewin' no tea here, are you, matey?' said the man, leaning forward. 'I can sell you some. Sixpence.'

Albert stepped up and placed sixpence on the table.

The man reached out and pocketed the coin. 'You can have it tomorrow.'

'I think I'd like it now,' said Albert, in a quiet voice.

'Well you ain't getting it now. So, you can fuck off.'

Albert nodded his head and without saying a word, he turned and walked out of the kitchen. I followed behind him, the laughter from the men ringing in my ears.

The creaking wooden staircase we found at the end of the passage led to a long, unlit room with maybe twenty or thirty rickety beds placed in single lines along the walls, most of them occupied. I followed Albert to the right corner of the room which contained two single beds. Each of the beds had a thin, dirty mattress spread across the top, stained with, what I assumed to be, urine and excreta. It was beyond disgusting. Even at my lowest ebb, I had never encountered anything quite as bad as this.

I sat on the bed and found myself gasping for breath. The air in the room was foul, compounded by the appalling lack of ventilation. Most of the occupants of the house never washed, never changed their clothes and the grossly stained floor boards testified to the men's habit of chewing tobacco and expelling the disgusting residue wherever they pleased. The pungent aroma of cheap tobacco smoke pervaded the senses and caused a feeling of sickness and nausea. It was not going to be an easy night.

As ever, tiredness prevailed, and at some point, I must have fallen into a light sleep. I awoke disorientated and fearful, before quickly remembering where I was. I felt suffocated, as though a thick blanket encompassed my whole body. I lay still for a minute or two and allowed my eyes to grow accustomed to the inky darkness that surrounded me. Suddenly, I sensed movement within the room. A swirl of fetid air passed over me as several indistinguishable shapes passed through the darkness and approached a bed to my left.

The sudden shriek of pain startled me and I sat upright, my back pressed against the brick wall behind me. Somebody was being beaten and robbed, and it was probably a nightly occurrence, as nobody in the room seemed keen to intervene.

Albert, who had been in the bed to my right, suddenly appeared by my side. He placed his hand on my shoulder. 'If we don't do something, we'll be next,' he whispered. 'It's the young lad we saw in the kitchen. Those three louts are attacking him. Are you ready?'

I could not guarantee that I was ever going to be ready for conflict, but I reluctantly nodded my head. We moved silently through the darkness until we stood behind the three men. Two of them were holding the young man down on the bed, the other punching him repeatedly about the face.

I moved behind the vicious thug who was orchestrating the assault and tapped him on his shoulder; it was the bald man with the loose bandana tied around his neck. One thing I had learnt from watching Cull punch several people, was that the ferocity of the punch one landed on the victim's jaw was irrelevant. It was all in the timing. Something my father had neglected to mention.

As the man turned his head, I landed a perfect left cross to the point of his jaw, and he sank slowly down beside the bed. I moved towards the man on the left side of the bed, and swayed gently back out of range as he launched a wild swinging punch in my direction.

The sound of a skull cracking made me wince. Unbeknown to me, Albert had brought his old police truncheon with him, and he had used it rather effectively to nullify the first ruffian. He then moved across the top of the bed, and laid the truncheon across the head of the man facing me. Although it was too dark to note the man's facial expression, I expect he was somewhat surprised to receive the thick end of a Metropolitan Police truncheon above his left ear. He'd have plenty to reflect upon when he eventually woke up.

'That has to be worth more than sixpence, hasn't it?' said Albert, dropping the truncheon back into his trouser pocket. 'I suggest we leave here as quickly as possible. I'll wager the manager knows all about these assaults. Probably takes a cut from these louts to look the other way.'

I glanced down at the sobbing young man. 'What do we do with him?'

'He comes with us. We leave him here, they'll kill him.' Albert leaned forward, grabbed the young man by his collar and raised him up. 'What's your name?'

'Edward,' he said, trying to regain his breath.

'Edward, you're coming with us.'

We grabbed the surprised young man from the bed and moved toward the stairs with undue haste. A gas burner on the landing provided a weak light, which cast deep shadows down the stairs.

'What the fuck's goin' on 'ere?' said the manager, suddenly appearing on the top stair. 'Think you can just walk away like that, do you?' He tapped a cudgel into the palm of his hand to emphasise each word.

Albert was right. It was obvious that the man standing before us was taking a cut of the proceeds from the louts, and he did not appear best pleased with our actions. To my left I could feel Edward shaking uncontrollably, almost as though he were having a fit. I placed my arm firmly around his shoulders and pulled him gently into my side.

The manager stepped forward, raised the cudgel and brought it down in the direction of Albert's head. Fortunately, Albert nimbly sidestepped the blow, rammed the truncheon deep into the man's midriff, causing him to double up, and then laid him out with one sickening blow to the man's forehead.

'Good night,' said Albert, stepping over the prone body.

We followed Albert down the stairs and out of the house. I was not looking forward to facing Cull and explaining why we had gleaned no information, or why we had not even managed to stay the night in the lodging house.

Little did we know that Edward was about to surprise us all by inadvertently supplying information that would change the course of our investigations and lead to the unmasking of the man terrorising the East End of London.

We were about to learn the identity of Jack the Ripper.

Friday
October 12, 1888

As I had anticipated, Cull was not best pleased.

'So, you learned nothing at all,' he said, dropping a piece of lemon into his teacup. 'And the name of the fifth prostitute remains a mystery. Not your best night's work, John.'

'I'm sorry. Events conspired against us,' I said sipping my Earl Grey. 'We did rescue Edward, though.'

'Yes, you did. How old are you, young man?'

Edward sat up straight in his chair and stared intently at Cull. 'Seventeen, Sir.'

'Why in God's name were you staying in a place like that?'

'My parents live in Devon. I came up to London to…' He paused for a moment as his eyes filled with tears.

'Seek your fortune,' I said, feeling a pang of sympathy for him. It wasn't too long ago I was doing something similar, if under slightly different circumstances. 'And now you do not have the wherewithal to get back home.'

Edward nodded his head. 'I lost my job in the City last week. I was staying in a respectable boarding house in Batty Street, but I couldn't afford the rent, so I left Wednesday evening. The doss house in Flower and Dean Street was all I could afford. I have no savings,' he said, inhaling a deep breath. 'Don't worry about me, sir. I'll get another position and find somewhere decent to live.'

'No you won't,' said Cull, reverting to his stern army voice. 'You will send a telegram to your parents telling them you're on your way back home.'

135

'But I...'

Cull raised his hand, placed a pound note on the table and slowly pushed it across to Edward. 'And you'll send that telegram today, young man. Use the money for your train fare.'

'Thank you very much, sir, I'm obliged,' he said, picking up the banknote and placing it into his pocket. 'That's the second kindness I've been shown since arriving in London. Perhaps it's not such a bad place after all.'

Albert, who had been tending to Domingo, entered the kitchen, washed his hands at the sink and sat at the table. 'What's that about London?'

'Edward said he's been shown kindness on two occasions since he arrived here,' I said, pouring Albert a cup of tea. Despite him bathing for the best part of an hour, I could still detect a pungent whiff of horse manure about his person.

'Salt of the earth, Londoners,' said Albert, sniffing his sleeve. 'I think I got the smell of horseshit off me clothes. Anyway, two acts of kindness, eh? What was the first?'

Edward took a deep breath. 'There was another lodger at Batty Street; a Dr. Frank Townsend. Claimed he was Irish-American. When he heard about my misfortune, he offered me a job as his assistant, and I probably would have accepted except he was...' Edward paused for a moment. 'Well, he was just a bit odd.'

'Odd?' said Cull. 'In what way?'

The young man's face burned brightly. Before he answered, he ran his finger around the inside of his grubby collar. 'I think he preferred the company of gentlemen.'

'Are you saying he was homosexual?' said Cull, in a matter of fact tone, although his brow remained furrowed.

'Yes, but there was something else.' Edward paused and took another deep breath. 'I couldn't sleep one night, worrying too much, you know, and I heard Dr. Townsend and his friend come in. I opened my door slightly and saw them entering the Doctor's room. The blood was everywhere. On their hands, their coats, everywhere. I assumed they'd been in an accident of some sort. It wasn't my place to ask questions.'

Nobody spoke for several seconds. We all stared intently at Edward, which seemed to unnerve him.

The young man appeared bemused. 'What?'

'Can you remember which night this was, Edward?' said Cull, leaning forward. 'Think hard, lad, it's important.'

'Oh, that's easy. It was a Sunday morning, the thirtieth. I know because I'd lost my job the day before.'

'What time did you see them on the stairs?' I asked, my stomach muscles tightening. I suddenly felt very nauseous.

Edward shrugged. 'I can't be certain, but around two-thirty.'

'I'm going describe Doctor Townsend to you, Edward,' said Cull. 'Just say yes or no after each part.'

Edward nodded.

'He was a man in his late 40's, early 50's,' said Cull.

'Yes.'

'Quite tall.'

'Yes.'

'Bushy black moustache, waxed at the ends.'

'Yes'

'Smoked a white, clay pipe?'

'Yes.'

'He often wore a long dark overcoat and a hard felt hat.'

'That's an exact description of Doctor Townsend. How did you know?'

Cull ignored Edward's question and banged his fist on the table. 'Doctor Frank Townsend is Mister Pipe-Smoker. He stood in the shadows and watched as the man in the blue peaked cap cut Liz Stride's throat. Fortunately, the engaging and lovable Michael Kidney arrived on the scene, and the good Doctor could not do what he normally did; butcher dead women. So, they moved on to Mitre Square and Catherine Eddowes. I suspect the location was a deliberate ploy to involve the City Police as well as the Met.' Cull paused and stared intently at Edward. 'How often did the Doctor's friend stay at Batty Street?'

Edward shrugged. 'He stayed about three or four times. I heard some noises during the night. Quite disgusting, really.'

'Can you describe this other man?' asked Cull, patently ignoring Edward's obvious discomfort.

'He was in his mid-thirties, short, with a fair complexion, and a neatly trimmed moustache. He was very abrasive and not very friendly. I didn't like him at all.'

'What sort of hat did he wear?'

'It was a blue peaked cap. Quite distinctive, really.'

Cull glanced across the table, his eyes boring into me. 'Who does that sound like, John?'

'No, surely not.'

Cull nodded. 'George Lusk.'

'If you're correct,' said Albert, looking confused, 'then Polly Nichols, Annie Chapman, Liz Stride and Catherine Eddowes were all killed by these two men.' He paused for a moment. 'Why would they do that?'

'Because the women knew something important,' said Cull, his mouth tightening into a thin line.

Albert shifted uncomfortably in his chair, his face a picture of concentration. 'No, I didn't mean that. I meant they could have killed these women and quietly disposed of the bodies. Nobody would have noticed, or even cared. Why attract so much attention by bringing a Masonic connection into it?'

Cull shrugged his shoulders. 'Maybe the women were killed in this brutal manner to undermine police authority. Maybe they wanted to cause unrest among the lower orders, who knows?' He paused and then glanced at Edward. 'What's the landlady's name at Batty Street?'

'Mrs Maurer, a German lady. She speaks a little English.'

'That's good. Maybe we can confuse her,' said Cull, staring directly across the table at Edward. 'What's your surname?'

'Wilson,' said Edward, an expression of bewilderment slowly spreading across his face.

Cull tapped the table. 'This is what we are going to do.'

Number 22 Batty Street was one street east of Berner Street. The lodging house was a pleasant, well-appointed, detached building. It backed up against Dutfield's Yard, the place where Liz Stride was brutally murdered. It was too much of a coincidence, and I could feel the expectation and tension rising as Cull and I approached the front door and entered the house.

I glanced around the depressingly gloomy hallway, noticing, as ever, the dusty and neglected décor. Despite the shabby interior, it appeared to be a quietly serene house, and we waited expectantly at the bottom of the staircase for several moments. Eventually, I cleared my throat in an extravagant manner, attracting the attention of a very plump lady, who emerged from a side room.

'May I be helping you, gentlemen?' she asked in a strong German accent.

I stepped forward and inclined my head. 'Good morning. Are you Mrs Maurer?'

'Ya,' she said, frowning slightly as she folded her arms across her ample chest. 'Why you need to know this?

'We are bailiffs,' I said, sticking exactly to the script Cull had outlined. 'We would like to talk to one of your guests. Edward Wilson.'

She slowly shook her head. 'He pays his bill and he goes. A nice young man, Edward. Pity he leaves. Why would bailiffs want to talk with him?'

Cull stepped forward. 'What day did he leave?' he asked, ignoring her question.

'Wednesday.'

'Have you cleaned his room?'

'Not always have time. Today, maybe.'

'Mrs Maurer,' I said, smiling broadly at her. 'We would like to check Edward's room. It's a Court matter. Would you mind?'

She shrugged her shoulders, indicated we should follow her, and waddled slowly up the stairs with some difficulty, her breath escaping in short rasping bursts. We followed her along an unlit corridor. A vague odour of cheap cologne or pomade hung in the air. Mrs Maurer stopped suddenly halfway along the corridor, grasped an ornate brass door handle and pushed a door open. She ushered us both in to the small room and then, surprisingly, left us alone.

Cull and I stood silently behind the closed door for a moment as the woman's footsteps receded down the stairs.

'How are we going to do this?' I asked.

Cull raised his finger to his lips, slowly opened the door and glanced up and down the corridor. According to Edward, Frank Townsend's room was directly opposite. Cull moved slowly across to the adjacent door and listened, his ear pressed hard up against the wood. When he was satisfied nobody was inside, he grasped the handle and pushed the door open. I followed him across the corridor and into Townsend's room.

Cull tugged one of the heavy drapes across the window, allowing bright sunlight to flood into the shabbily furnished room. There was an unmade double bed in one corner, the grubby sheets and crumpled blankets lying haphazardly across the top of the mattress. A single wardrobe and a small writing desk, which had several pieces of paper scattered across the top, filled the rest of the room.

I opened the wardrobe and studied the interior. It contained several jackets, shirts and other items of apparel, although the sickly sweet odour of cheap pomade emanating from inside made me feel quite queasy.

'Why would a professional man stay in an establishment such as this?' I asked, closing the wardrobe door and glancing around the room.

'It's a bolt hole. We wondered how the murderer always managed to disappear into thin air. Now we know. After every murder, Townsend and Lusk moved swiftly through the back alleys and sought sanctuary in here.'

I nodded. 'What are we looking for?'

Cull sat at the writing desk, opening and closing various drawers. 'Anything.'

I glanced around the room. Mrs Maurer's cleaning abilities were not immediately apparent. I noted the thick layer of dust coating the tops of the skirting boards; except for a small section that ran behind the wardrobe. I knelt down, placed my left hand on the skirting board, and took a deep breath. I dreaded to think what I might find. With some difficulty, I ran my hand along the board behind the wardrobe and into the darkness.

My fingers rested on a bundle of crumpled material stuffed behind the wardrobe. 'Dear God, look what I've found,' I said, holding up a man's white dress shirt.

Cull rose from behind the desk, walked across the room and stared at the item in my hand without saying a word. Words seemed redundant at a time like this.

Dried blood stained the right half of the shirt, indicating that the victim's blood had spurted upwards splattering the right cuff and upper arm of the shirt.

'Very careless,' said Cull, handing me a document. 'Maybe he thinks he is above suspicion. Arrogance is a great leveller.'

'What shall I do with this?' I said, holding up the shirt.

'Replace it where you found it.'

I carefully replaced the shirt behind the wardrobe and then read the document Cull had given me. It was confirmation of a booking at the Adelphi Hotel, Liverpool, for three nights starting that day. It was booked in the name of Dr. Francis Tumblety, MD.

I glanced up from the piece of paper. Cull moved across the room and stood in a shaft of sunlight, a thoughtful expression twinkling in his eyes. A slight smile creased his mouth.

'What's the matter?' I asked.

He extended his left hand and slowly uncurled his fingers. Two small brass rings lay in the centre of his palm, gleaming in the light. 'I found these in the desk drawer. They're the rings that were taken from Annie Chapman's fingers.'

'How can you be sure?'

'I removed the other one from Annie's finger. Remember?' Cull slowly uncurled the fingers of his right hand, revealing a single brass ring. 'Look, all three rings are identical.'

I slumped down onto the bed feeling an overwhelming sense of detachment; it was almost too much to take in. 'What shall we do now?'

'Leave everything as we found it. The doctor's arrogance will be his undoing. There is no necessity to reveal ourselves just yet.'

Inexplicably, the obscure trail now led to Cullen Moffat's hometown. We had uncovered two suspects heavily involved in the Whitechapel murders. We knew who they were and we knew how they did it. What we did not know was *why* they did it? A clear motive still eluded us. We quickly realised that the answers to this conundrum lay in the city of Liverpool.

And we had no time to lose.

Saturday
October 13, 1888

The first person I saw in Liverpool was James Maybrick.
Cull and I had alighted from the train at Lime Street Station
feeling slightly the worse for wear after the gruelling five-hour
journey. Albert was the lucky one, having opted to remain at
the house in Whitechapel. If anything untoward happened, he
had instructions to send a telegraphic message to the Adelphi
Hotel.

Young Edward, seemingly unaffected by his misadventures
in London, had returned to his family in Devon. He had no
idea how much he had contributed to our investigation.
History would reveal all.

'What's *he* doing here?' I asked, glancing across the smoke-
filled concourse at Maybrick, who was standing smugly beside
his barouche carriage, complete with a uniformed driver. I'd
only known Maybrick for a short time, but the barouche, a
two-horse, four-seat extravagance, was exactly the sort of
ostentatious vehicle I would expect him to use around town.
The man was consistent, if nothing else.

'I sent him a wire. He knows some of the details,' said Cull,
with a shrug of his shoulders. 'He's a dabbler and an irritant,
but we need his local knowledge.'

'Surely to heaven you have local knowledge?'

'It's been more than forty years since I lived in this city.
Things change.'

I couldn't argue with that. We picked up our bags and
walked toward Maybrick, who greeted us like lost friends. He

obviously had a very short memory, as the last time I saw him he was scuttling out of our Whitechapel living room in a state of acute embarrassment. The man had the skin of a dead rhino.

'Mister Moffat, Mister Batchelor, welcome to Liverpool. I hope you are both well.'

Neither Cull nor I responded, other than a brief inclination of the head. Maybrick beckoned his driver, who carefully stowed our luggage at the back of the vehicle. We drove through the billowing clouds of smoke engulfing the station concourse and out into Lime Street, gradually picking up speed to a gentle trot.

'Gentlemen, I hope you do not think me presumptuous,' said Maybrick, lighting a cigar and leaning back into the buttoned leather seat with practised ease, 'but I have instructed Florence, my wife, to make ready two guest rooms at my home in Aigburth. I trust you have not arranged alternative accommodation.'

'I would prefer to stay at the Adelphi hotel,' said Cull, his voice betraying no emotion. 'We have to watch this man with increased vigilance. He has travelled to this city for a purpose. We believe him to be the Whitechapel murderer.'

'Interesting,' said Maybrick. He paused for a moment before continuing. 'I have a suite retained at the Adelphi hotel for business purposes. You are free to use it any time. Room 132; just ask reception for the key. They do know me. Now, tell me about your enquiries. I'm intrigued.'

Cull, once again, outlined the details of our investigations, albeit a slightly longer version than the one related to Uriah Garrett at Hyde Park. I glanced through the window as we trotted down Lime Street, amazed by the abundance of handsome buildings contained in such a small area. It was plain to see that Liverpool, the second city of the British Empire, fully justified its distinguished reputation.

We turned right into London Road, travelled up a slight incline and then veered left into Gildart Street, my eyes focussing quickly on the street signs as they flashed passed. The carriage eventually stopped in a narrow back street. The handsome buildings had quickly given way to rows of dilapidated terraced houses and tenements. Hordes of children, hands and faces covered in grime, played in the filthy gutters, most of them oblivious to the vehicle that had parked in their street.

'Excuse me, but why are we here?' I asked. I leaned back in surprise as a blackened face pressed up against the window of the carriage, leaving a greasy smear across the glass. It was hard to distinguish whether the face of the child belonged to a boy or a girl.

Cull sighed and stared out of the window on his side. 'I asked Mister Maybrick to make a detour. This is Bidder Street. I was born in that house over there. My mother still lives here. She's 79-years-old next month, that's a good age.'

'Are you going to call upon her?' I asked.

Cull shook his head. 'It's been too long. She wouldn't know who I was.'

'That's no way to treat your mother, Cull.'

'I know.'

'You should be ashamed of yourself,' I said, adopting a sharp tone of voice that irritated even me.

'I am.'

'Good.'

Cull turned his head away from the window and stared directly at me. 'This is why I sent her an allotment from my army pay every month for the past forty years. How much have you ever sent your mother?'

I shrugged and glanced out of the side window at the children gathering beside the coach. Both Cull and Maybrick were staring intently at me. No matter. There are times when it is better to remain silent, and, after due consideration, I deemed this to be one of those times.

The lounge bar of the Adelphi hotel, with its swirling velvet drapes, elaborate crystal chandeliers and mahogany topped tables, was a rather superior place to sip a Martell and Hennessy cognac. The overt pretensions of this provincial hotel were such, that my mother, a lady who practised self-aggrandisement as a spiritual discipline, would have spent her time making copious notes before rushing off to visit her interior designer in Knightsbridge.

In reality, I found it difficult to contemplate the horrors of the Whitechapel murders whilst sitting in such grandeur and I would have preferred to be elsewhere. I had assumed that Doctor Tumblety would adopt some form of disguise and endeavour to remain incognito. As ever, I was wrong. The odour of cheap pomade assailed my nostrils some seconds before the good doctor put in his appearance. A more flamboyant and unrestrained entrance into a room would be hard to imagine.

The description Cull and I had been given was, if anything, understated. Doctor Tumblety, tall and broad shouldered, strode imperiously through the lounge bar, his black cape with red velvet collar and gold fastening chain, swirling in his wake. The green cravat with diamond pin, floppy wide-awake hat and gold-topped ebony cane were rather an extreme fashion statement for a man in his mid-fifties.

'Jack the Ripper?' I whispered, glancing across the table at Cull. 'Are you sure?'

Cull continued to stare at the floor. He answered me without looking up. 'Oh yes, I'm sure. This is our man, without a doubt.' He paused for a moment. 'Did you expect him to be disguised as a Limehouse villain in a penny dreadful novel?'

'Of course not, but I expected him in a disguise of some sort.'

'He is,' said Cull, raising his glass of brandy. 'You're looking at it. Is that the persona of a crazed murderer you see over there?'

Of course, it wasn't, but before I could reply, James Maybrick entered the room, nodding to various people as he passed their tables. He sat facing me and placed his glass of rum on the table in front of him.

'Don't turn around,' said Cull, addressing Maybrick, 'just look in the mirror; the far corner to your right. Do you know who that is?'

Maybrick looked up at the mirror behind my head. 'Yes, of course, that's Doctor Tumblety. He's a regular guest at the hotel. He stays here when he's in the city on business.'

Cull nodded. 'Really? What line of business would that be?'

'Medical supplies, I believe.'

Cull slowly sipped his drink. 'Do you know which part of the city he visits when he's here?

'Yes. He frequents The Beltaine club in Whitechapel.'

I glanced across the table. 'There's a Whitechapel area in Liverpool?'

'It's a road, not an area,' said Cull. 'Rather more salubrious than its namesake in London.'

'Perhaps we should visit this Whitechapel club.'

'It's not an establishment I would visit,' said Maybrick.

'Why not?' I said, somewhat taken aback by Maybrick's forceful response.

'It's not appropriate.'

'We may gain some information if...'

Cull interrupted me in mid sentence. 'Do you want him to spell it out for you in large letters?'

'What?'

'It's a club for homosexuals. We would not be welcome.'

Maybrick drained his glass, turned to face Cull and handed him a room key. 'It's yours for as long as you need it. I've taken care of the bill.'

'Do you know any local cabbies you can trust?' asked Cull.

Maybrick nodded. 'There is one I use when I don't have the carriage. Thomas. He's very good, but there's no need to use a cab, you can use my carriage for as long as you need it.'

'Too obvious,' said Cull. 'I'd like to hire Thomas for three days. Can you arrange that?'

'Of course, anything else?'

'Yes. You said you had influence in this hotel?'

'That's correct.'

'I'd like the room next to Doctor Tumblety. Do these rooms have connecting doors?'

'Yes, they do.'

Cull smiled mischievously. 'Would there be spare keys to these doors?'

Maybrick clasped his hands together and leaned forward. 'With the right contacts, anything is possible.' He paused for a moment, obviously considering his options. 'I'd like to make a request.'

'Yes,' said Cull.

'I want to be involved in the investigation.'

'Of course, you have every right to be involved.'

Maybrick leaned across the table and shook our hands. 'After I have concluded my business, we can meet here later this evening. Shall we say nine?'

I waited until he had walked out of earshot. 'You want *him* involved in our investigation?'

'No.'

'You just agreed to his request.'

'I lied,' said Cull, raising his glass. 'Cheers.'

It was a couple of minutes after nine o'clock the same evening that we found ourselves sitting in the damp Liverpool air. Thomas the cabbie tethered his horse and cab to a hitching post directly opposite the Adelphi and smoked endless paper cigarettes. Cull and I had been inside the cab, staring at the hotel entrance for over half an hour, and the light was beginning to fade.

During this time, Thomas, a slightly built man in his early thirties, left the ceiling flap open and had attempted to converse with me on several occasions. Unfortunately, I understood little of what he said. His accent appeared to be a mixture of Irish and a nasal version of Russian. The only words I grasped were *mate* and *fuckin'*, which he used in every sentence. Cull, on the other hand, seemed to have no difficulty understanding Thomas.

I reached up, grasped the leather handle and closed the ceiling flap. 'I'm sorry. What language is he speaking?'

'He's a Liverpudlian. That's the way we talk.'

'*We*? You don't sound like that.'

Cull shrugged. 'I used to.'

'I don't understand a word he says.'

'That's your fault, not his.'

'Begging your pardon, I'm sure. Perhaps you could translate his pearls of wisdom into the Queen's English for me.'

'No time for that now. Look.'

I glanced through the side window. Tumblety, cane in hand, was standing on the white marbled steps of the hotel chatting amicably to the liveried doorman. A cab eventually entered the in-and-out driveway that served the hotel entrance and reined to a halt, allowing Tumblety to board. The vehicle moved smoothly out of the hotel driveway, the horse picking up a gentle canter, and headed down Ranelagh Street towards the city centre.

Cull moved forward in the seat and spoke to Thomas who was now leaning against a hitching post smoking yet another cigarette. 'Follow that cab, Thomas.'

'Orrite, mate,' said the cabbie, in a language that surely could not have been English. He flicked the cigarette away, unhitched the horse and climbed up into the driving position.

The cab pulled smoothly away and followed Tumblety towards Bold Street, a central thoroughfare. Thomas may have lacked linguistic skills, but by God, he could drive. He kept an even distance behind the cab in front, negotiating bends and curves with consummate skill. Even as we picked up speed along Church Street, the cab remained steady and well balanced, the horse responding instantly to every movement of the reins.

Thomas drove the cab into a sharp right turn at Castle Street, and continued down a roughly cobbled side street without either of us shifting a single inch in our seat. Cull turned to me and slowly nodded his head in appreciation; which was the best endorsement anybody was ever going to get from him.

We eventually stopped some thirty yards behind Tumblety, who had left his cab and entered a shop. The sign hanging above the door proclaimed it to be a Chemist shop.

'It makes sense,' said Cull, leaning back in the seat.

'What does?'

'This visit to a chemist. If he deals in medical supplies, where else would he go?'

'It doesn't make sense to me,' I said, feeling one of my logical revelations coming on. 'Why would anybody need to travel to a Liverpool chemist to collect supplies? Are there no chemists in London?'

'Good point, I suppose.'

'And why is this particular chemist open for business so late on a Saturday evening?'

Before Cull could answer, two ruffians appeared and heaved a large travelling trunk onto the back of the cab. The men glanced around and then disappeared back into the shop. Without warning, the cab took off at a gallop.

'Damn it,' shouted Cull, jumping from the cab and dragging me after him.

I stumbled on the uneven pavement before steadying myself. Tumblety's cab had disappeared into the darkness, the sound of clattering hooves echoing through the warehouse buildings that surrounded us.

Cull looked up at Thomas. 'Follow that cab everywhere it goes. I want to know what happens to the trunk. An extra ten bob if you can get me that information. Go.'

Thomas cracked his whip enthusiastically. The vehicle lurched away from the kerb at speed and rattled into the evening gloom. He was out of sight in seconds.

'Oh, jolly good,' I said, glancing around at the less than inviting surroundings. 'We have no means of transport and no idea where we are. What an excellent way to spend a Saturday evening. I mean, all we need now is a couple of itinerate footpads for company.'

'You know, John, I feel sorry for your late father, who was probably an officer and gentleman. No doubt he despaired of your uncanny ability to find negative qualities in...'

Again, I had overstepped the mark with Cull, but luckily, Tumblety's appearance spared me the usual verbal mauling. The doctor stood at the front of the chemist shop shaking hands with an unseen figure hidden within the confines of the doorway. A moment later, Tumblety walked off into the distance, and the lights in the shop went out.

We followed the good doctor through several darkened, rubbish-strewn alleys that eventually led out into a brightly illuminated street. Cull informed me that we had entered Lord Street, which was quite as impressive as any London location. A variety of shops, their candy-striped awnings providing stylish cover, bordered the street on both sides.

Despite the surprising number of people wandering around, we managed to trail Tumblety without incident. He strolled along, occasionally stopping to look in a shop window. This was a man without a care in the world; death and suffering obviously meant little to him. I could see the scowl on Cull's face tightening as we meandered through the centre of Liverpool. But for me, it was a most pleasant experience, even under these trying circumstances.

We eventually turned left into another wide, well-lit street. Cull did not have to inform me of the street name as it was quite clearly sign posted on a nearby wall. It was beyond irony that we should follow the man believed to be Jack the Ripper into a street bearing the name *Whitechapel*.

We searched the stinking alleyways that led off the main road for half an hour. The area was a baffling maze of converging passages and narrow roads, and it didn't take us long to get lost.

Tumblety had simply disappeared from sight. Cull surmised that he had entered the Beltaine Club, which for obvious reasons did not advertise its location. Try as we might we could not find the entrance to this club. Eventually, we gave up and walked back to the Adelphi hotel, which was less than ten minutes away.

Back in our hotel room, the first thing I noticed was the small brass key placed on the table near the connecting door. James Maybrick had not lied this time; he really did have influence in this hotel.

'Is it wise to enter Tumblety's room?' I asked.

Cull picked up the key, inserted it into the lock and slowly pushed open the connecting door. 'He won't be back until the early hours. He's with his special friends.'

I followed Cull into the adjoining room. The lingering odour of familiar pomade confirmed the ownership of the room. 'Why does he use such inexpensive cologne? It is rather vulgar.'

The room looked odd. It was untidy and in need of the maid's attentions, and yet it looked empty and devoid of life. I could not see any personal items anywhere in the room.

Cull was standing in the middle of the room looking disturbed. 'There's something wrong here.'

He was right. We searched the room thoroughly, quickly discovering that all the wardrobes and drawers were empty. The writing desk situated under the large window was devoid of paperwork, except for the hotel menu and a writing pad.

'Damn,' said Cull, striding back into our room. 'He's gone.'

The desk clerk at reception was singularly unhelpful when we asked about Doctor Tumblety. Indeed, he refused to answer any questions at all.

Cull leaned across the desk. 'You do realise we are residing in this hotel as guests of Mister James Maybrick?'

'No, sir, I did not,' said the clerk.

Cull placed his hand behind his back and covertly beckoned me forward. I stepped up to the desk, understanding exactly how he wanted me to address the clerk. I stared at the man for several seconds before speaking. 'I believe Mister Maybrick would be quite disturbed by your unhelpful attitude,' I said, lapsing into my best Knightsbridge patois. 'If we relay this encounter to him, I expect he will call for your immediate resignation.' I paused briefly to allow the full implications to sink in. 'We are meeting Mister Maybrick shortly and unless you wish to be dismissed from your position this evening, I suggest you answer my colleague's questions. Thank you.'

The clerk swallowed hard and glanced nervously around the reception area. 'I'm so sorry. How may I help?' he asked, in a faltering voice.

James Maybrick's name was obviously more influential than we realised.

'When did Doctor Tumblety check out?' asked Cull.

'More than two hours ago, around nine o'clock, I believe.'

'Did he take any luggage with him when he departed?'

The clerk shook his head. 'No, sir. It was forwarded on for him.'

'Would you give me that forwarding address?'

'The Beltaine Club, Whitechapel.'

'Thank you.'

'You're welcome,' said the clerk, not very convincingly.

We moved away from the desk and stood forlornly in the centre of reception. 'What now?' I asked.

'I don't know,' said Cull. 'A very large whiskey, maybe.'

'Excuse me, sir. Mister Moffat is it?' said a booming voice. It was the imposing figure of the Concierge.

Cull nodded. 'Yes?'

'I'm sorry to trouble you, sir. There's an excitable cabbie outside ranting and raving; says he has a message for you. Sounds like a cock and bull story to me. Shall I inform the police?'

'No, we can deal with it,' said Cull, surreptitiously pressing a half crown coin into the man's palm.

We exited through the main door and out on to the hotel steps. Thomas was sitting bolt upright in the driving position of his cab silently fuming. We climbed into the vehicle without saying a word and fell back in our seats as he pulled out of the Adelphi driveway at some considerable speed.

Half way down Ranelagh Street the ceiling flap opened and an angry looking Thomas glared down at us. 'Fuck me; you two are 'ard to gerold of. I've bintryin to gerrer a fuckin' message to yers for over a fuckin' hour. Yer pair of fu...'

I stopped listening and glanced through the darkened window. Personally, I didn't understand a single word the man said; every syllable just merged into the next. To my ears, it was complete nonsense. Luckily, Cull *did* understand, and he kindly translated as we went along.

The gist of it was that Thomas had followed the cab to Lime Street Station, where the trunk was booked into the freight office. And that was it.

A torrent of words, a simple message.

Oh, and according to Thomas, the Beltaine Club was not a homosexual meeting place, it was an Irish club - Beltaine means *bright fire* in Gaelic - and Mister James Maybrick was a member.

And had been for years.

The man had lied to us yet again.

Fifteen minutes before midnight and Lime Street Station was surprisingly busy as numerous porters and assorted staff milled around the station concourse. Cull paid Thomas the extra ten shillings for his efforts on our behalf, and he dropped us off at the freight office adjacent to platform One. He bid us both a muted farewell before clattering off into the night muttering something about southern fairies.

The man standing before me at the freight counter wore a grubby muffler, a flat cap, and a waistcoat with obligatory gold chain and fob. A posh accent would not intimidate a man like this.

'I'm checking my trunk in,' I said, smiling ingratiatingly at him. 'It's London bound.'

'Name?' asked the man, puffing slowly on his pipe.

'Doctor Francis Tumblety, MD.'

He ran his finger down an ink-stained list in front of him. 'The trunk is booked on the midnight post train. Departs in ten minutes, arrives Euston Road Station 0600 hours tomorrow morning.'

'Would it be possible to travel on that train?'

The man slowly shook his head. 'No.'

Cull stepped forward and laid a pound note on the counter, which was probably a weeks' wages to this man.

'Would you reconsider?'

The man glanced at the counter and then back up at Cull. 'You would have to travel in one of the luggage vans and it's not very comfortable.'

'I've travelled in worse, lad. I was in the Crimea.'

'My father was at the siege of Sevastopol,' said the man, pausing for a brief moment. 'Didn't make it.' He opened a pad and wrote something quickly in pencil. 'If anybody challenges you, show them this travelling pass. The train is standing at platform One. Your trunk will be in the third van down.'

Cull nodded. 'I'm sorry to hear about your father. I expect he was a brave man.'

'He was that. It was a while ago now, but he did his little bit for Queen and Country. '

'Of course he did. You should be proud of him,' said Cull. He leaned forward and shook the man's hand. 'Will you send a telegraphic message for me?'

'Yes sir.'

Cull scribbled several words on a scrap of paper using the man's own pencil. He wrapped the message in a ten-shilling note and pushed it across the counter. 'As soon as you can, it's important.'

The man nodded and placed the note into his waistcoat pocket.

In the distance, we could see the waiting train standing at the platform, clouds of steam belching from the engine in several directions. We walked through the platform gate in full view of anybody who cared to notice, and nobody challenged us. I pulled open the door of the third freight carriage, stepped aside to allow Cull to enter and then stepped in after him.

The interior was gloomy, but not pitch black, and my eyes grew accustomed to the darkness very quickly. Tumblety's distinctive trunk stood out among the crude wooden crates that filled most of the van. 'There it is,' I said, pointing to the left corner.

The trunk, crafted from a particularly fine maple wood, had two highly polished metal bands running across the top of the lid, reinforcing it. Measuring roughly 21 inches tall, 32 inches wide and 20 inches deep, it was a handsome item, indeed. A small brass plate on the front of the trunk read: *John Baker & Co, Kensington.*

I pulled at the sturdy padlocks. Securely fastened, they looked impregnable.

'How do we open it?' I asked.

'I don't know. Can you pick locks?'

I shook my head. 'No. Can you?'

'I've never tried,' said Cull, sitting down on a wooden crate. 'And we certainly can't break it open.'

I ran my hand around the top edge of the trunk. 'There is something we can do. Find out the destination.'

The writing on the label was barely visible in the gloom. 'Good Lord,' I said, straining my eyes to make out the words.

'What?'

I read aloud: 'Dr. Francis Tumblety, Whitechapel Vigilance Committee, 127 Whitechapel High Street, London E.'

It was at that moment that the train lurched forward, its wheels spinning against the track as they fought for traction. The dense smoke from the engine poured into the carriage, forcing us both to cover our faces.

Cull waited until the cacophony of noise had died down; he glanced at the trunk, shook his head and sighed. 'All we have to do now is open the bloody thing.'

I glanced at the trunk. It looked quite solid to me.

Damn it. It was going to be a long night.

Sunday
October 14, 1888

Although there were no windows in the freight carriage, shafts of early morning light filtered through the various ill-fitting boards on the roof and sides of the carriage. The rhythmic sound of the wheels passing over the rails was quite soothing, especially in my early morning state of fragility.

I blinked and raised myself on one elbow, having managed to get a few hours sleep draped unceremoniously across an oblong crate. Cull was kneeling beside Tumblety's trunk.

'Morning,' he said, without turning around. 'I thought you said you couldn't sleep in such trying circumstances. You've been dead to the world for the last three hours.'

'It was hardly restful.' I said, sitting upright on the crate. 'Did you manage to open the trunk?'

'No, but I did discover something of interest.' Cull inclined his head. 'Would you come over here for a moment?'

I clambered from the packing case and knelt expectantly beside the trunk.

'Can you smell anything unusual?' asked Cull.

'I haven't bathed since yesterday but...'

'No, can you smell an odour around the trunk?'

I leaned forward, placed my nose against the trunk and inhaled deeply. 'Rotten eggs?'

'That's sulphur. Anything else?'

I repeated the process. 'Yes. Quite a sharp odour.'

'Ammonium nitrate, to be precise.' Cull laid his hand gently on the lid of the trunk. 'There's also nitro-glycerine in there.'

'Tumblety paid a visit to a chemist. He's a doctor. He would surely have picked up an array of chemicals.'

'These are not just chemicals,' said Cull leaning forward. He placed his nose against the trunk and inhaled deeply. 'Mix sulphur, ammonium nitrate and nitro-glycerine in the correct quantities and you have *Swedish Blasting Oil*; it's used by British Army Ordnance as a high explosive. In a manufactured state, it's perfectly safe.

'Thank God for that,' I said, breathing a sigh of relief.

'Unfortunately, these particular chemicals have not been manufactured. I believe they are in a raw state.'

'But they would need a detonator to explode them. Right?'

Cull paused for a moment, a look of anxiety crossing his bewhiskered face. 'No. Nitro-glycerine explodes when shaken. A violent movement will detonate it. So, if this train should brake suddenly...'

He didn't have to finish the sentence. Even I could work out the ramifications of this situation.

'What time do you have?' asked Cull.

I glanced nervously at my pocket watch. '5:15 am.'

'We're forty-five minutes from Euston.'

'I think we should consider jumping from the train.'

Cull didn't even look at me. He was still staring at the trunk, which seemed to have acquired its own malevolence. 'You can, if you wish, I'll take my chances with the explosives.'

'We could be blown to Kingdom come.'

'Leaping into the unknown from a train travelling at fifty miles per hour is hardly a sane alternative. Unless you have a death wish, of course.'

I didn't. So I moved to the far end of the carriage and squatted down behind a large upright crate. It seemed the right thing to do.

Cull's gruff voice floated eerily down the carriage. 'If this trunk explodes, everything within fifty yards will be reduced to firewood.'

'What would you suggest?'

'A prayer, perhaps' said Cull, sitting on the crate beside me, 'there's not much else available.' He sucked on his pipe and contentedly blew a stream of acrid smoke from the corner of his mouth.

Even as I contemplated an early death, dispatched to a better place after disappearing through the roof of a freight train, I still couldn't escape his foul Afghani tobacco.

'Of course, there are several other lines of thought,' he said.

'And what would they be?'

'Why did James Maybrick lie about his membership of the Beltaine Club? Why is a trunk of explosive material consigned to *The Whitechapel Vigilance Committee*? And what do George Lusk and his friends intend to do with it?'

'Good questions.'

Cull tapped the smouldering pipe against his heel. 'Indeed. And, if we can find answers to these questions, we will solve the Whitechapel murders.'

The train pulled into to Euston Road Station at 6:02 am, just a couple of minutes behind schedule. Never in my life have I been more relieved to arrive anywhere. And I was off the train before it juddered to a halt and half way down the platform before Cull's raised voice halted my flight to safer ground.

'What?' I said, stopping some thirty yards away from a freight carriage carrying enough explosives to reduce all and sundry to bundles firewood at any moment.

Cull leaned out of the open door. 'We're taking this trunk with us.'

Despite my trepidation, I still did not have the courage to say no to him, and for the next couple of minutes I shuffled backward along the platform holding up my end of the trunk with trembling fingers. My whole life, such as it was, flashed before my eyes. Cull, for his part, puffed on his pipe while holding up his end of the trunk, his face a picture of unconcerned serenity.

Uriah Garrett and another man I had never seen before were leaning against a two-horse Landau at the end of the station concourse. Garrett managed to appear even more slovenly dressed than I remembered. As for the other man, he was just an unkempt East End ruffian.

'You obviously received the telegraph,' said Cull, placing the trunk down. I lowered my end and quickly stepped back.

'Yes. Unfortunately, I couldn't find a locksmith at this ungodly hour on a Sunday morning.' Garrett stepped forward and glanced down at the trunk. 'However, I have with me an acquaintance who does not wish to be identified.'

The ruffian strutted forward, a sneering expression lingering at the corners of his mouth. 'Mornin', gentlemen, you want this 'ere trunk openin', is that right?'

Cull nodded. I took a closer look at the ruffian and moved three steps further back.

The man knelt beside the trunk and carefully examined the lock. 'Tricky job this. It's goin' to cost you thirty bob, matey.'

Without saying a word, Cull showed the money to the man, but did not offer it. The man remained on his knees by the trunk, looking puzzled. He shrugged, produced a large ring of keys, and tried several in the two locks before they both sprung open. It had taken him less than a minute.

'Thirty bob for that,' I said, looking down at the man who was still on his knees. 'I thought you said it was a tricky job.'

The man smiled at me, revealing a mouthful of blackened and broken teeth. 'Could you open it?'

Cull moved forward, saving me from more embarrassing exchanges, and stood over the man. 'We'll need you to lock it after we have checked the contents.'

'No problem, me old son, that'll be another thirty bob.'

'No, it won't,' said Cull. He held up the two bank notes in front of the man's face. 'If you want payment, you'll lock that trunk when I tell you to. Thirty shillings is more than enough for this job. Understand?'

The man looked Cull up and down, obviously trying to work out if he should challenge the rather large person standing over him. After a couple of seconds of deep thought, the ruffian shrugged his shoulders. He stood up, and moved across to the Landau, where he stood moodily picking his nails with a long bladed knife.

Cull slowly lifted the lid of the trunk to reveal a row of silver-topped bottles, neatly packed onto a wooden shelf. A single spring either side of the trunk held the shelf in place.

'Quite ingenious,' he said, nodding his head as he examined the shelf. 'It's all here, as I expected. Sulphur, ammonium nitrate and nitro-glycerine. Impressive.'

Garrett looked down into the trunk, frowned and then reached forward. He removed a piece of notepaper from under the shelf and held it up. 'Instructions?'

'Quite possibly,' said Cull.

Garrett sat down beside the trunk and studied the piece of paper closely. 'It looks like measurements. 827 by 84 by 20. There's a fractional figure - $4/7^{ths}$ - and a number written at the bottom of the page which reads, 11101415. Interesting.'

'Would you make a copy of that?' asked Cull. 'We can then replace the original and leave the trunk undisturbed.'

'Of course, it will only take a few minutes to transcribe it,' said Garrett, standing up and walking towards the Landau. He sat in the back seat, placed a notepad on his knee, and began writing.

I glanced at the shafts of diffused morning light streaming into the station through the glass roof of the concourse. It was a beautiful morning. All we had to do now was discover exactly what George Lusk and friends intended to destroy.

How many public buildings were there in London?

Cull paid off the ruffian who quickly slunk away, no doubt looking for more poor souls to gull. We loaded the securely locked trunk onto the Landau and arrived back at the house in Church Lane a little over forty-five minutes later.

Albert was rudely awoken and despatched to deliver the trunk to *The Vigilance Committee*, mainly because he was unknown to the people at that address. I brewed a large pot of Earl Grey tea and placed it on the table between Cull and Garrett.

'The truth is, gentlemen,' said Garrett, slowly shaking his head. 'We can't make a case against them with the evidence we have. It's mostly circumstantial. Tumblety may or may not be *The Ripper*. George Lusk may or may not be the second man involved in the murders.'

'The descriptions appear to fit,' I said, feeling quite deflated as I listened to Garrett's summation.

'The descriptions of *Jack the Ripper* suspects are many and varied. And what about Superintendent Cutbush? Is he really a corrupt officer, or is that just your perception?'

Cull, who had been silent for some time, glanced across the table at Garrett. 'I believe the contents of the trunk are quite incriminating, wouldn't you say?'

Garrett shook his head. 'No. Tumblety could argue that as a Doctor he requires such chemicals as part of his practice.'

'What about the instructions?' I asked.

Garrett placed the copy of the instructions on the table in front of him. 'If we misinterpret these measurements we could go careering all over London and not find a thing.' He paused, glanced at Cull and pushed the piece of paper across the table. 'What do you think these measurements represent?'

'It has to be something large like Buckingham Palace, or even the Houses of Parliament. I've no idea what the other numbers might represent.'

'Before we rush off in all directions, we must make sure we're taking the correct actions.' Garrett paused and placed a document on the table. 'We need hard evidence. Over the last week, I've done a little research into the various suspects. It makes interesting reading, but nothing that would stand up in court.'

Cull poured himself another cup of tea. 'Even if we did gather hard evidence, who would we give it to? If Cutbush is corrupt he would manipulate everything.'

'That's something we'll have to address at a later date,' said Garrett. 'You may find this interesting. Mister George Lusk served as a Second Lieutenant in the British Army 1871-1881. His army record shows a dishonourable discharge from the Royal Engineers April 1881. No further details are available.'

Cull scowled and slowly sipped his tea. 'He was probably discharged for displaying Anarchist tendencies. It has been quite prevalent recently.'

Garrett tapped the table. 'This is the most interesting piece of information. Charles LeGrand, alias Grand, alias Grant was convicted in 1877 for a series of robberies and demanding money with menaces from wealthy females. Quite an odious crime sheet. He served an eight-year prison sentence.'

'How did he ever become a Private Investigator?' I asked, feeling slightly foolish having believed everything LeGrand had said.

'The terms of his sentence stipulated that he reported under police supervision for at least seven years. But he disappeared, emerging some time later in London as *LeGrand of the Strand*, Consulting Detective to the gentry. Totally bogus, of course.'

I shrugged. 'So, what do we do?'

'Let's start with LeGrand. May I suggest you wait until he's out for the evening, break into his rooms and see what you can find,' said Garrett.

I glanced at Cull. 'Tonight?'

He slowly nodded his head.

We hitched the cab to a standing post opposite the familiar building in the Strand and waited. It was now 8:15 pm, and if LeGrand intended going out this particular evening, it would surely be any time soon.

Using the Hansom cab for various activities had proved inspirational. It was a vehicle that could be parked anywhere without attracting undue attention. Cull had reluctantly agreed to let Albert drive the cab through the London traffic, but only after intense persuasion, and several prolonged demonstrations of Albert's driving skills and control of Domingo, which was quite impressive.

I glanced to my right as a carriage drew up against the opposite kerb. The imposing figure of LeGrand emerged from the building some minutes later, resplendent in top hat, white tie and tails. I tapped Cull on the shoulder and he leaned forward in the seat. He gazed across the road, his face devoid of expression except for a persistent twitch above his right eye.

We allowed fifteen minutes to pass before exiting the cab. Albert, who was sitting proudly atop the Hansom in the driving position, mischievously doffed his cap as Cull and I crossed the road and entered the building. We made our way up to the third floor without incident. Still attached to the door of number 138 was the polished brass plate I had used to examine my battered face on my first visit to these premises.

I found myself savouring this particular moment. Whilst in his employ I had noted that Charles LeGrand considered himself to be of superior intellect to most people. Fortunately, and despite his ostentatious entrance into our sitting room in Whitechapel with dismissal notices and paltry final salaries, LeGrand's superior intellect that day did not extend to asking for the return of his room key. Gaining entry to his rooms was now a matter of inserting the key and hoping LeGrand had not changed the lock.

He had not.

The sitting room was as I remembered it. The ornate desk piled high with documents, the upright Regency chair still faced the bookcase; nothing had changed. When I had first entered this room all those months ago, I had suggested that something was amiss with the décor in the room, something that evoked an atmosphere of expense without style. It was now obvious. Knowing that Charles LeGrand was a fraudulent impostor and a convicted criminal explained his expensive and one might say vulgar, lack of taste.

I moved to the window and opened the heavy brocade curtains slightly, allowing some of the ambient gaslight in the Strand to filter into the room; it was enough light to aid us in our search.

Cull gently placed his hand on my shoulder. 'Remember the position of everything. If there's any incriminating evidence here it will be in this desk.'

I nodded and began searching through the drawers on the left side of the desk. The top drawers contained receipts and statements, but nothing pertaining to our investigations.

I glanced at Cull who was carefully searching through the other desk drawers. 'Anything?'

'Not yet, but remember, this man is not as clever as he thinks.'

I reached the third drawer down and tried to pull it open. It refused to move. 'Damn, this drawer is locked. We can't force it, LeGrand would know. Another dead end.'

'Not necessarily,' said Cull, gently moving me out of his way. 'Fortunately, I know how to get into a locked drawer. A misspent youth, I'm afraid.'

'Really?' I said, slumping down into the familiar Regency chair. 'You do surprise me.'

Cull pulled the second drawer open to its fullest extent, waggled it slightly and then slowly removed it, leaving a gaping hole. It was now possible to access the drawer below.

He reached down into the locked drawer and removed a small cardboard box, which he set down on the desktop. 'How interesting. It's addressed to George Lusk.'

I placed my hand over my nose and mouth as Cull slowly removed the lid. Wedged inside the box was a disgusting piece of rancid offal. Dark bloodstains splattered the bottom and sides of the box. The odour was nauseating.

'What in God's name is that?' I said, gasping for breath as the putrid smell assailed my nostrils. Even when I'd worked in the Lambeth Bone Works rendering week old carcasses, I'd never smelt anything quite as bad.

'It's half a kidney. A couple of weeks old, I'd wager,' said Cull.

'Is it human?' I asked, not really wanting to contemplate the reality that it might be.

Cull shrugged. 'Hard to tell. I would imagine it's more for effect. Shock value.'

The possibility that it might have been Catherine Eddowes' organ was even more revolting. How could any sane person do something like this?

Cull cautiously retrieved a bloodied piece of writing paper from within the box. As he read the contents, a wry smile creased the corners of his mouth and he slowly shook his head. A childish hand had scrawled the words across the paper in glutinous red ink. It read:

> From hell
>
> Mr Lusk
> Sor
> I send you half the Kidne I took from one woman prasarved it for you. tother piece I fried and ate. it was very nise. I may send you the bloody knif that took it out if you only wate a whil longer
> Signed
>
> Catch me when
> you can
> Mishter Lusk

I handed the letter back to Cull, who had sat down facing the desk. He stared thoughtfully at the desktop and then replaced the letter and the bloodied box back into the drawer. 'Now we know for sure that Jack the Ripper does not exist.'

'Anything else in there?' I asked, somewhat reluctant to plunge my own hand into the unknown.

Cull shrugged, leaned forward and delved into the depths of the drawer. He retrieved a bundle of papers and placed them on the desktop. Even from where I was standing, I could see the original draft copies of the *Dear Boss* letter published in the *Evening News*.

'I couldn't put my finger on what bothered me when I first read that letter,' I said, tapping the papers. 'Look, the fifth line down reads, *Grand work the last job was...*'

Cull nodded. 'LeGrand, Grand work. I didn't see it either. I think we are dealing with a master egotist.'

I reached forward and picked up a receipt that had fallen from the pile of papers. It was a bar bill for twelve pounds and fifteen shillings, dated March 3rd 1888. 'That's a hefty bill. Obviously likes a drink, does Charles,' I said, passing the receipt to Cull.

'There's no company name, but the address is 19 Cleveland Street, London, W.' Cull paused for a moment. 'Why does that address sound familiar?'

We both remained silent for a moment. I took a deep breath. 'I don't understand why they are complicating the issue. Why indulge themselves in a woeful series of melodramatic letters, and Masonic murder rituals? It's a worse plot than one of those penny dreadful novels you read.'

'It makes perfect sense, John. Let's suppose you wanted to blow up a prestigious building in London. It would help your cause if the attentions of both the Metropolitan and the City of London Police were diverted away from your activities, wouldn't it?'

'Of course.'

'A series of murders occur, each one more brutal than the last. Senior officers resign, questions are asked in Parliament;

even the Queen is concerned. A mythical character emerges, *Jack the Ripper*, disrupting normal life and causing havoc in a huge swathe of East London. Officers from both police forces flood the area in search of a homicidal maniac.'

I slowly nodded my head. 'Leaving other parts of London light handed.'

'Exactly,' said Cull, rising from the chair. 'It is imperative that we find the fifth woman Elizabeth Stride spoke about.'

'Why is that so important?'

He paused for a moment. 'Because she knows the truth.'

The evening traffic trundling along the Strand was relatively light, allowing Albert to make good time as we headed back to the East End.

'I think Albert is rather a good driver,' I said, leaning back into the leather seat. 'You are a bit harsh on him.'

'His control of the reins leaves a little to be desired,' said Cull. 'And his approach to that last corner was unacceptable. Most horses sense when a beginner is behind them, and they don't like it. Domingo knows his position on the road and he probably feels very confused. Poor old bugger.'

The ceiling flap flipped open and Albert stared down at us. 'Excuse me, I may be a novice driver, but I'm not deaf.'

'Don't talk to the passengers, driver. The best cabbies are seen but not heard.'

'I'm not a damned cabbie. I'm doing you two a favour,' said Albert, indignantly. 'Right. I'm doubling the fare.'

Cull reached up and closed the flap. 'Cheeky pup. Youth of today don't know their place.'

A muffled voice drifted down from the driving seat. 'I can still hear you.'

Nothing more was heard from Albert as he concentrated on his driving, doing rather a sterling job, I thought. We arrived back at the Church Lane house some fifteen minutes after leaving the Strand.

Cull turned to face me. 'We need to get the information about the letters and that vile kidney to Uriah Garrett as soon as possible. Did he say he would call on us tonight?'

'Yes, I believe he did. Around 10:00 pm.'

'What time is now?'

I glanced at my pocket watch. 9:35.'

Cull nodded.

Albert jumped down from the driving position and pulled up the cab doors. 'There you go, guv'nor,' he said, touching his cap in mock reverence. 'That'll be three and six pence for you and your friend, without tip.'

'If you're not careful, lad, you'll be getting the thick end of my boot up your jacksie.'

'In that case, I think I'll go in and make a nice pot of tea,' said Albert, turning on his heel and walking quickly towards the front door.

'To hell with tea,' said Cull. 'I fancy a very large…'

It is difficult to describe with any accuracy what happened next, as I didn't see anything. I just felt it. A blast of hot air and debris hit the side of the cab, smashing the door shut and blowing in the right side window. The vehicle turned over onto its left side, the shafts dragging the horse over with it.

Cull's body cushioned my fall as I tumbled sideways. He grasped the leather handle on the right side of the cab, which immediately broke off in his hand. He smashed against the left side window, which shattered into razor-sharp shards of glass, several of which pierced his left shoulder. Although my breathing was laboured in the dust-laden atmosphere, other than a throbbing ache in my ears, and a stinging sensation on the right side of my face, I felt no pain.

Cull had risen to his knees and he was running his hands over my legs and arms. 'I can't feel any obvious breaks. Do you have sharp pains anywhere?'

I shook my head. He grasped my collar and dragged me out through the front of the cab, which was lying on the road at a crazy angle.

We both sat down on the edge of the pavement and stared at the carnage in front of us.

'Don't touch your face, John. There are several shards of glass embedded in your right cheek.'

'Are you all right?' I asked, not knowing what else to say.

He paused for a moment and then glanced down at his left shoulder, which was soaked in blood. 'A flesh wound isn't going to kill me, but I may have just retired from cabbing.'

The left wheel, blown off the cab's axle by the force of the blast, now lay in the middle of the road, slowly spinning. The main structure of the vehicle was an unrecognisable heap of wood and metal, held together only by a tangle of reins and bridle. The tears suddenly welled up into my eyes.

'Cull...'

'I know.'

Domingo was lying on his side, surrounded by an ever-widening pool of blood. Part of the shaft had broken off and pierced his right side.

He was dead.

Cull's face was ashen, his hands shook uncontrollably, but he still managed to stand up and pull me to my feet. 'Albert. We must find Albert.'

The blood was running freely down my face, and I could now feel the shards of glass sticking out of my cheek. The throbbing had turned to intense pain. 'How bad is it? Tell me.'

'You'll live,' he murmured, moving unsteadily towards the house and what remained of the front entrance. The whole door frame, part of the facade and most of the hallway had gone. It was possible to see right through into the kitchen and beyond.

Albert's broken body was lying on the right side of the path. The explosion had blown both his legs and his right arm off, leaving just bloodied stumps. Strangely, his face, although pitted with small splinters, appeared undamaged by the blast; he looked as though he'd fallen asleep.

Cull removed his own jacket, wincing as he pulled it over his bloodied shoulder and placed it across Albert's face. He stared down at the body for a moment, took a deep breath and then staggered slowly down the path, looking neither right nor left. He stood on the pavement among the debris swaying from side to side. He stood like that for a minute or more, just staring into the distance. Eventually, he knelt down on one knee and gently stroked Domingo's bloodstained head, before tipping forward and slumping into the gutter next to the dead animal.

At that point, I had no idea if Cull was dead or alive.

Thursday
October 18, 1888

The slovenly, unkempt figure of Uriah Garrett was the first person I saw when I opened my eyes. He was slumped on the side of my hospital bed noisily eating a grape. When all this was over, I fully intended to take him to my tailor and forcibly dress him in attire that was more suited to his position in life – whatever that was. And a few culinary manners aimed in his direction would not go amiss, either.

'Matron will not be pleased with you, Mister Garrett. You are not supposed to sit on the bed.'

He shrugged. 'This happens to be a private room paid for by my newspaper. I'll sit where I please.'

I glanced to my right. Cull was lying in the next bed, asleep and snoring with his usual intensity. At least some colour had returned to his cheeks. 'How is he?'

'He's as good as anybody is ever going to be with a hundred stitches in their shoulder. He also suffered severe concussion. It could have been worse. He's not a young man.' Garrett paused, popped another grape into his mouth, and chewed noisily. 'You were severely concussed too. You've both been drifting in and out of consciousness since the explosion. We've all been quite concerned.'

'What day is it?'

'Thursday the 18th. You have been here five days. Don't worry; I've been busy following up numerous leads.'

I felt my face. It was swathed in heavy bandages. 'Damn, how bad is it?'

'Fifty stitches, I'm afraid. I won't lie to you, John. You will have heavy scarring on the left side of your face. The surgeon did his very best, but, you know...'

I nodded. 'As Cull would say, don't fuss yourself with things you can't change. I'll just have to get on with it, won't I? No choice really.'

'You may not be quite as philosophical when you read this,' said Garrett, holding up a newspaper. 'This is an edition of *The Times* printed the day after the explosion, Monday the 15th. Apparently, it was an unfortunate accident.'

'*What*?'

'Reported as an accidental gas explosion. Look here.' He tapped the front of the newspaper. 'The City of London Gas Company has accepted responsibility. A Metropolitan Police spokesman stated that a section of fractured piping led to a explosion that killed one man and seriously injured two others in Church Lane, Whitechapel.'

'Is the police spokesman named?'

Garrett's eyes narrowed and he slowly nodded his head.

'Oh, let me guess,' I said, feeling the anger rising within me. 'It wouldn't be Executive Superintendent Charles Henry Cutbush by any chance?'

'It would,' said Garrett, laying down the newspaper and picking up another. He pointed to the main headline. 'On a different tack, this is yesterday's edition of *The Times*. George Lusk received a bloodstained letter headed *From hell*, and a box containing half a human kidney. Quite disgusting, but I'm not convinced it has anything to do with *Jack the Ripper*.'

I nodded. 'And you would be right. We found that letter and the kidney in LeGrand's desk the night we broke into his rooms. We are definitely on the right track.' I paused for a moment, trying to recall the details. My brain felt extremely woolly. 'There was something else.'

Garrett stood up and moved towards me. 'What?'

'I can't remember.'

'Well, try,' he said, rather sharply.

'I'm not a well man, Uriah.'

'Pair of damned Jessies,' said Cull, his strident voice rising from the bed to my left. 'We need to know about 19 Cleveland Street.'

Garrett opened his notebook. 'What do you want to know?'

'Several things. Is it a Masonic club? Homosexual? Who visits? Names? Times? It's the key to finding the fifth woman because I believe she worked there, and when we do find her we'll gain a better idea of what these people intend to do.'

I turned to face Cull. 'I thought you were concussed.'

'I am, and I can still remember more than you.'

Garrett sat down on the edge of Cull's bed and opened his notebook. 'Any thoughts about motive? I mean, what do these people have to gain? I'm thinking of Lusk, Tumblety, etc.'

Cull slowly raised himself up in the bed and leaned back against the headboard. 'Of course we've thought about it. We just haven't reached any significant conclusions.'

'Right,' said Garrett, glancing through his notebook. 'I have reached a conclusion. I'm not quite sure how close to the truth I am, but what do you think of this? The whole episode boils down to Irish-American hatred of the British Empire in general and Great Britain in particular. George Lusk is of Irish descent *and* an anarchist. If he can destroy this Government, he will certainly try. I believe that both he and Tumblety have connections to *The Fenians* and several other anti-British organisations and I'd wager they were not best pleased with the defeat of the Irish Home Rule Bill.'

'How would damaging the British Empire help their cause?'

'I don't know,' said Garrett, irritably. 'I'm just speculating, please bear with me.'

I shrugged. '*The Fenians* blew up Scotland Yard in '84. That didn't make much difference to anything.'

'No, but this time their actions might incite armed rebellion in Ireland,' said Garrett, reading from his notebook. 'Don't ask me how they intend to do that. I have no firm ideas, but we have to find out. And quickly.'

'I understand what you're saying about Lusk and Tumblety, but what has Charles LeGrand got to do with this?' asked Cull.

'I believe he's their banker. He may provide all the finance. I doubt if he cares what happens in Ireland, or anywhere else for that matter, as long as he gets a good return on his investment. He's an opportunist who places expediency above principle. He's also the weak link.'

'Why did he send us to Whitechapel? Doesn't make sense,' said Cull.

'Oh, but it does,' said Garrett, tapping the notebook in front of him. 'Initially, he probably thought your presence would cause confusion and create unrest in the East End. He didn't know about your background as a Military policeman and once you began to uncover uncomfortable facts, he had to remove you from the equation.

'And Cutbush?' I said, feeling slightly light-headed.

'While you gentlemen have been resting here, I have been quite busy,' said Garrett, smugly.

'Will you just get on with it,' said Cull.

'Superintendent Cutbush has no interest in Governmental or Irish matters whatsoever. He's just an officious buffoon who goes about his business in the East End of London annoying all and sundry.'

Cull nodded. 'We did notice. Please get to the point; if you have one.'

'I've researched Superintendent Cutbush extensively and I've discovered some rather interesting information.' Garrett paused for a moment, flicked through his notebook and then continued. 'He has a nephew. Thomas Haynes Cutbush.'

'Why is that important?' said Cull, becoming more agitated.

'Young Thomas Cutbush led an idle and useless life before being committed to the Broadmoor mental institute, where he was certified. Apparently, he liked to go out *Jobbing*.'

'Jobbing?' I asked, unfamiliar with the word.

'It means stabbing young ladies in the rear end with a sharp implement,' said Garrett. He paused and then glanced at each of us in turn. 'Gentlemen, I believe Superintendent Cutbush is being blackmailed by Lusk, LeGrand and Tumblety. It may have started around the time you two arrived in Whitechapel. If the information about his lunatic nephew enters the public domain, Cutbush's police career will come to an abrupt end and he will lose a substantial pension. He has to do exactly what he's told, whether he likes it or not.'

Cull nodded. 'Interesting. But there are still two questions that need answering.'

Garrett popped another grape into his mouth and chewed noisily. 'And what would they be?'

'How do we find out who or what they intend blowing up?'

'And the second question?'

Cull leaned back in the bed and closed his eyes. 'How in God's name do we stop them?'

Friday
October 19, 1888

They buried Albert today. His handsomely carved headstone, paid for by Uriah's newspaper, stated that he was just twenty-two-years-old and had died in a tragic accident. Other than the three of us, Cull, Uriah and I, there were no other mourners present at the burial. No flowers or messages of condolences arrived, and we suspected Executive Superintendent Cutbush had advised Albert's friends and ex-colleagues in the police service not to attend the funeral.

Cull and I were discharged from hospital some hours earlier and we listened in a dazed silence as the vicar performed what I thought was rather a perfunctory service. He eventually closed his bible, shoved it under his arm and strolled away to indulge himself in matters of more importance.

We continued to stare at the marble headstone for several minutes, all of us deep in thought; words seemed redundant. Cull eventually broke the prolonged silence.

'He would have made a good soldier. Rest in peace, lad.'

'Excuse me, gentlemen.'

A tall, well-dressed man in his early forties appeared from nowhere and stood behind us. He removed his hat and paused for a moment before continuing. 'I know this is inconvenient for you, but we need to talk.' The man's tone of voice was quiet and understated, and he had an air of confidence about him that was unnerving. 'Chief Inspector John Littlechild. Metropolitan Police. I'm head of the *Special Irish Branch*.'

'Are you alone?' asked Cull, scanning the immediate area.

'No, I have several officers with me.'

I glanced around the graveyard. If there were several officers in the vicinity, I couldn't see them.

'Perhaps we should enter the church and pay our respects to young Albert,' said Littlechild, walking away towards the main entrance. 'One never knows who is observing.'

Cull shrugged his shoulders and we followed him and the officer down the narrow path that led through an array of headstones and into the gloomy church. We sat in a pew staring straight ahead, to all intents and purposes, paying our last respects to the deceased.

'The explosion in Church Lane was not an accident,' said Littlechild, staring down at the tiled floor. 'You have come to my attention because you are now targets, gentlemen. I would like to talk to you about various matters.'

We remained unresponsive, each of us apparently unmoved by Littlechild's words. The heavy, uneasy silence hung in the still air like a dark thundercloud.

'I understand your reservations,' said Littlechild, ignoring our ill-mannered reticence. 'I am aware what is happening within the Metropolitan Police, including the unacceptable behaviour of a certain officer. I have noted the incompetent investigation of the Ripper murders. Rest assured these matters will be dealt with at a later date.'

Cull finally took a deep breath. 'Maybe if you'd acted sooner, young Albert would still be with us.'

'My brief is dealing with Irish terrorism, Mister Moffat, which, fortunately, we now have under control thanks to the sustained efforts of my men. At this present time, *The Fenians* are a spent force.' Littlechild paused, giving greater emphasis to his words. He was clearly a master inquisitor. He continued in the same reasoned tone of voice. 'However, we believe that Lusk, Tumblety and LeGrand are operating as free agents, possibly for an American based anarchist group. We also believe they intend to commit an outrage that could bring down this government and throw the British Empire into chaos.'

'What sort of outrage could destabilise something as strong as the British Empire?' I asked, once again revealing my innate naivety.

Littlechild continued to stare ahead, but he spoke in a soft, almost inaudible voice, which seemed to imbue his words with even greater authority. 'The assassination of Queen Victoria would destabilise the British Empire.'

'I don't understand that,' I said. 'The Queen has been a virtual recluse for nearly thirty years. Her passing would be greatly mourned, of course, but I doubt if the Empire would collapse.'

Littlechild nodded. 'That is quite an astute assessment, Mister Batchelor. However, it is not the Queen's death that would cause destabilisation; it is the reputation of the heir to the throne that causes concern.'

'The Prince of Wales?' I said, not grasping the significance of Littlechild's argument.

'Yes. Unfortunately, Prince Edward is vain, frivolous and indiscreet. His gambling and sexual proclivities, most of which have been secretly covered up by the establishment, would shock the nation. The government does not want the Prince of Wales to succeed to the throne at this particular time.'

Nobody spoke for several moments, all of us contemplating the shocking relevance of what the Chief Inspector had said.

'Why don't you just arrest the plotters now?' asked Uriah.

'We don't have enough evidence,' said Littlechild, shaking his head. 'And they are extremely cunning men. As Chairman of *The Vigilance Committee*, George Lusk is the archetypal pillar of society. Charles LeGrand roams around Whitechapel in the guise of a Private Investigator supposedly working for the public good, and Francis Tumblety is a respected, if somewhat eccentric, doctor of medicine. A competent solicitor would have them free within the hour.'

'Maybe so,' said Uriah, once again clearly sensing the impact of the front-page headlines should anything untoward happen to the monarch. 'But it cannot be that difficult to protect the Queen. You have unlimited resources.'

'The Queen is protected,' said Littlechild, 'but no amount of security, however tightly controlled, can be guaranteed against extremists.' He paused and then half-turned to face Cull. 'As an ex-soldier, Mister Moffat, I am sure you are well aware of that.'

Cull nodded his agreement before speaking. 'Do you know who planted the bomb in Church Lane?'

'We can't prove anything, of course, but George Lusk is the only one trained to use explosives,' said Littlechild. He paused for a moment and took a deep breath before continuing. 'The question I need answering is why they suddenly needed to eliminate you. What has changed?'

We remained silent, deep within our own thoughts. I was first to speak. 'It surely has something to do with the trunk we opened at Euston Station. There is no other explanation.'

'Gentlemen, the Liverpool Police have had James Maybrick under surveillance for some time. Did you know his wife Florence is American?' Littlechild stared in the direction of the exquisitely carved wooden altar, his eyes unblinking. 'He has also spent time in America lately and we believe he is the instigator of this scheme. But, once again, we have no hard evidence. We do, however, know that he informed Lusk and Tumblety of your activities in Liverpool.'

'I should have guessed,' said Cull.

'Gentlemen, your input into this case has been extremely important, and I congratulate you on your efforts, but I would suggest you now leave it to the professionals.'

'Like Executive Superintendent Cutbush,' said Cull, still agitated. 'Police officers do not come any more professional than that man, do they?'

'I understand your frustrations, Mister Moffat. The question is, are you willing to share what you know with me?'

Cull turned and stared directly at me. 'John?'

Personally, I didn't think we had any choice. Littlechild had an air of authority that suggested honesty and integrity, very much like Cull, in my opinion. I nodded my head.

Uriah Garrett leaned forward in the pew. 'Chief Inspector, I'm the chief crime reporter for the *Evening News*.'

'Yes, I am aware of that, Mister Garrett' said Littlechild, maintaining his unruffled air of superiority.

'When these events reach a satisfactory conclusion, I intend to write the story for the *Evening News*. Can you guarantee my newspaper the exclusive rights?'

Littlechild smiled. 'That can be discussed in due course.' He paused and stared at Cull. 'What about you, Mister Moffat? Are you willing to assist my enquiries?'

Cull continued to stare ahead. He eventually nodded his head. 'For Queen and country, Chief Inspector. What else is worth fighting for?'

'Thank you. I expected nothing less.' Littlechild rose and stepped out into the aisle. 'I'm sure you realise that your lives are at risk. They have tried to kill you because they believe you have information about their activities. They may well be right.'

On Littlechild's signal, three burly plain clothed police officers appeared from the shadows and stood in the aisle. It was an impressive display,

Littlechild continued. 'My men will protect you twenty-four hours a day. We have a safe location in central London and I want you to move there immediately. I have to say, gentlemen, the interrogation will not be an enjoyable experience. I need to know everything, and I do not have the time for pleasantries.'

'We lost everything in the explosion,' I said. 'All we have is the clothing we stand up in. I would be grateful if you could supply some toiletries.'

'I'm sorry, but I'm not interested in damned toiletries,' said Uriah, surprising nobody. 'Could you get me a typewriter and plenty of copy paper, Chief Inspector?'

'You will be provided with whatever you need, including your typewriter, Mister Garrett,' he said, wearily. He turned and faced Cull. 'And what about you, Mister Moffat, what do you require?'

'Peace of mind, Chief Inspector.'

Littlechild glanced at Cull as though expecting a further comment. Nothing was forthcoming, although the feeling of mutual of respect that passed between the two men was quite heartening. Littlechild eventually nodded. 'We really have to go now, gentlemen.'

What I didn't know at that time was that Cull had lost all his army service and gallantry medals in the explosion; something he failed to mention. This information, when revealed, put my own selfish requirements in prospective.

Number 37 Brewer Street, Soho, was indeed a safe house, being located on the second floor of The Duke of Argyll public house. Although the apartment, if that was the correct term for a place such as this, was clean and well maintained, it was rather small for three people to share, under what were exceptional circumstances. It comprised of a small, sparsely furnished sitting room, a functional kitchen and one large bedroom fitted with three uncomfortable looking beds.

I quickly realised that Cull's snoring would be detrimental to any hope I had of sleeping peacefully. Apparently, one of his men once informed him that his snoring had reached such a crescendo, the noise drowned out the Russian bombardment at Balaclava. I hoped that particular story was an exaggeration.

As expected, the Chief Inspector led the interrogation, and he fired his first question at me less than thirty minutes after our arrival, barely giving the pot of Earl Grey time to brew.

We sat around the dining table, and for reasons best known to Cull and Uriah, they nominated me to answer Littlechild's endless questions. My stomach immediately began churning as I recalled each unsavoury event I had witnessed in the previous months. It became apparent I was in for a hard time when Littlechild removed his jacket and hung it carefully on the back of the chair. His charming gold cuff links were representations of four leafed clovers, presumably an ironic gesture aimed at *The Fenians*, or at least one hoped it was.

'Who is the Ripper?' was the detective's opening gambit. This was obviously not a man who wasted time on small talk.

'Jack the Ripper is not one man. George Lusk uses his army training to kill the victims quickly and cleanly and Tumblety butchers them.'

'Evidence?'

'We found a bloodstained shirt and two brass rings at a Batty Street lodging house; that evidence may still be there. We also discovered the timings of the murders coincided with their movements, especially on the night of the double murder when they entered the lodging house in a bloodstained and distressed state. The descriptions we obtained, particularly from Elizabeth Stride's boyfriend, Michael Kidney, indicated beyond reasonable doubt that Lusk and Tumblety were responsible.'

'What about the writing on the wall in Goulston Street?'

'That was street theatre, probably organised by Tumblety, who strikes me as a frustrated actor. He likes the limelight of centre stage. He paid Michael Kidney ten shillings to chalk those words on the wall. The best conjurers use misdirection as an art form, Chief Inspector.'

Littlechild nodded, raised his cup and sipped the tea. 'This is rather a good dish of Earl Grey, Mister Batchelor.'

'One tries one's best,' I said, sounding like a member of my mother's afternoon sewing circle, as previously suggested by Cull. The smirk on the big man's face made my resolution to lose this damnably annoying accent even more of an incentive than usual.

'I think I can guess the motive, gentlemen,' said Littlechild, looking thoughtfully around the table at each of us in turn. 'Tie up both the Metropolitan and City Police resources by creating what is perceived to be the world's first serial killer, who perpetrates several murders, each one more brutal than the last. The Masonic rituals were particularly inspired, if somewhat melodramatic.'

'They have committed four murders to date,' I said, trying desperately to collect my thoughts into some semblance of order, 'although I'm sure they'd be quite happy to accept responsibility for all the others that occurred in Whitechapel over the past several months. We know that a certain Nathan Bromley was responsible for the early murders. Lusk and Tumblety probably thought it a good idea to continue what Bromley started.'

Littlechild paused for a moment as he sipped more of his tea. 'Is there any reason why they would select those particular four women?'

I nodded. 'Five women shared a space in a Flower and Dean Street common lodging house. Whatever they discussed led to the deaths of four of them. We have been unable to trace the fifth woman.'

'If we follow that logic, Mister Batchelor, then the fifth murder will be the most horrific of all.'

'Why?' I asked, once again trying, but failing miserably, to conceal my gullibility.

'To arouse public abhorrence and unrest. This would force the police to raise their profile in the East End to an even greater extent. Manpower in the rest of London would be depleted giving the perpetrators the opportunity to implement their outrage.'

Littlechild was meticulous in his questioning; repeatedly asking me to clarify times and dates until my brain was in a whirl. He seemed particularly interested in the fifth woman scenario and continued to gnaw away at me like a dog with a bone, asking the same question in several different variations. It was at this moment that Cull came to my rescue, and not before damned time, either, if I might say.

The big man picked up the bottle of whiskey, recently delivered by one of Littlechild's men, and poured a large shot into a glass. 'The fifth woman was employed in a Cleveland

Street club. Whatever she overheard, she shared with the other four women. That's the crux of this whole story.'

'Why don't you just raid the club, Chief Inspector?' I asked, once again displaying my penchant for naïve rhetoric. 'That's where the answer to this conundrum lies.'

'We are aware of the establishment in Cleveland Street. Unfortunately, its members consist of wealthy businessmen, members of parliament and peers of the realm. There is also a member of the Royal family who is a frequent visitor to the establishment. The resulting scandal that would ensue does not bear thinking about.'

I shook my head wearily. 'Then it is unlikely you will locate this particular woman, because everything leads back to Cleveland Street.'

'There are clandestine methods of obtaining information that involve stealth and intelligent reasoning, rather than the obvious ploy of smashing through doors with sledgehammers. If the fifth woman is still in London, my men will locate her.'

I felt chastised. Never once had I suggested that it would be a good idea to smash through doors with sledgehammers, indeed, that was an activity more suited to my late father's temperament. He enjoyed nothing more than smashing down doors in the farthest outposts of the Empire, particularly if there were hostile warriors on the other side. Perhaps I should learn to rephrase my words in a more conciliatory manner. Either that or just keep my mouth shut and continue to brew the Earl Grey.

Cull picked up his whiskey glass, emptied it in one gulp and then refilled it to the brim. Unfortunately, one of the few things Cull had not lost in the explosion was his pipe and supply of Afghani tobacco. He packed the pipe and lit it, blowing a stream of foul smelling smoke up into the rafters.

'How much more of that tobacco do you have left?' I asked.

Cull shrugged. 'Not very much at all, but I have written to an army friend serving in Afghanistan who has promised to procure me another batch as soon as possible.'

'Oh, that is good news,' I said, coughing slightly as I slumped back into my chair. The interrogation had been going on for over an hour and I still didn't think Littlechild had finished.

'Is there anything else that could assist my investigations?' he asked, discreetly wrinkling his nose as the foul odour of Afghani tobacco reached his nostrils. Of course, he was too much of a gentleman to mention it.

Cull reached into his pocket and withdrew a piece of paper from his wallet; it was the copy of the item obtained from the trunk. He slid it across the table to Littlechild, who studied it for some moments before speaking.

'Interesting. 827 x 84 x 20, $4/7^{th}$ and 11,101,415. What do we think, gentlemen?'

Uriah shrugged his shoulders. 'A building, perhaps.'

'No,' said Littlechild. 'I suggest these numbers pertain to a corridor within a building.'

'What sort of a building has a corridor 827 feet long?' said Uriah, glancing at me for support.

I shook my head. What did I know?

Littlechild leaned back in his chair and slowly twisted the ends of his moustache. 'There are several buildings that meet those requirements including, Buckingham Palace, Windsor Castle, Hampton Court and Osborne House. Take your pick, gentlemen. All of them have corridors of that length or longer. Particularly the Palace.'

'Chief Inspector, if you supply us with outlines or blueprints of those buildings, we will study them,' said Cull. 'We don't have much else to keep us occupied.'

In life, I have found, there are certain statements that should remain unsaid. As we were about to learn to our cost, Cull's last statement fitted that category exactly.

Friday
November 9, 1888

Chief Inspector Littlechild provided several plans and outlines of the various Royal buildings, and we studied them avidly from all angles, until we were blue in the face. The hours turned into days, the days turned into weeks and no matter how hard we tried, we could not find a corridor that fitted the damned measurements we had in front of us. In fact, we couldn't find anything at all that came even close to the measurements, be it a corridor or not. Cooped up in the apartment for more than twenty-two days, we were just about ready to kill each other.

Cull's foul tobacco ran out eleven days previously and he now smoked pipe after pipe of a normal, sweeter smelling tobacco; for which we were all truly grateful. Unfortunately, now lacking his pungent foreign weed, he became extremely tetchy and short tempered to the point of petulance, which was most unlike the big man.

As for Uriah, he just sat and bashed away at the keys of the new Remington typewriter provided courtesy of the *Special Irish Branch*, and judging by his demented facial expressions and contorted body positions, he was writing either a painful series of memoirs, or the longest suicide note in history.

And Chief Inspector Littlechild, with the resources of the Metropolitan Police available to him, still hadn't found the fifth woman. Perhaps a sledgehammer through the front door of 19 Cleveland Street, despite the obvious consequences and resultant scandals, may have been the best option after all. My late father, despite his penchant for unbridled bravado, would not have hesitated. He would have acquired the details within hours, solved the Whitechapel Murders before luncheon was served, paid his mess bill, avoided his tailor and still found time to play a successful round of croquet before Tiffin was served on the veranda; or so I am led to believe.

Perhaps the most disheartening episode had happened two days previously. Late on Wednesday evening, November 7th, Littlechild visited to inform us that Francis J. Tumblety was under arrest. We could barely contain ourselves. Indeed, Uriah was so quick off the mark he was in his *work* chair, as he called it, and speedily typing up the lurid story of the Whitechapel murders before Littlechild had even finished speaking. It was hard to believe that finally, despite their best efforts to the contrary, the Metropolitan Police had *Jack the Ripper* in a cell. Obviously, judicious questioning would lead to the imminent arrest of all the other miscreants who would find themselves in police custody before the evening was out. And then, it was only a matter of time before the whole convoluted and atrocious story became public knowledge.

Unfortunately, our euphoria lasted about as long as it took Littlechild to relate the circumstances. Even Uriah stopped typing and slumped forward in the chair, his head in his hands.

Apparently, Dr Francis Tumblety faced charges of gross indecency and using force against men between 27 July and 2 November. These charges were euphemisms for homosexual activities and amounted to a total of eight separate offences. Unfortunately, by the time Littlechild heard the news and had arrived at the police station to interrogate him, Tumblety was gone, inexplicably bailed out in his own recognisance. Of course, he quickly disappeared into the London underworld without a backward glance. Once again, the finger of blame pointed directly at a certain Executive Superintendent, who had arranged bail almost immediately.

I spent the next couple of days thinking about Littlechild's revelations regarding Tumblety, and just became angrier. All I could do was stare forlornly through the window, and just watch life flow along a very busy Brewer Street; prostitutes, flower sellers, pickpockets, market traders and elegantly dressed merchants passed below the window, all engrossed in their everyday activities, and all unaware that an outrage was about to occur somewhere in London. Whether it would affect the ordinary person in the street was a moot point. I suspected it would affect us all in some way; it was just very difficult to image how.

Cull spent his time slumped in an easy chair with his feet up smoking pipe after pipe until the sitting room resembled Euston Road Station concourse on a particularly busy day. I waved a newspaper around occasionally, wafting the clouds of dense smoke up into the rafters, but he simply ignored me, and continued to blow streams of the stuff in all directions. It also appeared as if he had ceased trying to fit the measurements to the plans some days ago, but he stoutly maintained that he was still thinking about it. I'm glad he was, because both Uriah and I had given up completely and now thought about other things, such as how to live one's life in something other than a rabbit hutch.

It was around 8:00 pm when Littlechild burst into the sitting room, surprising all three of us with his intense manner. He stood in the centre of the room, tapping his mahogany cane on the floor. He took a deep breath and attempted to regain his composure. 'We think we've found the fifth woman.'

Cull glanced through the rising fug of tobacco smoke. 'You *think* you've found her. Could you be more specific, Chief Inspector?'

'Sergeant Godly has a lady downstairs in the Landau. We also arrested her boyfriend on unrelated charges. His story fits the times and dates that all the women lived together at the doss house,' said Littlechild, pacing breathlessly up and down the room while repeatedly tapping his cane against his shoe. He eventually stopped and stared directly at Cull. 'She, on the other hand, will not talk to the police under any circumstances. However, she may well speak to one of you gentlemen.' He walked across the room and opened the sitting room door. 'You simply have to get the information from her, and I don't care how you do it.'

'Don't worry, Chief Inspector, we'll beat her to a pulp if we have to,' I said, attempting to inject an ironic tone into my voice.

Cull leaned forward in his armchair, shook his head and slowly rubbed his eyes. Uriah glanced across the top of his typewriter, an expression of disgust lingering on his face.

'For God's sake, what's wrong with you two? I was joking.'

'This is no time for schoolboy humour,' said Cull, standing up and stretching his arms above his head. It was the first time in at least four hours he'd moved from the chair.

'You seem to have a penchant for the mistimed comment,' said Uriah, continuing to tap away on the typewriter.

'Unlike journalists,' I answered, 'who make a living out of ill-judged comment, mistimed or otherwise.'

'A little decorum, gentlemen, please' said Cull, lighting yet another pipe full of tobacco. 'Constantly bickering among ourselves will not improve the situation.'

Indeed. I turned and walked towards the window. At some point in the future, I intended to register a complaint about smoke pollution in a confined environment. I would probably have to be in a state of intoxication to do so, but I would confront him.

Eventually.

I stared through the window at the glowing gaslights that lit up Soho. Brewer Street looked particularly busy tonight. If London was the centre of the Empire, then this small section was the centre of London and I was proud to be part of it, whatever happened.

The lady who entered the room with a flourish surprised me with her appearance, which was a contradiction in terms. She was probably in her mid twenties, but looked older. She was tall, five feet seven inches or more, and quite stout, which made her look dumpy. Her blond hair, blue eyes and fair complexion were appealing, but she was not beautiful by any stretch of the imagination. She was bareheaded with a red shawl pulled loosely around her shoulders, which gave her the appearance of a common flower girl. If she was a prostitute, she was a several rungs above the normal Whitechapel street walker. She had a hard faced coarseness about her that was off putting but I suppose, in a good light, she could be loosely termed *attractive*.

Cull stood up and indicated that the lady should sit in his armchair. She brushed passed him, sat down and glanced at each of us, her eyes betraying neither fear nor intimidation.

'Why do you want to talk to me? I don't know anythin',' she said, pulling the shawl up around her shoulders. 'Wouldn't mind a drink, though.'

'What would you like?' I said, stepping forward and standing by the side of her chair, rather like a subservient wine waiter at the Ritz hotel. I really would have to learn how to adjust my behaviour to circumstances. This strict adherence to politeness, when dealing with members of the lower classes simply would not do. I dreaded to think what my mother would make of it all. As for my father...

'Gin,' she said, without even looking up at me.

'We don't actually have any gin. We have Irish whiskey or Earl Grey tea. Shall I brew a pot of tea?'

'No. Whiskey, if that's the best you can do,' she said, and then glanced at Cull. 'He's a bit posh. Is he the butler?'

I poured a whiskey and handed it to her, a look of quiet disdain engraved across my face. She quickly swallowed a large mouthful without blinking an eyelid.

'What's your name?' asked Cull.

'What's yours?' she replied, downing the remainder of the whiskey in one gulp. She leaned forward and passed me the empty glass, clearly expecting a refill.

Cull glanced at me and slowly shook his head. 'My name is Cullen Moffat,' he said, opening his wallet and placing a pound note on the table in front of him. He carefully smoothed it out before pushing it in the woman's direction. 'And that's yours if you answer some questions.'

'Mary Kelly is my name. What do you want to know?' she said. A slight touch of the Gaelic lingered beneath her broad cockney accent.

'You worked in Cleveland Street, is that right?'

'Yeah. I worked in a shop.'

Cull shook his head. 'I'm not interested in the shop. You were also employed in a Cleveland Street men's club, weren't you?'

'Bunch of perverts, they were. You wouldn't believe what they get up to in that place. Really, you wouldn't.' She paused for a moment, clearly disturbed by the memories. 'I served the drinks, did a bit of cleaning, that sort of thing. They paid good money because no other bugger would do it.'

'Why did you leave?'

She shrugged. 'Sacked.'

'Why?'

'No idea, I'm serving drinks one minute, next I'm out on me arse. Bastards. Call themselves gentlemen, they do. That's a laugh, eh?'

Cull leaned forward in his chair. 'This is important, Mary, so please think carefully.' He paused to allow his words to sink in. 'Do you know the names of the men you were serving directly before you were sacked?'

She nodded her head without hesitation. 'Doctor Tumblety and Charles LeGrand, not likely to forget them in a hurry.'

'Why?'

'Do I get that pound note yet?'

Cull picked up the note and handed it across to her. She shoved it down her blouse. 'They always sat together, always whisperin' about somethin'. They just looked a bit shifty, if you know what I mean. Dressed like a pair of circus clowns, especially that quack doctor. He was a Yank, you know.'

'What did you hear them say that particular day?'

'Just bits and pieces, none of it made much sense. Could I have another drink, mouth's a bit dry.'

Cull nodded at me. I poured a large whiskey and handed it to her.

'Me ears pricked up when I heard the bit about Irish home rule. I was born in Ireland, you know,' she said, swallowing a mouthful of whiskey. 'Didn't understand what they were goin' on about. Tumblety said somethin' about the Empire. Didn't say which one, could have been the one in Leicester Square, I suppose. Said they were goin' to knock it down.'

'I think they meant the British Empire, Mary. Could they have said *bring it down*?'

She nodded. 'Suppose so. LeGrand said if they timed it right, they could get all three of them together, a late birthday present for the bastard. They both laughed at that. Then they saw me standin' there, accused me of ear wigging and threw me out.'

'So, you then moved to a lodging house and met four other women?'

Mary nodded.

'Did you tell them this story?'

'Yes, but they didn't understand it either, or care. I mean, who is really bothered if they knock a bleedin' theatre down? Got better thing to worry about.'

Cull reached for the whiskey bottle and poured himself a large shot. 'Did you know that all four of the women you lived with are now dead?'

'No, I didn't. Bit of a shame, eh?'

'They were murdered.'

'I weren't really friends with any of them. Didn't keep in contact, or anythin'. After staying at the doss house I went to France for a few months, had a good job there, so I can't even remember all their names. Sorry to hear about what happened, of course I am, but life goes on, doesn't it? It's bleedin' tough out there, you know.'

Cull paused and then swallowed the contents of his glass. 'You're next.'

'Get away. Who'd want to murder me? I ain't done nothin' to nobody. Well, not recently, anyway.'

Cull refilled both his and Mary's glass. 'Unfortunately, you heard something you shouldn't and then you told the other women.'

Mary shrugged. 'So what? I can't even remember what I said. Weren't that important.'

Cull handed her the piece of paper with the measurements on it. 'Do those numbers mean anything to you? Think back to what you may have seen in the club.'

She studied the piece of paper for several moments. 'Don't know about the measurements, but I do recognise that bottom number 11-10-1415. Tumblety wrote a number like that on his drink receipts.'

'What does it mean?'

'Date and time.'

Cull banged his fist down on the table. 'Damn it, of course it is. 11 October, 1415. They used military time because they were open twenty-four hours a day. 1415 equates to 2:15 pm.'

'Well, whatever they had planned has happened,' I said, stating the obvious, 'because we are now in November.'

Cull nodded and leaned back in his chair.

Uriah filled a glass with whiskey and drank it down in one swallow. 'I haven't heard about any outrages recently, not a damn thing, unless, of course, we are completely wrong about the ripper murders. Oh my God, I have to explain this to my Editor. He won't be best pleased.'

Mary shook her head. 'The quack doctor used to write the date the American way, month first. Took me ages to work it out. 11-10 means November 10.' She paused and finished the whiskey in her glass. 'That's tomorrow.'

Cull stood up. 'Of course it is. Mary, I want you to stay here for a couple of days, at least.'

'I can't do that; I've got things to do. Family matters. Why should I stay here?'

Cull paused for a moment and then grasped Mary by her shoulders. 'Because they intend to murder you tonight.'

Saturday
November 10, 1888

I awoke relatively early the following morning, with the uncomfortable feeling that it was going to be a very long and fraught day. Cull's snoring, which for some reason did not appear to bother Uriah in the slightest, was particularly noisy, especially as I was enduring my usual early morning fragility. To avoid disturbing Mary, who had agreed to stay at least overnight, I stealthily bypassed the sitting room, went into the kitchen and brewed up a pot of Earl Grey. Even somebody as vulgar as Mary could not possibly want to drink whiskey at 8:59 am, although nothing surprised me these days. I took a bottle of whiskey and glass in with me, just in case.

I knocked on the sitting room door before entering, and set the tray down on the table. To my surprise, the settee was empty, the blankets strewn across the floor. She had gone, although I quickly noticed that she had scrawled a message across the piece of paper bearing the measurements. It was an address in Dorset Street, 13 Millers Court, and some vague message about having to meet her sister.

I raised both Cull and Uriah from their slumbers and quickly apprised them of the situation. Although he hid it very well, it was obvious that Cull was still annoyed with himself for missing the date and time reference. He indicated that we should sit at the table.

'We have to treat this like a military operation. Therefore, we are going to use 24-hour military time. So, what time is it now, John?'

I glanced down at my pocket watch. 'Ten minutes past...' I paused for a second. 'Sorry, er, 0910 hours.'

'Right, if we believe this event is going to occur at 1415 we have five hours. We shall split up. Uriah, you'll have your own specific objectives, John and I will pursue different lines of enquiry, and we'll meet back here at 1200 hours.'

I raised my right hand, once again feeling like an errant schoolboy. 'If they didn't kill Mary last night, will they still go ahead with whatever they intend to do this afternoon?'

Cull nodded his head. 'That's a good question. If their intention is to create a horrific murder scene that causes chaos and panic among the police and local population, then they still have time. They *need* to engineer a diversion. We have to find Mary before they do.'

'What else do you need to know?' asked Uriah, taking out his ubiquitous notebook and pencil.

Cull stared purposefully across the table at Uriah. 'Mary gave us some useful information. They intend to destroy the British Empire, so it has to be something really outrageous. She also mentioned about *getting all three of them together*.' Cull raised his hands. 'Who are the three? Why are they so important? That's what you have to find out.'

Uriah continued to scribble in his book. He spoke without looking up. 'She also mentioned a late birthday present for the bastard. Whoever *the bastard* might be.'

Cull lapsed into silence, slowly stroking his moustache. It was two or three minutes before he spoke. 'I also want you to check if there were any birthdays within the last week? Royal birthdays, government ministers, anybody of importance.'

I glanced across at Uriah. 'What is the Prime Minister's birth date? Or Queen Victoria's birth date, for that matter?'

He shrugged his shoulders, more than a little embarrassed. He was supposed to be a journalist, why didn't he know these things?

'Queen Victoria was born 24 May, 1819,' said Cull, quietly. 'Most military men know that. So, I suppose we can rule her out. I doubt if even these people would refer to the Queen as a *bastard.*'

'What about the Prime Minister?' I asked.

Uriah looked up from his notebook. 'Robert Gascoyne-Cecil, Marquis of Salisbury, is the worst Prime Ministers this country has ever suffered. His death would not bring down the British Empire. In fact, it may even improve our standing in the world.'

'It depends who is sitting next to him when the bomb goes off,' said Cull, leaning back in his chair.

Uriah slowly nodded his head. 'Now that's a very good point.'

Sergeant Godly, the officer who was supposedly guarding us against physical harm, had organised a rather comfortable setup for himself on the ground floor. He sat in an amply padded chair behind a small table, presumably so he could survey the entrance; it also enabled him to stuff his face with food at the same time.

When Cull and I confronted him, he placed a large mutton pie onto a plate beside him and stood up, chewing vigorously.

'Good morning, gentlemen,' he said, wiping his hands on the sides of his trousers. 'What can I do for you?'

'What time did Mary Kelly leave this morning?' asked Cull, his eyes focussing on the officer's dishevelled appearance.

'About eight o'clock.'

'Why didn't you stop her? She's a material witness.'

'She wasn't under arrest, sir,' said Godly, licking a blob of gravy off his forefinger. 'She was free to do as she pleased.'

'We are going out now, Sergeant, and Mister Garrett, who is upstairs at this moment, will follow presently,' said Cull.

'I'm afraid I can't allow that without the Chief Inspector's permission.'

Cull turned on his heel and walked towards the front door. He grasped the handle and pulled the door open. 'And just how do you intend to stop us?'

Sergeant Godly appeared bemused. I followed Cull through the open door, slammed it behind me, and followed him up Brewer Street without hearing another word of protest from the officer.

We walked briskly through the narrow confines of Soho, eventually entering Regent Street, just below Oxford Circus. I had tramped these very same streets many times when I was down on my luck, and I recognised virtually every square inch of pavement.

'Where are we going? I know a few short cuts around here.'

Cull shook his head and continued walking along Regent Street towards Piccadilly. He eventually paused at the cab rank outside *Mason & Peacocks* department store. A group of cabbies had gathered next to their cabs and were chatting amicably with each other.

One of the cabbies suddenly stepped forward and grasped Cull's proffered hand. 'My word, as I live and breathe, Cullen Moffat. I haven't seen you for months. Where have you been? A lot of the clients have been asking about you.'

Cull half turned to face me. 'Jimmy Payne. Took me under his wing when I first started cabbing. What he doesn't know about driving these cabs isn't worth knowing,' said Cull, his accent broadening slightly. 'This is John Batchelor, Jimmy. He's a good lad.'

I stepped forward and shook hands with the man, although I refrained from saying anything, just to be on the safe side.

'Still cabbing?' asked Jimmy, patting Cull on the shoulder. 'You're one of the best I've seen. 'Ere, how's old Domingo?' Jimmy stared across at me and pushed his cap to the side of his head. 'I'll tell you, John, he was one of the craftiest horses on the rank. Didn't need reins with him, knew his way all over London. Ain't that right, Cull?'

'He's gone, Jim,' said Cull, his face betraying no emotion.

'Well, he was getting on a bit, poor old bugger. Old age was it?'

Cull nodded. 'Yeah, it was something like that.' He paused and removed a pound note from his wallet. 'I need a favour, Jim, no questions asked. How would you like some time off? I need your cab for a few hours.'

The expression on Jimmy's face never changed, he just took the pound note and slipped into his inside pocket. 'You know old Bessie. She pulls towards the kerb in heavy traffic, but she's not too bad, although you might have to hold her back at times, she's a bit frisky. Just give her a touch of the whip now and again.'

'She'll be back on the stand by six tonight,' said Cull.

'I know she will. Never known Cullen Moffat let anybody down. Ever.' Once again, Jimmy turned to face me. 'I could tell you a few stories about this man, John.'

I nodded. So could I.

It was strange being in a different cab. Although it was the same build and make as Cull's old one, it didn't quite feel the same, or ride as smoothly. It was clean, but not *as* clean; the seats were highly polished and shiny, but not *as* shiny. And to think that I had actually complained about that. Perhaps it was just nostalgia on my part; maybe I was getting old before my time. Perhaps I was trying to avoid thinking about what happened outside the Church Lane house.

We reached Whitechapel at 1005 hours, and then discovered we really didn't have a plan of action. Although the area was familiar to us, it was impossible to guess where Mary might be. We travelled up and down various streets, but it was highly unlikely we would chance upon her just strolling along.

Cull pulled up the ceiling flap. 'Where do you think she'd go?'

'If she has any sense she won't go near Millers Court.'

'Maybe she has to go there. Didn't she say something about sorting out family matters?'

I paused for a moment trying to recall Mary's words. 'Yes, it was something about her sister. Maybe we should just wait in Dorset Street and see if she shows up.'

'Can't wait too long. We have to get back to Soho before midday. I'm sure Uriah will uncover something.'

Dorset Street was less than a three-minute ride away and we parked up outside the alley that led to Millers Court. Cull hitched Bessie to a holding post and disappeared down the alley. I stood by the cab, feeling extremely vulnerable. This was the same street where we met Michael Kidney in his hovel, and nothing much had changed since that day. I could still feel various unseen eyes boring into me.

The big man returned a minute later, leaned against the hitching post, and slowly stroked Bessie's nose. 'I knocked on the door but I don't think there's anybody in there. Mary is bound to turn up here sooner or later.'

Cull was right. At exactly 1025 hours, Mary appeared at the top of Dorset Street, strolling along as though she didn't have a care in the world. She was wearing the same clothes as the night before, including the red shawl. As she approached, she threw back her head and attempted to ignore us.

Cull, who usually managed to hide his emotions better than most, angrily stepped out in front of her, effectively blocking her path. 'Where the hell have you been?'

'It's none of your bleedin' business. I told you I had family matters to sort out. Just leave me alone.'

'Have you been home?' asked Cull, his expression softening slightly.

Mary shook her head and pulled the red shawl up around her shoulders. She brushed past Cull and turned right into Millers Court. 'No time for idle chit chat. Things to do.'

We followed her down the dirty alleyway that led to a small decrepit looking building, which was actually an extension of one of the houses that faced out onto Dorset Street. Even

202

though the small windows were filthy beyond belief, it was possible to see that one had been broken and not replaced, probably a regular occurrence in this area. Mary inserted her key into the lock and pushed open the door.

'You two can wait here, I have private matters to discuss with my sister.' She entered the building, leaving the door slightly ajar.

Cull looked at me, raised his eyes and sighed. 'Five minutes and that's it. I mean it.'

It was actually less than five seconds before we heard the muffled sobbing. Cull quickly pushed the door open and entered. I followed him into the small room and recoiled in horror at the sight before me. Mary was kneeling on the floor, her right hand covering her mouth. My vocabulary is simply inadequate to convey the extreme heartlessness and cruelty that had occurred in this room. Despite what I could see before my eyes, it is probably the odour that will stay with me. The sweet sickly smell of putrid meat pervaded the whole room.

The body of Mary's sister lay on the single bed, inclined towards the left side. Chunks of flesh had been crudely hacked out of her left thigh and simply thrown onto the floor like scraps of offal. An incision sliced through the abdomen from the pubic area to the sternum, leaving a gaping hole. Various locations around the room contained the internal organs ripped from the body and slung into the corners. The breasts had been hacked off, one placed under the head the other rested by the right foot. Yet again, the murderer had taken the time to arrange the intestines around the left shoulder of the body.

The previous Ripper murders were overt attempts to convey ritualistic practices, this was different; this was butchery taken to such a degree as to be almost indescribable. The killer had slashed the victim's face up and down with crude strokes of his blade, partially removing the nose, cheeks and eyebrows, leaving the facial features of the woman unrecognisable.

Cull was correct. This was not just murder; this atrocity would, undoubtedly, create panic and hysteria among the residents of Whitechapel. Nobody would feel safe.

Cull grasped Mary by her shoulders and gently led her out of the room. He took the door key from her and passed it to me. As he held her closely, and she sobbed silently into his shoulder, he glanced at the door. I understood immediately what he wanted me to do. If we locked the door and nobody found the body before 1415 hours, the chaos the bombers wanted would not materialise and their plan would not come to fruition, at least, not in the way they expected.

We walked quickly back to the hitching post, Mary and I entered the cab and sat back as Cull urged Bessie away from the kerb and into a gallop, the willing horse pulling the vehicle noisily across the cobbles towards the top of Dorset Street.

Mary lay her head against my shoulder and sobbed gently. Being unfamiliar with this sort of situation, I was unsure how one consoles a distraught woman. Indeed, is it possible to comfort somebody who has just witnessed such an atrocity? How would I have reacted had the mutilated body been that of my own sister? In truth, Mary had handled the situation very well. She hadn't screamed and wailed, but perhaps there are things outside the realms of human understanding. Maybe this was a situation beyond trauma. I now had a greater respect and a feeling of deep sorrow for Mary Kelly. Her grieving, when it came, would be overwhelming.

We left Dorset Street and Whitechapel behind and headed at speed towards central London. I thought we had dealt with the situation very well under the circumstances.

As usual, I was wrong.

Just nine minutes later at 1045 hours, Thomas Bower went to Millers Court to collect the overdue rent from Mary Kelly. After receiving no response to his knocking, he pushed the curtain aside, stared through the broken window and saw the mutilated body lying on the bed. At exactly 1049 hours, all hell broke loose in Whitechapel and surrounding areas as the news of the ghastly murder spread like wildfire across a vast grassy plain.

The bombers were back within their time frame.

The congested traffic in the West End of London reduced our journey back to Brewer Street to almost walking pace. We arrived back at the safe house at 1225 hours.

Sergeant Godley's table and chair still occupied the ground floor entrance, his half-eaten pie sitting forlornly in the middle of the plate. He, however, was missing. It looked as though he might have left in a hurry.

Mary hadn't said a word for some time. She just trembled uncontrollably as I led her up to the first floor. Cull made her drink a large whiskey, wrapped her in a blanket and gently laid her down on his bed.

He joined me at the table in the sitting room. 'I'm afraid there's nothing we can do. She's suffering from acute shock. I've seen hard men, and I mean *hard* men, curl up into a ball and lie shivering on the floor. Shock can cut down the most dedicated soldier. What chance has a young woman got?'

'Will she recover?'

'Some do.'

I poured two cups of freshly brewed Earl Grey, passed one cup across the table and decided to keep quiet. There was nothing further I could add, and small talk would not improve the situation. I wandered into the bedroom to check on Mary, who was still sleeping fitfully on Cull's bed. The sympathy I felt for her was overwhelming, and I found it difficult to contain my emotions as the tears welled up into my eyes. We knew something was going to happen, something outrageous, and we knew what time it was going to happen. We just didn't know where or to whom. And all I could do was stand in a Soho bedroom and watch a young woman suffer mental anguish.

At exactly 1305 hours Uriah burst into the room all of a fluster and dumped a carpetbag in the middle of the table. He could barely contain himself.

'Sorry I'm late; I'm supposed to be in Whitechapel. You can update me with your details later. Listen, every newspaper in Fleet Street is flooding the area with reporters; the world and his dog are heading towards the East End of London.' He paused and tipped the contents of the carpetbag onto the table. 'In the meantime, I've uncovered some interesting information from my newspaper's record files. Any chance of a cup of tea, John?'

He knew how to pick his moments. Once again, acting out the role of unpaid butler, I went into the kitchen, returned with a cup and saucer and poured our intrepid reporter a cup of Earl Grey. 'So what have you discovered?' I asked, placing the cup and saucer in front of him. He could put the lemon in himself.

Uriah opened a file lying in front of him and pulled out a bundle of papers. 'Albert Edward, Prince of Wales, was born 9 November, 1841, and he celebrated his forty-seventh birthday yesterday. He is, gentlemen, *the bastard* who will be in receipt of a late birthday present from the potential assassins.'

Cull nodded his head. 'Well done, but there's more, isn't there?'

'There certainly is. You won't believe this.' Uriah picked up a piece of paper and slowly read the contents aloud. 'Prince Otto von Bismarck-Schönhausen, Duke of Lauenburg will arrive at Waterloo station today at approximately 1400 hours on a private visit to this country. The Prince of Wales and the Prime Minister are meeting him at the Station in an informal capacity. They will then be conveyed in the Royal coach to Buckingham Palace for a series of meetings with the Queen.'

'Erm, who is Otto von Bismarck-Schönhausen?' I asked, again feeling like the bored schoolboy sitting at the back of the classroom. Unfortunately, I could write my entire knowledge of world affairs on the back of a postage stamp.

Uriah seemed more than eager to impart his knowledge. 'Prince Otto von Bismarck is the president of Prussia. He also happens to be the Chancellor of the German Empire and a distant relative of Queen Victoria. He is the most powerful man within the German Confederation. Von Bismarck has created peace and stability in Europe by addressing political conflicts through skilled negotiations.' Uriah paused for a moment, placed the file on the table and leaned back in his chair. 'If he were assassinated in Great Britain, Europe would fall into chaos. The prospect of a full-scale war between the British and German Empires would be highly likely, leading to world war as other nations fulfilled their treaty obligations. We are looking into the fires of hell, gentlemen.'

I felt numb. It was the worst possible news. How could we stop something as well organised as this? The whole operation had probably been months, if not years, in the planning. We had stumbled onto something of momentous proportions, and I wasn't entirely convinced we were equipped to deal with it.

'I'm sorry, gentlemen, there is more,' said Uriah, opening another file.

I refilled each of our teacups. 'Could it get any worse?' I said, to nobody in particular.

Uriah slowly nodded his head. 'I'm afraid it can. Queen Victoria has enjoyed a long and successful period as monarch of this country. But even the staunchest of royalists must realise the Queen's reign is reaching a conclusion. Sometime in the very near future she will be succeeded by the heir to the throne.'

Cull leaned forward in his chair. 'Edward, Prince of Wales, will become King Edward V11. Chief Inspector Littlechild said that the Prince indulged in gambling and other morally degrading activities. Apparently, the establishment feels that Edward is unfit to rule the county at this time.' Cull's brow wrinkled and he slowly stroked his moustache. 'If Edward is assassinated along with the Prime Minister and Von Bismarck, who succeeds to the throne upon the death of Victoria?'

'Take a deep breath,' said Uriah, opening yet another file. 'Should Edward die, the heir to the throne would be none other than his son, Prince Albert Victor, Duke of Clarence.'

Cull shook his head. 'The establishment think the Prince of Wales would be unsuitable to rule. My God, what would they make of his obnoxious son?'

The facts and figures were now flying around my head very quickly. I found it increasingly difficult to connect the various scenarios laid out by Uriah. I closed my eyes and attempted to concentrate. Chief Inspector Littlechild had mentioned that peers of the realm, members of parliament *and* Royalty would all be involved in the unsavoury scandal that would erupt, should the police decide to raid a certain establishment. 'Is the Duke of Clarence the same person who frequents the brothel at Cleveland Street?' I asked, trying not to sound completely stupid.

Uriah nodded. 'The Cleveland Street brothel is just one of his many nefarious activities. The Duke of Clarence is twenty-four-years-old, and has created a reputation and disposition totally unsuited to the demands of high office.'

Cull stood up. 'I would die for this country. But I will never serve under a monarch with the morals of an alley cat.'

'Oh, and I forgot to mention,' said Uriah, tapping one of the files, 'that the measurements we have, more or less fit the dimensions of the platform at Waterloo station. 800 feet long by 84 feet wide. I suspect the height of a train is around 20 feet. 4/7th is probably the fourth coach of seven.'

'Well done, that was good work,' said Cull.

I glanced across at Uriah as he closed the carpetbag. 'Does that mean…'

He interrupted me in mid sentence. 'Yes, John, that means they intend to blow up the train as it enters Waterloo Station in exactly,' he checked his pocket watch, 'forty-five minutes.'

Uriah decided to stay in Soho to type up his story, while making sure that Mary's condition did not deteriorate any further. We outlined what we had seen at Millers Court and he decided to file his report as though he had actually been there, which told me all I needed to know about the morals and ethics of newspaper reporters.

Meanwhile, Cull and I were stuck in Piccadilly Circus for what seemed an inordinate length of time. The Saturday afternoon traffic through London was horrendous. By 1345 hours, we still hadn't managed to cross over to the south bank, where we needed to be in order to reach Waterloo Station. Cull was weaving the cab through the traffic with great skill, but we still did not make good time, and there was absolutely nothing we could do about it.

I glanced up as Cull raised the ceiling panel above my head. 'There's something I don't understand, John. The time on the piece of paper is 1415, but Uriah said the train was due to arrive at 1400. That leaves a discrepancy of fifteen minutes. Why?'

I shrugged my shoulders. 'Perhaps they are going to have a ceremony or something. Brass bands and the like. That would take about fifteen minutes, and they would all be standing on the station platform. Ideal moment to set off a bomb.'

'No, Uriah said it was a private visit. They will probably move from the train to the Royal carriage.' Cull paused for a moment before continuing. 'There's something wrong here, and I just can't put my finger on it.'

We drove onto Waterloo Station concourse at exactly 1358 hours, and parked the cab haphazardly against the kerb. Cull left Bessie unfettered and we both dashed along the concourse and onto the platform. It occurred to me even as we sprinted passed the huge engine, which was still belching out steam and smoke, that running straight into a potential explosion did not seem the wisest course of action. However, to our surprise, all seemed remarkably quiet in the vicinity of the coaches.

The lone porter leaning against a luggage cart watched us warily as we approached. I expect he'd seen more than his fair share of mental cases in his time.

'Is this the Royal train?' asked Cull, breathing heavily. 'Due to arrive here 1400 hours?'

The porter nodded. 'Aye.'

'So, where is everybody?' I asked, peering through one of the train windows.

'They've gone,' said the porter, scratching the back of his neck. 'The train arrived five minutes early. A couple of posh types, foreigners I think, got off, climbed into the Royal coach and left. Not much fuss, considering.'

'How long ago was that?' asked Cull, trying to regain his breath.

'Only a few minutes. Five at the most. You probably passed them as you came in.'

Cull turned and walked quickly back to the cab. I thanked the porter and followed behind the big man. We were out of the Station and travelling along York Road within seconds. Cull induced Bessie to a gallop, expertly weaving her in and out of traffic. I grasped the leather handle to my right and hung on for dear life as the cab rolled from side to side with an alarming instability. Two minutes after leaving the station, we passed the Royal coach, which was clopping along at a gentle pace.

I pushed up the ceiling flap. 'Can we stop them?'

Cull shook his head. 'No. There will be two guards onboard, both armed. We try and stop them, they'll shoot us.'

Bessie was still galloping at full speed and we had left the Royal coach so far behind, it was now out of sight. As we approached Westminster Bridge, something caught my eye. If I live to be a hundred years old, I will never be able to explain why I noticed it.

I pushed up the ceiling flap and directed my words through the gap. 'Look at the bridge, Cull. How many arches does it have?'

'Seven.'

'Correct,' I said, keeping my eyes locked on the bridge. 'There are three arches leading from the south bank, then one in the middle, and then another three leading to the north bank on the House of Commons side of the river. That makes the arch in the middle four of seventh. Does it not?'

Cull slowly nodded his head.

I continued. 'I'm not very good at guessing distance, but I would now gamble everything I have that Westminster Bridge is 827 feet long by 84 feet wide.'

'And the missing fifteen minutes between 1400 and 1415 is the travelling time from the station to the bridge,' said Cull staring out across the Thames. 'Good God, they're going to blow up Westminster Bridge as the Royal coach crosses the fourth arch.'

The Saturday afternoon traffic flowing over the bridge on both sides was extremely heavy. Cull suddenly pulled the cab to a halt halfway across the bridge, causing irate drivers to verbally assail him from all sides. He simply ignored the swearing and cussing aimed at him, walked from the cab and stood in front of the blue painted metal railings, and stared down at the Thames.

'How on earth are they going to do this?' I asked.

'As soon as the Royal coach is seen approaching from the south side, the bomber gets a signal from somebody situated on the bank, primes the bomb and makes his getaway in a boat,' said Cull, slowly shaking his head. 'By the time the bomb detonates, he is far enough away to be safe.'

'But that means everything else on the bridge at that time goes up too. That's mass murder.'

'Do you think they care?' He paused for a moment. 'Well, look who it is.'

George Lusk was standing at the rear of a steam launch that had drifted out from under the bridge. In the wheelhouse of the boat, I could see the portly figure of LeGrand navigating the boat into the tidal stream. Lusk raised his eyes and saw us, grimaced and then scrambled along the boat toward the small wheelhouse.

Cull grasped hold of the metal railings with both hands. 'He's primed the bomb. The Royal coach will be on the bridge in less than three minutes.'

'You've got to stop him,' I said, without a single idea of how either of us might achieve that.

'Over you go, son,' said Cull, indicating the bridge parapet.

'*What*?'

'The bomb is on a timer. You have to go down there and defuse the thing.'

'*Me*?' I said, incredulously. 'I know nothing about bombs.'

'Then it's time you learnt.'

I paused for a moment and considered the options. There weren't any. It was a do or die situation. I climbed up and stood on one of the narrow metal balustrades that jutted out of the bridge, and stared down into the dark, choppy waters of the Thames. I'd been here before, except last time I had intended to commit suicide. I couldn't do it then, and I wasn't sure I had the courage to jump now.

The Royal coach was trundling along the south bank; it would be on the bridge in less than two minutes. I glanced up at the cloudless blue sky. What would my father have made of this? He always insisted I never had the guts to do anything except whinge.

He may have been right.

The first bullet whistled passed my left ear, missing me by inches. I glanced down. Lusk was standing at the back of the launch pointing a service revolver at me. The second shot hit the metal balustrade below my feet and ricocheted away into the distance. To hell with it or to hell with me; it wasn't my choice anymore. I closed my eyes, held my nose and leapt into the unknown. The water was freezing and it took my breath away as I entered the Thames feet first. As I broke the surface,

I took a deep breath and swam towards the small platform under the fourth arch, which was only a couple of feet away.

There were two bombs sitting on the small brick platform, both about the size of large, square tea caddies. One of the bombs had an intricate clock face on its front side, and the hand on the dial had reached twelve. I was sixty seconds from oblivion.

Another shot rang out. The bullet struck the bridge slightly to my right and tore a chuck of masonry away. George Lusk was standing in the back of the boat, less than sixty feet away from me. He surely wouldn't miss with his next shot.

And he didn't miss.

The bullet grazed my left arm, ripping through the sleeve of my jacket and searing the flesh underneath. Thankfully, no pain, just a stinging sensation and the smell of burning flesh. I ignored it. The pain would come later, no doubt about that.

I looked up. 'There are two bombs here, Cull. What shall I do?'

'Is one counting down on a timer?'

'Yes. Thirty seconds left,' I shouted, wondering if I should just pull the wires out. I didn't know it at that time, but the Royal coach had just entered the bridge. 'I'm going to pull the wires.'

'No, don't do that,' was the calm answer that floated down to me. 'Grab the one with the timer and throw it as far away as you can.'

I picked up the bomb, closed my eyes and hurled it away with all the strength I could muster. The end of Cull's whip suddenly appeared in front of my face. I grasped it and climbed, hand over hand, up the bridge. Still no pain in my left arm, just a dull ache. Cull grasped me by the collar and heaved me over the edge and onto the pavement.

It was at that moment the Royal coach passed. Cull stood rigidly to attention and saluted. I just stood there dripping water all over the place; God alone knows what the coach passengers thought they were looking at. Should they have chosen to glance through the coach window at that precise moment they would have seen a tall, fifty-five-year-old man with a pronounced military bearing, wearing grey side-whiskers and a heavy grey moustache, who knew how to salute very important people. And standing alongside the old soldier was a young man, wearing a sodden, bloodstained suit of clothing, hair plastered flat to his head, dripping filthy Thames water all over Westminster Bridge.

Welcome to Great Britain Herr Bismarck.

Both Cull and I turned, leaned against the bridge and stared out across the Thames. The steam launch was making slow progress away from the bridge, and was now about fifty yards downstream. Even from that distance, I could see George Lusk desperately scrambling around the stern of the boat. I had tossed the bomb as far away from me as I could and it had landed on the boat. Just like the bowler coming in from the pavilion end at Lords, I did get the occasionally one right on line and rip out the leg stump.

The explosion reduced the boat to firewood, lifted a plume of water twenty feet in the air, and sent a large wave washing along the river in the direction of Chelsea. The steam launch simply disappeared from sight.

Cull turned and stared at me, his face expressionless. 'Damn it to hell, John. So many senseless deaths.'

I nodded. 'Including Albert, of course, a young man who had everything to live for. I think he would have made a good soldier.'

'You're right,' said Cull, extracting a grubby sugar lump from his pocket and tossing it into the Thames. 'We've all lost something.'

We both turned and faced the roadway. Nobody seemed to have noticed the explosion out in the middle of the Thames. The passing traffic continued to berate Cull for blocking half of the bridge with his cab.

If only they knew the circumstances, ungrateful beggars.

Sunday
November 11, 1888

Mary Kelly went to Ireland to stay with relatives, courtesy of the Metropolitan Police, who paid her passage. Cull, Uriah, Chief Inspector Littlechild and I gathered around the table in the sitting room of the safe house in Soho. We thought we were about to be praised for our work in solving not only the Ripper murders, but also saving the British Empire from disaster. What the chief Inspector said shocked us.

'I'm sorry, gentlemen, you are bound to secrecy. That's just the way it has to be,' said Littlechild, looking very sheepish. 'I have spoken to the Commissioner and he is adamant that he will not allow this incident to enter the public domain. There's absolutely nothing more I can do.'

Uriah looked the most displeased. He tapped his fingers on the table, as he always did when he was irritated. 'So, I can't write the exclusive story? I can't reveal the truth about the Ripper, or the bomb, or Bismarck, or Westminster Bridge, or even Mary Kelly?' He paused for a moment. 'Can I write about anything to do with this incident?'

'I'm afraid not, Mister Garrett. If you publish that story, or anything pertaining to it, the Metropolitan Police will deny all knowledge of everything you write. Your newspaper will look ridiculous.'

I leaned forward and topped my cup up with more Earl Grey tea. 'Why can't the story be published, Chief Inspector?'

Littlechild sighed gently. 'Gentlemen, we know the identity of *Jack the Ripper*, and we know why the crimes were committed. And my investigations *will* continue. However, for reasons of national security, we cannot admit how close Otto von Bismarck came to assassination. Which means details of this investigation will remain on the classified files list in perpetuity. Certain details of the events in Whitechapel *will* be released, but only you gentlemen will know the whole truth.'

'You do realise my newspaper will sack me,' said Uriah. 'They've incurred a lot of expense in the expectation of an exclusive story concerning the Whitechapel murders.'

'I'm sorry, Mister Garrett.' Littlechild paused for a moment before continuing. 'Gentlemen, there is some good news,' he said, glancing around the table. 'The *Special Irish Branch* would like to make you an offer in lieu of services rendered to the country.'

'A monetary reward?' I said, vowing to refuse anything less than a hundred pounds.

'Yes, it is a valuable offer' said Littlechild, producing some documents from a briefcase. 'There is a ninety-nine-year lease on this building, which includes all three floors and the public house below. I am prepared to sell the lease to you for just one pound. There are, of course, conditions.'

'Well, there's a surprise,' said Uriah.

Littlechild ignored the sarcasm and continued. 'If any details of the Whitechapel investigation should leak out within the next twenty years, the lease on this building will revert back to the Metropolitan Police. If you wish to abide by that condition, gentlemen, then each of you sign the lease.'

Of course, we all signed the lease and became the proud owners of an acceptable three storey building in Soho. I was so excited I brewed another pot of Earl Grey.

When he failed to write the Ripper story Uriah's newspaper did indeed sack him. He wasn't too disappointed because we decided to set up a Private Investigation business in our newly acquired residence in Soho, and Moffat, Garrett and Batchelor began trading above a public house in January 1889. And, at that point, I really thought our troubles were over.

They weren't.

One morning a package arrived on the doorstep. Consigned from a barren outpost in Afghanistan; addressed to Colour-Sergeant Cullen Moffat, I should have guessed the worst.

The damned package contained *twenty-five* pounds of prime Afghani tobacco.

Only one of us was pleased.

This last entry dated: November 11, 1888.

J.H.B

Notes and observations:

Wednesday
March 15, 1950

Cullen Moffat

Cullen Moffat served his country for more than thirty-five years in various branches of the armed services. He spent his last twenty years as a successful Private Investigator with Moffat, Garrett and Batchelor, solving several high profile Victorian and Edwardian cases. He died peacefully in his sleep on 23 April, 1908, aged 75.

Uriah Garrett

Uriah Garrett never published any works connected with the Jack the Ripper enquiries, either fiction or non-fiction. He retired from Moffat, Garrett and Batchelor in 1908 after many years of sterling service, in which he brought to bear all his experience as a Senior Crime Reporter. He died of natural causes on 14 May, 1913, aged 70.

Chief Inspector John George Littlechild

John Littlechild resigned from the Metropolitan Police in 1893 and worked as a consultant for Moffat, Garrett and Batchelor for several years. He retired in 1908 and died 4 January, 1923, aged 75.

Francis J. Tumblety

On 24 November, 1888, Francis Tumblety jumped bail in London, and using the alias Frank Townsend, fled to Boulogne, France, and then on to New York. In the early 1890's there were several unsolved murders of prostitutes in the New York area. He died in St. Louis, Missouri, on 28 May, 1903 of heart failure, aged 73.

George Lusk

George Lusk, erstwhile Chairman of *The Whitechapel Vigilance Committee*, disappeared, presumed drowned, while travelling along the River Thames in a small steamboat. The Metropolitan Police steadfastly refused to confirm or deny reports that a steam launch exploded close to Westminster Bridge. The police never recovered George Lusk's body.

Charles LeGrand

Charles LeGrand spent several weeks in hospital after receiving injuries in an undisclosed incident close to Westminster Bridge. When he recovered, he faced several charges. On 27 February, 1889 an Old Bailey jury found him guilty and he served ten years solitary confinement in various prisons. One hour after being released from prison on 12 March, 1899, he was knocked down and killed by a hit and run driver while crossing a London street. The Metropolitan Police never traced the driver of the hansom carriage.

James Maybrick

Both The Metropolitan Police and The Liverpool City Police questioned James Maybrick on several occasions. They never charged him with any crime. He died in Liverpool, on 11 May, 1889 of arsenic poisoning. His wife, Florence, convicted of his murder, served a sentence of fourteen years in British prisons, before returning to America upon her release in 1903. She maintained her innocence until the day she died. James's Maybrick's fictional diaries of the Whitechapel murders remain unpublished.

Executive Superintendent Charles Henry Cutbush

Despite his unprofessional and incompetent behaviour during the Whitechapel murder investigations, Executive Superintendent Charles Henry Cutbush never faced any charges. An 1891 enquiry into the miserable performance of the Metropolitan Police during the Jack the Ripper investigations failed to reach a conclusion. Cutbush continued to serve as an officer in the Whitechapel district of London.

However, in 1896, whilst sitting with his family in the kitchen of his home, he produced a gun and shot himself in the head. The coroner's verdict was that Charles Cutbush took his own life while the balance of his mind was disturbed.

Or perhaps he just couldn't live any longer with the knowledge of his own actions during the autumn of 1888.

Otto von Bismarck

Otto von Bismarck was a diplomat who displayed his excellent manners and politeness on a world stage. Other than his native German language, he was also fluent in English, French, Russian and Polish. In the role of *honest broker*, he was responsible for maintaining peace in Europe during the years he was in office, particularly during a successful private visit to Great Britain in November 1888.

Emperor Wilhelm 11, who disliked Bismarck's popularity, forced him to resign all his political offices in 1890. Otto von Bismarck, a broken and unhappy man, died of natural causes on 30 July, 1898, aged 83.

Prince Albert Victor, Duke of Clarence

Prince Albert was the eldest son of Edward, Prince of Wales (later King Edward V11) and he was second in line of succession to the British throne after his father. Speculation and conspiracy theories concerning the Prince's intellect, sexuality and sanity abounded in late Victorian society.

In July 1889, the Metropolitan Police under intense public scrutiny raided a male brothel in Cleveland Street, London. The resulting scandal implicated many high-ranking figures in British society including Prince Albert Victor, Duke of Clarence.

In the wake of the scandal, the government despatched the errant Prince to India where he continued his scandalous ways by having an affair with a married woman, Margery Hadden. The Prince died of pneumonia on 14 January 1892. Rumours still persist that he actually died of a morphine overdose, deliberately administered to him to prevent him succeeding to the British throne.

Edward V11 (Albert Edward)

Edward was the son of Queen Victoria and first in line of succession to the British throne. Before his accession to the throne, he held the title of Prince of Wales, and has the distinction of having been heir apparent to the throne longer than anybody ever has in British history.

During Queen Victoria's widowhood, Edward represented his mother at public gatherings, but never had an active role running the country. Several incidents, including a court appearance in a notorious divorce case, and a gambling scandal, damaged the Prince of Wales's reputation. The British government considered him unsuitable material for a future monarch.

However, following the death of Queen Victoria, Edward became King Edward V11 of the United Kingdom of Great Britain and Ireland. He reigned from 22 January, 1901 until his untimely death on 6 May, 1910.

J.H. Batchelor
Brookfield House
Tetbury
Gloucestershire.
March 1950

Editor's Note

Sir John Howard Batchelor Kt.

John Batchelor retired from *Moffat, Garrett and Batchelor* after Cullen Moffat's death in 1908 and was welcomed back to the family estate in Gloucestershire, which he inherited upon his mother's death in 1910. He contributed several thousands of pounds to worthy causes mostly in the Whitechapel area of London. On 18 April 1950, John Batchelor received a knighthood for outstanding services to the community.

The National Trust purchased John Howard Batchelor's estate in 1951. In 2004, a cleaner found several journals, hidden behind a filing cabinet.

The journals described in great detail some of the cases *Moffat, Garrett and Batchelor* investigated during their time in Soho. To date only two have been published; *The Whitechapel Murder Mystery* (2006) and *Seven Mile Avenue* (2007). Several other journals written by John Batchelor, some describing criminal investigations in the early Edwardian era, await publication.

On 27 April, 1951, Sir John Howard Batchelor Kt., aged 88 years, died peacefully in his bed whilst drinking a cup of Earl Grey tea. He passed away without spilling a single drop. His mother would have been proud of him...

...his father less so.

1972377R00114

Printed in Great Britain
by Amazon.co.uk, Ltd.,
Marston Gate.